CHRISTMAS WISH LIST

HARTBRIDGE CHRISTMAS SERIES BOOK TWO

N.R. WALKER

COPYRIGHT

BLURB

In need of work and a change of scenery, Aussie ex-pat Jayden Turner agrees to a short-term chef position at a Bed and Breakfast over the Christmas holidays. After all, how hard could it be in a small town in the mountains of Montana? What he finds is a grand old house in a beautiful town, and his new boss is gorgeous, gay, and single.

After his divorce, Carter "Cass" Campion bought his great-aunt's rundown country manor in his home town, and he's determined to get it ready for the busy holiday period. Recently out as gay, he's been focused solely on his business and hasn't had time for a man. Not that many gay men come through Hartbridge . . .

As his new clients arrive, and being away from his two kids, celebrating Christmas is the last thing on Cass's mind. But his new chef has other ideas. And if there's one thing on his Christmas Wish List this year, Jayden can make it come true.

CHRISTMAS
Wish List

N.R. WALKER

CHAPTER ONE

JAYDEN TURNER

I WASN'T sad about leaving Missoula, Montana, behind. Sure, I'd miss *some* of the folks I'd worked with over the last year, but when my co-worker-with-benefits decided he wanted benefits with the boss instead, I knew it was time for me to leave.

I saw an ad online for a temporary chef position in a small town over the Christmas period and decided to apply. Temporary suited me. It'd get me through the holidays until I figured out where I wanted to go next, so I could start somewhere new in the new year.

That was the plan.

So I packed up my car, loaded the town into my phone maps, and without so much as looking back, I headed northwest on I-90.

Was it always so easy for me to just pack up and go?

Kinda.

I'd been in the US for twelve years. I came here with my folks at fifteen when my dad was offered some great job to move his family from Australia to LA. It was so great that he then moved us from LA to Vegas to Denver in the space of three years.

I'd moved so many times trying to graduate high school, in the end I scraped by enough to graduate and enrolled in culinary school. My dad's great job gave way to an even better job back in Melbourne, so when they moved back to Australia, I decided to stay.

Not even twenty years old and completely on my own, but I liked it here. I had a job I enjoyed, a good teacher at culinary school, and figured why not give it a crack by myself.

Since then, I'd lived and worked in Denver, Salt Lake City, and then Missoula. I didn't move for any reason other than wanting to find somewhere that felt right.

I wanted somewhere that felt like home.

Not that I really remembered what *home* felt like, and I was beginning to wonder if I should just pack up one final time and move back to Australia.

I didn't really want to do that.

I was twenty-eight. I was sick of moving around and packing everything I owned into a car. I needed to find somewhere that felt right and find some permanence. I was sick of being alone, sick of working all the time just to get by, sick of feeling so . . . disposable. I wanted more in life. I wanted better.

As I drove, the elevation got higher and the passing scenery got prettier. There was a thick blanket of snow over almost everything, though the skies were blue, the sun was out, and the roads had been cleared. Traffic was fine, conditions were good.

Admittedly, when I first got to the States, driving in snow hadn't been my favourite thing. But after so many years, it was no longer a big deal now. The key was to be prepared and to be cautious. The truth was, I loved the snow.

I loved American winters in the mountains. I could have chosen somewhere south like Florida and avoided all chance of snow, but there was something amazing about snow on the mountains, on the trees, the biting air . . . I was drawn to it.

As long as there was heating and my feet weren't wet.

And as I turned onto a road called Hartbridge Main, the snowbanks were taller, the mountains steeper, the roads slipperier. But trusty old Google Maps hadn't let me down yet, and before I knew it, I turned the corner and drove into what must have been the prettiest town in America.

Hartbridge.

There were old-fashioned shops with awnings, Christmas decorations, the cutest street lamps, planter boxes with trees and most likely flowers come spring time. People were talking in the street, smiling, shopping, waving to someone in a passing car. Even the snow clumped on the sidewalks was still pristine white, not slushy grey.

Idyllic was an understatement. I felt like I'd gone back in time.

I was tempted to pull over and stretch my legs, maybe grab a coffee, but figured I should go sort out my employment first. Considering it was also my accommodation, it was kind of a priority. I was early, but I'd take early over late any day.

I drove down the main street, which was actually called Main Street, past the diner, the barber, and the mechanic, and headed south. The map said Ponderosa Road was just one more mile out of town . . .

But there was no road.

There was the occasional driveway, by the looks of

them. Not that I could see the houses from the road. There was nothing but snow and trees, and the snowbanks made it difficult to see what was what, but there was definitely no road.

What the hell?

There wasn't really anywhere I could pull over but a driveway, so I found one and hoped no one came out to yell at me. Maybe if they did, I could ask them where the hell Ponderosa Road was.

Taking my phone, I zoomed in on the map, but cell reception chose this particular time to be sketchy and it wouldn't load correctly. Why didn't I download the map in case it went offline?

Ugh.

Carefully reversing out of the driveway, I headed back towards town, slowing down to a snail's pace to double-check there was definitely no road where the road should have been.

Nope.

I found myself back in Main Street and parked out the front of the hardware store. Certain someone in there would be able to help me with directions, I went inside.

The doorbell rang above my head and I was hit with the smell of wood shavings and paint. As strange as it sounded, it smelled like childhood memories. I saw rows of shelving with nuts and bolts and chains and saws on my way to the counter.

"Morning," a guy said. "How can I help you today?"

He was a big guy, burly build, but a friendly smile and kind eyes. He wore a dark red apron and a name badge that made him out to be Ren.

"Ah, yeah, I think I'm lost?" I said. "I'm looking for a Ponderosa Road. It's on the map and I drove out there, but there was no sign. Actually, there wasn't even a road from what I could tell."

Ren's smile widened. "Well, at least you didn't drive headfirst into a snowbank."

I blinked. Uh . . . "Pardon?"

"Your accent. You're Australian, right?"

Not many people picked it up straight away, given I'd been here so long, my accent was starting to fade. "Uh, yeah."

"Last time an Australian tried to drive up here, he almost died."

The way he was smiling, I was beginning to think I should have tried asking for directions at the diner instead.

Then Ren turned and hollered, "Hamish?"

"Um, I just need . . . you know, I can ask across the road . . ."

Just then, a guy appeared with a dark beard, holding a fluffy black dog. I assumed he was Hamish. He wore a pink beanie . . . The guy did. Not the dog. But the dog was wearing shoes. Little leather dog shoes, but still.

"Yes, I'm here. She took ages to pee. You know she doesn't like going in the snow," the guy said. He was looking up at Ren, who was smiling at me, and only then seemed to notice I existed. "Oh, is there something I can help you with?"

He had a very familiar accent.

Definitely Australian.

Ren spoke before I could. "I was just telling this customer of the last Australian guy who tried to drive in snow."

Hamish rolled his eyes. "It was three years ago. I've driven in the snow plenty since then and have never had an accident. Well, except when you moved the mailbox."

I was beginning to think I'd walked into an episode of *Eureka*. You know that TV show set in the small town where everything was weird? Maybe that was the reason why this idyllic little town had stayed so small.

Before I could back out slowly, Ren laughed. "This is Hamish," he said warmly.

"Hi," I said, trying to be normal. "You're Aussie, right?"

Hamish's whole face lit up. "Yes, and so are you? Where are you from?"

"Originally? Melbourne. Been here a while now though."

"Oh, nice. I'm from Sydney. Been here three years." He put the dog down and pulled off his beanie and held out his hand to shake. "Hamish Kenneally."

I shook his hand. It was actually nice to hear his accent. "Jayden Turner."

"What brings you up here?" Hamish asked.

"Work, actually. I was looking for Ponderosa Road but it's not where the map said it should be."

Hamish grimaced. "Directions, I'll leave to Ren." He put his hand on Ren's arm in a manner that was not just friendly. It was an affectionate touch. They were a couple? Hamish was definitely a little fem, but that didn't mean anything. And Ren was a big lumberjack kind of guy. They made a hot couple. "You don't want to take directions from me. There'd be no saying where you'd end up."

I smiled at that but took out my phone and showed them the map. I pointed to the road that wasn't there.

Ren nodded. "They closed North Ponderosa Road a few years ago," Ren said. "And those maps don't update too often. You just need to keep on the road you were on for four more miles and you'll see signs to West Ponderosa Road."

"Oh. Okay, thanks."

He gave me a curious look. "You said work?"

"Yeah," I replied, not sure how much I should give away to this albeit friendly stranger. "There's a B&B out there. I'm a chef. The owner's expecting me today."

"Nice," Ren said. "Yeah, the B&B's really coming along. Or so I've heard. The house was huge, from what I remember as a kid. We'd ride our bikes out that way in the summer, along the river."

The bell above the door rang and it was a good cue for me to leave. "Thanks so much," I said. "And nice to meet you, Hamish. It was good to hear a familiar accent."

"Same," Hamish said. "If you want to chat about how much you miss Chicken Crimpies or Twisties, or proper coffee, you can find me here. Not all the time, but some of the time. I don't actually work here. I'm just getting married to this lug." He gestured to Ren. "And this is his second home."

I found myself smiling at him. "I haven't thought of Chicken Crimpies in a long time."

Hamish sighed. "I need to find a supplier."

"Excuse me, Jayden?" Ren said. He was now standing with some guy at the side of the service counter. "The owner of the B&B who's expecting you? This is him."

Holy shit.

The guy he gestured to was in his mid-thirties, had short brown hair, slightly greying at the temples. He had greyish blue eyes, some stubble, and a dimple in his left cheek. He was wearing a blue jacket, dark jeans, and boots. And not just pretty boots for show. These were working boots, scuffed and dirty, which told me he wasn't afraid of hard work.

He looked like he stepped straight out of a magazine full of ruggedly handsome middle-aged country men.

He was sexy as fuck.

And he was holding his hand out to me. "Carter Campion," he said. "Most people call me Cass."

His touch was warm and strong, calloused. I somehow managed to stumble over my name. "Jayden Turner. Nice to meet you. I just stopped in here to ask for directions. I couldn't find the turn-off for your address."

Cass smiled at me, and I swear time seemed to do some weird little blip. He turned to face Ren and I needed a second to catch my breath. "That's what I came in for," he said. "Ren, I need some supplies to make a sign."

CHAPTER TWO

CASS CAMPION

MY TO-DO list was a mile long, and every time I crossed off one thing, I found another two things to add.

Eighteen months of planning and a lot of hard work was coming down to days, and while I was really excited to get started and finally see some income coming in, I was also dreading it.

Maybe dreading it was a harsh call. But I was nervous and worried sick.

I couldn't fail at this.

I'd thrown the last year and a half into this place, into this business. I'd also thrown a lot of money into it.

I needed it to work.

It wasn't my only income, but making it my only income was the long-term plan.

Renovating a once-grand old country manor and turning it into a Bed and Breakfast was no small plan, either. Some days I thought I had to have been crazy. Some days I was sure I was.

My parents sure thought I was.

But totally renovating my great-aunt's house to its

former glory to be my home and business, while being able to claim some of it back as a taxable write-off, wasn't crazy.

It was long hours, some back-breaking work, but it was rewarding to see my hard efforts pay off. I did almost everything myself. Of course, things like electrical rewiring and plumbing upgrades were done by professionals, but the rest was all me. I pulled up carpets, sanded floors, sanded back the walls, stripped ghastly wallpapers, put new stringers on porch steps, fixed fence palings, graded and gravelled the driveway, and painted.

So much painting.

And that was just to name a few of the jobs I'd done myself.

I could decorate the guest rooms just fine, and I could refurbish old pieces to new again, buy new linens to make it all match and look like a million dollars. But one thing I couldn't do was cook.

Well, I could cook a little. Your basic home cooking to ward off starvation, I could do. I'd advertised this holiday period to include all meals, not just breakfast. I figured it was a good draw card for a brand-new business that had no reviews.

Breakfast, I could stumble through. Cook fancy lunches and dinners for a number of people, I could not. Especially Christmas Eve lunch and dinner. They were special events, and there were no DIY videos or magazines that were going to get me through that.

And I had to get the food right. If guests loved the food and ate well, they'd be happy. So I did what any sane and savvy business person would do.

I asked Carl at the diner if he wanted to cater for me. I mean, I knew he was busy . . .

Anyway, after he stopped laughing, he suggested I advertise for a temporary chef for the holidays.

So that's what I did.

I narrowed the applicants down to a few, called their references and past employers, and I pared it down to two. I spoke to both of them on the phone and settled on the guy with the accent.

He was young, experienced, and eager to work. And he was also arriving this afternoon.

Which reminded me . . .

I was going to have the sign fixed before he got here. I was supposed to have had the sign fixed a year ago—I had asked the Department of Transportation to do it, as they should have—but it never was. Then it became a non-priority on my to-do list, and then with customers arriving in the next few days, like most things, it became urgent.

Well, it wasn't *urgent* urgent, because the first customers weren't arriving for another three days. But my newest, and only, staff member was arriving today, and if he couldn't find the place . . .

So I drove into town and pulled up at the hardware store. I kinda hoped Hamish wouldn't be there, which was stupid. I liked Hamish, Ren's fiancé. Everyone in Hart-bridge loved Hamish; he was funny and charming, and he made Ren ridiculously happy. I just had the feeling Hamish didn't like me. Actually, I was sure he didn't. He wasn't very good at hiding it.

Not that we'd ever really had the chance to clear the air between us, either.

But anyway, into the hardware store I went. And, of course, Hamish was there, but Ren welcomed me with a smile.

"Morning," he said. "We were just talking about you. Well, kind of."

Oh. That didn't bode well. "Really?"

"Yeah." Then he turned to Hamish and the guy Hamish was talking to. "Excuse me, Jayden. The owner of the B&B who's expecting you? This is him."

I was expecting him?

Jayden . . .

Oh shoot. The chef. My first employee.

I put on my best smile and held out my hand. "Carter Campion. Most people call me Cass."

He seemed a little stunned at first, but he quickly snapped out of it. "Jayden Turner. Nice to meet you. I just stopped in here to ask for directions. I couldn't find the turn off for your address."

His accent was cute. Kinda faded now. A bit American, a bit . . . something else. English?

Then what he said dropped in my head. He'd tried to find the place already and had to ask for directions. The sign, yes . . .

"That's what I came in for," I said. "Ren, I need some supplies to make a sign."

"They still haven't fixed that yet?" Ren asked.

"Nope. Still just a post in the ground. And I've got my first clients turning up in a few days. I best get something sorted out so they can find the place." I turned back to Jayden and Hamish. "Jayden, if you want to wait a few minutes while I get this sorted out, you can follow me to the house."

"That'd be great," he replied.

I gave him a nod and looked at Hamish then. I gave him my friendliest smile. "Morning, Hamish."

"Carter, what kind of sign are you making?" Ren called

out from the lumber section, "The hanging kind with a cross post?"

It was a good excuse for Hamish not to answer, and I wondered if Ren had called out deliberately to intervene. I smiled at Jayden. "Will just be five minutes, if that's okay."

He nodded. "Sure."

I followed Ren into the lumber section and, with his help, quickly got everything I needed. He helped me carry it out to my truck and I followed him back inside to pay. By the time all that was done, Hamish was trying to take the shoes off their dog, and Jayden was waiting for me.

"I'm all done if you're ready?" I asked. "Did you need to grab anything while we're in town?" Then I gave that another thought. "Actually, we'll probably have to make a list and come back in later, if that suits you?"

He gave a nod. "Yeah, that'll be fine." He then turned to Ren. "Thank you. Please tell Hamish I said goodbye."

Ren replied with a broad grin. "I will." Then he turned that killer smile my way. "You two have fun. Oh, and there's the Christmas Tree Night thing, four days from now. Be sure to bring Jayden in."

Well, that was a little weird. The way Ren smiled and nodded suggestively from me to Jayden gave me flashbacks of when Ren and I were in high school and would fool around after football practice.

Wait a minute . . .

Was he implying that me and Jayden . . . ? That we could . . . ? That Jayden was . . . ?

No.

He was an employee, and I needed these next ten days to go smooth and professional. That was all.

Even if Jayden was cute as hell.

"What's the Christmas Tree Night?" Jayden asked.

"Oh, they light up the Christmas tree in the main street, by the park," I explained. "Well, they actually light it on the first of December, but they hold a night where they re-light it and cut a ribbon, and they block off the street and make a festival out of it."

Ren was doing that smiling thing again. "Everyone comes. There are carollers and a snowman building contest, and Santa brings little gifts for the kids. Carl from the diner puts on a food stall. The whole place is lit with fairy lights and lanterns and it's a lot of fun."

"Oh," Jayden said with a bit of smile. "That actually sounds kinda nice." He blanched and glanced at me. "I mean, if I'm done working for the day, I could come in after . . ."

Why did I feel so put on the spot? I wasn't prepared for being a boss in front of other people. "Yeah, sure," I said. What he did outside of work was of no concern to me. If our clients had had dinner and the kitchen was tidy, Jayden was free to do what he wanted.

Ugh. This was weird.

I tapped the service counter. "Thanks again for your help with the sign, Ren. But I should get back to it."

He waved us off. "My pleasure. See you both again soon. If you need some help putting the sign up, give me a call."

"Will do. Thanks again." I gestured toward the door and Jayden followed me out of the store and onto the sidewalk. "Well, this is me," I said, nodding toward my truck.

"And that's me," he said, gesturing to the dark SUV next to mine. It looked packed full and I had to wonder just how long he thought he was staying for. "I'll follow you, yes?"

"Sounds great. Just try not to get separated by the traffic rush."

I tried to joke. It was lame . . .

He looked up the very empty street. I think it was old Barney Durnell's Dodge turning two blocks up. "I'll certainly try." But then a car went through the intersection, driving all of five miles per hour, and crossed the bridge. Jayden put his hand to his heart. "Phew. That was close. There was almost a collision."

I snorted because those two cars were half a mile apart. "Almost." Glad he added his own lame joke to mine, I got in my truck and he followed me out down Main Street toward home.

As I pulled into my gate and headed up the long driveway to the house, I was acutely aware that he was following me and also that he was seeing my pride and joy for the first time.

The front pastures were covered in snow, a large frozen pond sat centred before the house. There was an open field behind the house, with gardens and a barn before the land began to incline, and the sheer mountain and trees behind the property completed the picture worthy of a painting.

It was hard not to be impressed, even if I did say so myself, and I loved seeing people's first reactions.

I drove around the back to the barn and Jayden slowly followed me and parked. He got out of his car smiling and looking up the mountain peak that disappeared into the low cloud. "Wow."

I grinned, a little proud. "It never gets old."

"And the house," he said. "It's huge. And beautiful."

"Come on, I'll help you get your stuff inside. You must have had an early start and probably want to rest."

"I was a bit early," he admitted, and opening the backseat, he pulled out two large duffle bags and some kind of toolbox. But then he closed the door.

"Oh, did you want to bring the rest of your stuff in?" I asked. There were some boxes and bags in the back, from what I could see.

"No, that can stay for now," he said. "But if you'd like to carry this, that'd be great." He handed me the toolbox, which was odd, but I took it. He picked up his two bags and smiled at me as if he was waiting for me.

Right. Yes.

Take him inside the house, you idiot.

We trudged through the snow to the long porch at the back of the house. "Weather's actually been really good this year," I said. "No huge snow dumps so far, no blizzards. It's supposed to be a mild winter, apparently. Which, I have to admit, I don't mind."

"Haven't missed all that shovelling?" he said as he climbed the steps behind me.

"Not one bit." I grinned, unlocked the door into the mudroom, and led the way inside.

Boots off, I showed him the front family room and the dining room but guessed a formal tour could wait. "I'll show you to your room and let you get settled," I said. "I can show you the rest of the house later, and the kitchen, of course. I need to get a start on that sign before I lose daylight. And being on the side of the mountain means it gets dark pretty early."

"Oh yes, of course. You do what you need to do," he said. "I'll be fine."

I showed him to his room. It was down the hall in what I called the bedroom wing. It was tucked away down at the very end so it was quite the walk, but that meant it was private, and most importantly, it had its own bathroom.

He walked in, seemingly impressed, and put his bags on the double bed. "Oh wow," he said, pointing to the small fireplace in his room. "Does that work?"

"I closed the flue off, only because I'd never used it," I explained. "But yes, it does." I pointed to the heating unit on the wall, which I'd had installed. "But this works much better."

He smiled in a way that sent a buzz of warmth through me. "Well, it's great. I might need a map to get back to the kitchen though."

I chuckled, staving off my embarrassment at how I'd just reacted to him. "I'll show you the way."

CHAPTER THREE

JAYDEN

DRIVING UP TO THE HOUSE, I was lost for words. When Ren at the hardware store had called this a manor, I wasn't sure what to expect. And the photos on the internet did not do it justice.

First of all, it was huge. Nestled up on the hill on stilts with panelling to hide the under-house, it was grand but not over imposing. Clearly built in a different era, when builders were craftsmen; and this was a work of art. It had a veranda across the entire front, with wide stairs at the entrance down to the front grounds. The house itself had wood-siding, painted white, with ornate window frames. The veranda posts had those fancy brackets, and the balustrade under the hand railing was in some filigree pattern that made it all look very stately.

It reminded me of those old Queenslander homes back in Australia, only bigger.

I followed Cass's truck around to the back of the house where there was a covered parking bay for several cars and a huge barn. He'd clearly put a lot of time into getting the place up to scratch. Yes, the house was old, but it looked very well maintained.

It was certainly beautiful.

Cass showed me inside and to my room, which was unexpectedly lovely. I don't know why I was surprised, but the quality of everything was top tier. "Oh, wow" was all I could say.

I was a bit bummed that the small fireplace in my room didn't work, but I wasn't here to vacation. I was here to work. Which reminded me . . . I should go inspect the kitchen.

"I might need a map to get back to the kitchen though," I said, getting my mind back on track.

Work. That's what I was here for.

"I'll show you the way," he said. His smile was something else . . .

Wow.

Even as cute as Cass was. And he *was* cute. A few years older than me but certainly handsome.

I wasn't here for that either.

No, no. Nope. You're here to work . . .

"Here, I'll take that," I said, taking the toolbox Cass had looked entirely surprised to realise he was still holding.

His eyes went to the offending toolbox. "Does your car break down often?"

"What?" I asked. My car? "Oh no, this is my kit. It has my knives and gear in it."

"Oh!"

"A chef's knives are their pride and joy," I said with a bit of a smile. "And they're expensive as hell."

"I bet," he replied. "Come on, I'll show you around."

He led me back down the hall, this time explaining what was behind each door. Guest rooms, a communal laundry, a reading room with French doors that opened onto the front veranda.

A reading room? What kind of house had a reading room?

This one, apparently.

Cass gestured to the door after the reading room. "That's the door to the private quarters," he explained. "The attic was huge and so much wasted space, so I converted it to bedrooms and an office. And this was a second entrance to the veranda, so it became the staircase."

"You've done a lot of work," I offered.

"Oh yeah," he said, a mix of embarrassed and proud. "But this old place was built to last forever. She's as strong as an ox. There's still a bit to do though." He kept walking and we arrived back at the sitting room that came off the mudroom. It was then I noticed boxes beside some couches. And what looked like a shelving unit that needed putting together by the fireplace.

But the sitting room itself was massive, with great natural lighting; the front windows were huge, the view down to the road and river was spectacular. Some of the furniture was older, some of it new, but it somehow all matched and looked very welcoming. Whoever he had as his interior decorator had done a great job.

"Kitchen's through there," he said, pointing behind us. "But I'll show you this side of the house first." On the far side of the sitting room, on the same wall as the fireplace, was a set of double doors. "When it's just me here, I keep these closed. Half the house to heat that way."

He opened the doors to reveal what looked like another very large family room, more matching furniture with a huge TV and another fire.

Christ. How big was this place?

"This way is the dining hall," he said, going through another door. "It has a door direct to the kitchen." We walked into a room that was probably bigger than the last apartment I lived in. There was a table, antique by the look of it, that ran almost the length of the room, plus a matching cabinet at the end of the room. "This was my great-aunt's," Cass explained, running his hand along the back of one of the wooden dining chairs. "I considered taking it out, but well . . . I'd have to have the windows taken out or the roof lifted to get it out in one piece."

"I've never seen a table this long before," I said.

Cass smiled. "This place used to be a country club. There used to be tennis courts and they'd swim in the lake out front. People used to travel to stay here, with the mountains and the river across the road."

"There's a lake?"

He laughed. "Out front. It's frozen over at the moment. There's a dock in the summertime."

"I hadn't noticed when I drove in," I admitted. "I was too busy staring at the house." I paused. "Is house the right word? Or manor? Mansion?"

He met my eyes and nodded. "It's my home. So yeah, house is fine. It was called a manor a hundred years ago, but that term isn't used much in these parts anymore. I wanted to keep the original name though."

There were those warm eyes again. They cut a little deeper this time.

Oh boy.

Keep talking, Jayden.

"Did your aunt run it as a country club?"

"In the early days, yes. There's quite the story about how she came to own it when she was so young. It was quite the scandal that an unwed young woman came to own such a place. Apparently her uncle left it to her in his will. He had no children of his own, and my great-aunt was the only family he cared for. He died in 1944, in the war. She was very young and very single. She never married, never had kids. Rumour has it that she had many lady friends who would stay."

I raised my eyebrows. Was that look he gave me searching for information? Was he fishing for information? "*Ooh*, scandalous for that time."

"Very," Cass said.

"Good for her!" I proclaimed. "She sounds like an amazing woman."

He smiled then, before he went back out into the family room and through another set of double doors. "And this is the rec room."

A recreation room? Jesus.

And it was massive. It was basically the end of the house with windows on three sides.

There was a pool table in the middle of the room, a big TV on the wall closest to us, bean bags, and what looked like a gaming console of some kind. There was a Lego table I hadn't seen since I was a kid, which was cool. An old doll house that was as old as it was well-loved, by the looks of it. There were shelves of books and games and tubs of toys and dolls.

There were also some boxes shoved in one corner and what looked like rolls of linoleum and some planks of wood or something.

"This is basically for the kids," he said, nodding to the room in general. "I remember playing in here as a kid, and it felt right to keep it that way."

He was obviously sentimental, and I liked that.

"Well, I'm impressed," I said. He glanced at me and I explained. "With all of it. It's beautiful."

"Thank you," he said with such gratitude it took me a few seconds to understand where it was coming from.

Because he'd done all this on his own, and someone was finally appreciating his hard work.

That was what it felt like.

He started, then clapped his hands together like he'd just remembered something. "The kitchen."

"Ah, yes. The kitchen."

Truth was, I was now excited to see what he'd done with it.

So back we went through the far wing of the house the way we'd come and into the kitchen.

And what he'd done with it?

It was simply huge, like everything else in this house, but clean, functional, and it was definitely country charm themed, despite the industrial stainless-steel countertops. There were white cupboards and an island with storage compartments, which was great for prep. But the stove . . .

The stove.

"What is that?"

Cass grinned proudly. "Isn't it beautiful?"

"Oh, is this original?" I asked.

And I meant *original* from a hundred years ago. It was a large, pale-yellow enamel looking thing with little doors and old-fashioned lever handles and one door with an inbuilt thermometer. The stove top was . . . *my god, is that cast iron?*

What the hell?

"Oh yep. Original as the day she was made," Cass said. He was obviously very proud of this stove. Possibly emotionally attached to it. "She's wood fired and cooks a roast like you've never tasted."

He then realised I didn't share his enthusiasm.

"Is that okay?" he asked. "Have you never cooked on something like this before?"

"Well, no, because I'm not Fred Flintstone living in Bedrock," I said before I could stop myself. I covered my sarcasm with a laugh. "I mean, do you fire this up every night? Or for breakfast if you want to cook yourself some bacon and eggs, do you go to all that hassle to light it up?"

He chuckled and pulled open a cupboard door next to the wood fired stove. Except he didn't open it like a normal cupboard. He opened the door downward and slid it underneath the cabinetry to reveal an ultra-modern, very expensive-looking oven.

Then he lifted that section of the countertop like the hood of a car to reveal a cooktop. The hood clicked into place, and I couldn't believe my eyes.

"*What?*"

Cass laughed. "Pretty cool, yes?"

"Ah, that's amazing."

"I paid a fortune for it, so it would wanna be amazing." He shrugged. "I wanted to keep the original feel of the house where I could. I had to modernise a lot of it, but there was no way I was getting rid of Ernace."

"Ernace?"

"Yeah, Ernace the Furnace," he said, patting the hundred-year-old wood stove. "Under the house, there's extra bracing in the floor they had to put in to support the weight of it. Extra piers too, into the hillside. So when I say there was no way I was getting rid of it, there was no way I *could* get rid of it. It weighs a lot. I've only lit it up a few times."

I was still staring at the hidden oven and stovetop.

"That door is through to the dining room for easy service," he said, pointing to a door at the end of the counter before walking through another door at the end of the kitchen. "And in here is your pantry, fridge, and a chest freezer."

It was a pantry, yes. If you called a pantry another full-sized room with two whole walls of shelving and a fridge and freezer, like he'd said. There was also a lot of mess. Nothing was organised, nothing was set out in any kind of order. There were more boxes and a broom, a utility rack that was still unassembled and sitting on top of the chest freezer, along with a white board and a cordless drill with a box of screws.

"Oh, I was looking for that," he said, picking the drill up. He pressed the trigger and it whirred slowly, the battery in need of a charge.

So, I quickly deduced, some things were very organised, some things were not. But the kitchen was fine; I could have it whipped into shape in no time. Probably be best if I did it and not him, anyway.

"Anyway," Cass said. "It's a bit of a mess at the moment. I wasn't expecting you until later. I was gonna tidy it up a bit in here."

"I can do it," I said. "Won't take me long."

"You don't start officially until tomorrow, so if you wanna rest up or take a nap or watch TV, just go right ahead. There are some books in the reading room, if you like to read. Or whatever you want. You're not on the clock yet; free to do whatever you want."

I got the feeling he wasn't used to giving orders.

"I can potter around in here for a bit," I said. "Get a head start on tomorrow. And I like to organise things."

"Yes, well, tomorrow. I thought we could go over the menu you wanted to do, go over the equipment that I have, like pots and pans, and if there's anything you need, we can go into town. We'll need to do a grocery run as well. I've put in an order at the store. They agreed to wholesale prices, which is great. But you can check off what I've ordered with what you need."

"Sounds good."

"My aunt had a whole heap of pots and pans in here." He opened one cupboard, then another, to reveal stacked cookware. And not just any cookware, but these were vintage enamel or copper and some cast iron. An old pudding steamer toppled out and I picked it up.

"This is cool! I haven't seen one of these in years."

Cass eyed it. "What is it?"

"A Christmas pudding steamer."

He made a face. "Ew."

I laughed. "Well, not just Christmas pudding. Any kind."

He clearly wasn't sold.

"What about a warm gingerbread cake with caramel sauce? That's Christmassy."

"Now, that kind of cake is something I can get behind."

"Okay. Easy." I held the steamer up. "It might not even work because this is about a hundred years old."

He laughed and pulled out a cast-iron skillet. "So's this. It's old and heavy as hell. Might need to be cleaned up a bit, though," he said, taking it to the sink.

I let out a squeal. "No!"

He spun around. "What?"

I took the skillet from him. "What you're not going to do, is that." It took a second for me to breathe right. "No water. The cooking gods will strike you down." I turned the skillet over in my hands. "Lord, do you have any idea how valuable these are?"

He shrugged. "Uh, no. Apparently not." Then he smiled. "Thought you saw a cockroach or something. Which I don't have cockroaches, by the way."

I put the skillet down and took a ceramic pot out of the cupboard that I was pretty sure was made in the 1950s. "I can't believe you have a kitchen full of this stuff." People paid a lot of money for these. "I'm going to give these all a clean." I shot him a look. "The proper way. If that's okay?"

"Sure." I think he was a little embarrassed. "Like I said, I don't cook too often. And I've never used any of those." He made a face. "You don't have to do that today. You just got here."

"Would you believe me if I said I like to clean and organise for fun?" I chuckled. "I like things neat and tidy, plus it'll be a good way for me to see if we need anything."

"Okay. Well, I'll let you alone for a bit now. I gotta go get a start on this sign." Cass got halfway out the kitchen before he stopped. "Help yourself to anything in the fridge you want. Guess it's lunch time now. Make yourself something, and there's coffee. Look through the cupboards till you find what you need."

"Will do, thanks."

He left me alone then, and I heard him whistling as he walked outside and over to the barn.

The house seemed very quiet when it was just me.

And, because I just had to, I lifted the stovetop cover, and smiling, I shook my head. It was a ridiculous luxury when any normal kind of stove would have sufficed. But this hidden one, to match the cabinetry? Jeez.

How much money did this guy have?

I left my knife kit on the kitchen counter for now and

decided to poke my head in a few rooms while Cass wasn't here. The first bedroom was beautifully decorated; the wrought iron bed frame and white linens gave the room an elegant country feel. The second room was much the same, except it was a pale blue. The third room was a fawn colour with orange hints.

It was all beautiful. Like pages out of a magazine.

But the next room wasn't made up yet. The linens were still in their packaging. An old-fashioned dresser had a door taken off. What looked like new blinds were still in their boxes on the bed and tins of paint. Wait . . . the painting wasn't finished.

Was he not using this room?

The reading room was next, and my first glance was just wow. Tall built-in shelves along one wall were filled with books, two fancy looking chairs sat with a chess table between them. It was filled with natural light. French doors led out to the front veranda, a gorgeous cast iron and tiled fireplace took up one wall.

It was a stunning room, no doubt about it.

But there were boxes shoved in the far corner next to a display cabinet that looked like it was an original piece from when the house was first built. It was pulled away from the wall and there were newspapers and what looked like cleaning products in a basket next to it.

It seemed to me that there were little odds and ends left undone all over the house. Which was fair enough. If he was doing this all by himself, it was quite the undertaking.

I pulled the door closed and went back to the kitchen, figuring maybe some lunch was in order. And there, stuck to the fridge, which I hadn't noticed before, was a to-do list. It had about thirty things written down, some with lines through them, some had ticks, some had asterisks.

He still had a bit to do, and he was taking his first clients in three days. I tried not to think about how he was going to do it all.

But lunch first.

I had no idea where anything was or what food there was or what I could even use. Cass had said I could help myself.

His fridge was pretty well stocked. Well, it was stocked for personal use. Not for commercial use. I'd definitely need to stock up before guests arrived. A quick look in the dry storage and I decided tomato soup and grilled cheese sandwiches were on the menu.

A quick rummage through a cupboard next to the stove produced a saucepan and a frypan. I gave them a proper clean and set about heating a can of soup and making toasties in the frypan. I found some insulated travel coffee mugs and poured the soup into two of those, wrapped the sandwiches in foil, bundled them into an insulated carry bag I found in the storeroom, and trudged out into the cold to the barn.

I knocked on the big front doors and pulled it open. The yellow lighting inside was dull compared to the sun on the snow, and I couldn't see much. "Hello? Lunch delivery!"

Cass appeared from around his truck, wiping his hands and smiling. "Oh hey, you didn't need to do that."

"It's no problem. It's just soup and sandwiches," I replied. He shut the door behind me and my eyes adjusted. The inside of the barn was much like all barns. It smelled of timber, sawdust, and dirt. There was a space for his truck where we stood and shelves down the right side of the barn. A huge ride-on lawn mower was parked at the back, plus various wood tools and equipment I couldn't name. He had one of those big boards on the wall with pins that held hammers, wrenches, saws. He was obviously very handy.

"We can put it here," he said, clearing some papers on the wooden shelf. There were also some screws and a small tin of lacquer. Pretty sure I could smell turpentine.

"I love the smell of barns and work sheds," I said.

Cass grinned. "I'm liking the smell of whatever it is you cooked."

With a bit of a laugh, I opened the insulated bag and pulled out the travel mugs and unwrapped the sandwiches. "Tomato soup and cheese toasties," I explained. I handed him a cup of soup. "I didn't know what else to put the soup in, so travel mugs will have to do, sorry."

He sipped it, smiling. "This is perfect, thank you."

His voice was a little too soft, too warm. Like maybe he was genuinely touched that someone would make him lunch. It tugged at the part of me that liked to cook food for people, to make someone happy with a simple gesture, and I liked the fact my bringing him lunch made him smile like that.

I needed to change the subject.

I took a small bite of my sandwich. "How's the sign-making going?"

"Oh, good," he answered with his mouth half full. He covered his mouth with his hand and laughed. "Sorry. This grilled cheese is really good."

"Key is to do it in a frypan and not a sandwich press. And use butter."

"Well, it's worth every calorie." He sipped the soup, then walked over to a worktable of some kind. He needed both hands to lift up the sign. It was a fair size, like a miniature barn door with panels and Z-shaped bracing. "It's coming along. I was just giving it a final sanding, then I can paint it. I'll have to bring it into the house to dry tonight if I want to write on it tomorrow before I hang it. I might have to take Ren up on his offer of some help."

Ah. Ren from the hardware.

"He seems nice," I hedged. "And his . . . boyfriend, Hamish."

I wasn't sure how he'd react to the boyfriend word. I was about to find out if he'd turn his nose up or roll his eyes, or worse.

"Fiancé, now," he corrected. "They got engaged last Christmas. Hamish is a nice guy. The odds of meeting another Australian in this small town, huh?"

Well, that was a good reaction, right? To them being gay?

"Yeah, crazy odds. It was nice to hear the accent, to be honest. I don't hear it much. Though I'm losing mine, or so my folks tell me."

"Sound pretty Australian to me."

I shrugged, not sure if I should bring this up. "So, what did you ever do to Hamish?"

His eyes shot to mine. "Why, what did he say?"

"No, nothing," I replied quickly. "He was very nice and polite. He just seemed a little miffed when you got there."

The truth was, Hamish's whole demeanour changed when he first saw Cass. He went from being all smiles and hand gestures to having pursed lips and squinty eyes, and I knew that look. That was the gay equivalent to a *hell no*.

Cass shook his head dismissively, and he spoke while he packed up a few things. "I dunno. I've barely had two conversations with Hamish. But I've known Ren since we were in high school. We played football together. Maybe Hamish just doesn't like me. I dunno."

He didn't say anything else for a little while and I

wondered if I'd overstepped. I had only been in town for a hot minute. I sipped my cup of soup and Cass sipped his. He frowned, uneasy. "Ren and Hamish are a great couple," he blurted out. "I'm happy for them, and Ren deserves to be happy. He's one of the good guys, ya know? Just like his dad. His dad was a good man too."

Okay, so that was all a little weird.

But he'd called them a couple, blurted it out like he wanted me to know.

I could have very easily told him, right then and there, that I was gay. It was the subject of this conversation. But what would it achieve? I wasn't staying here. I was doing ten days' work, getting paid, and moving on.

This was a temporary position, nothing more.

So I didn't.

"The joys of a small town," I said instead. "Knowing everyone's family, like Ren's dad. Can't say I ever really had that growing up in Melbourne. Have you always lived in Hartbridge?"

"Nah, I moved to Billings for a while. Straight out of school, actually, then came back when I took this place on."

"Nice." I began to pack up our mess from lunch when I noticed one of the pieces of paper on the wooden shelf was another to-do list.

The list was shorter, with some crossed out, some ticked. It seemed like a good distraction. "The list on the fridge looks different to this one," I said, aiming for a smile.

He seemed embarrassed. He ran his hand through his hair and shifted his weight. "I, uh, I write lists. For most things."

"Same. I love lists."

He smiled. "Well, I start them but then I put the list down and I forget them. Then I have to make another one.

And I start to do the things on the list, because there's a hundred things that need to be done, and then I find something else that needs to be done and I get side-tracked doing something else, and the first thing I was doing ends up half done. And then the next thing. And the next."

I'd already guessed that much, not that I let on.

"And you'll probably find these lists all over the place. It's a habit."

I chuckled. "Easily distracted."

"Yep. And a to-do list that doesn't stop growing."

I finished my cup of soup and put the cup in the bag. "Well, you've accomplished a lot. But I better let you get back to your sign-making. I'm gonna take you up on that offer of a shower and get unpacked."

Cass shoved his hands in the back pockets of his jeans. "Okay then. I'll, um, thanks again for lunch. It was mighty kind of you."

I took the bag and his mug. "You're welcome."

I couldn't be sure because the lighting in the barn wasn't great, but I was pretty sure he blushed.

Well, that was unexpected.

CHAPTER FOUR

CASS

PAINTING the sign wasn't exactly easy when I was thinking about Jayden being in the shower. It was hardly fair, and not very boss-like, for me to be having such thoughts about him.

But he was cute.

And very kind.

He'd thought to make some lunch for me as well, and he brought it out into the cold and ate with me.

I couldn't remember the last time someone had done something like that for me.

I'd been alone a long time, and I missed that thoughtfulness, wanting to do something for someone else just to see them smile.

Not saying Jayden made me lunch so he could see me smile.

But it was nice of him, nonetheless.

And lawd ha' mercy, I almost told him I was gay. When we were talking about Ren and Hamish. The point of conversation was right there. I could have said it. I probably should have. Jayden certainly didn't seem the type to have an issue with it—he knew Ren and Hamish were together and didn't seem to care—but I'd known the guy for all of five minutes. And what was he supposed to do with that information, anyway?

The words were on my tongue, but I'd swallowed them down with my courage.

I'd never told anyone before.

Well, aside from Kendra, my now ex-wife. And my parents.

But I'd never said it to anyone else.

Not out loud.

I wasn't ready. Almost three years after that awful conversation with Kendra, where I'd realised I couldn't lie to her anymore, and then when I'd explained to my parents the reason for my broken marriage . . . Those were the only times I'd ever told anyone that I was gay.

I certainly never dated anyone or gave anyone in town reason to question me. I lived alone, I saw my kids every second weekend, and I spent every waking minute working on the house.

Sure, I'd been with men. I'd had encounters. I knew what I liked and what I didn't.

And aside from Ren, and assumedly Hamish, no one else in town knew.

Had I put myself back in the closet? I wasn't sure. I wasn't living a lie anymore, but I also wasn't exactly living my truth.

Maybe Jayden would be a good test.

Maybe I should see how I handle it, how it feels to tell someone. Maybe I could try telling him, because surely telling some random stranger who would be gone soon would be so much easier than announcing it to the folks in Hartbridge whom I had to see on the regular.

Maybe.

Shaking my head of stupid and wishful thoughts, I turned my attention back to the sign, and after finishing the sanding and priming, I painted the first coat of white paint.

But it was never going to dry out here in the barn. The temperature was supposed to drop tonight, so I carried the sign into the mudroom, careful not to smudge the paint, and went back out to put my truck in the barn and close up for the night.

I brought up some more wood to dry and then I noticed the snow shovel I'd left by the barn door so I had to reopen the barn, and of course, I'd left the paint and the brush on the shelf, so I grabbed that to take inside . . .

And I saw the to-do list Jayden had found. I shoved it in my pocket. Then I remembered the old pot I'd cleaned up so I grabbed it, and finally went inside.

"Boy, it's getting cold," I mumbled, shaking the few soft snowflakes from my hair before I pulled my boots off.

"Shouldn't you be wearing a proper coat?" Jayden asked.

He startled me. I was so used to being alone, I'd forgotten he was here. I'd forgotten about him being naked in the shower . . .

Except now he wore comfy track pants and socks with a hoodie. His brown hair looked freshly washed and almost dry.

I wish I'd seen it wet.

Okay, wow. That came out of nowhere.

"Sorry, didn't mean to startle you." He smiled. "I was just walking past, heard you mumbling."

I had my hand on my chest. I wasn't entirely sure it was because he startled me or if it was because he looked so good it rendered me speechless.

I cleared my throat. "Ah, yeah, it's a . . . I lost track of time, I guess. It got real cold, real quick. Are you warm enough?" Then because my brain was still stuck on him being wet, I said, "You showered okay?"

He stared.

My cheeks heated. "I mean, you found everything okay? You found the towels? Water pressure was fine?"

His slow smile became a grin. "Yeah, I found everything okay. Water pressure was great, actually. I wasn't sure on how long the hot water would last, so I made it pretty quick."

"There should be endless hot water," I replied. "The beauty of old houses like this is that they have those old boilers. They never run out."

His smile lingered until his eyes went to my hands. "What have you got there?"

"Oh." I'd forgotten I was holding it. "It's an old copper pot. It was in the barn. I meant to bring it in yesterday to put by the fire. It's old as hell but it looks good. They're popular again now, if you can find one. My great-aunt must have had it in the barn."

He glanced behind me, to the mudroom. "And the sign?"

"Oh yeah, that too. I need to get it dry and maybe put on another coat before I go to bed. Then tomorrow I can write on it and hang it up before the clients try to arrive and can't find the place."

"Sounds great."

"Oh, and we have to go through the menu. Did you want to do that now?"

"Uh." He glanced at the pot I was still holding, then to the sign behind me. "That can wait. How about I take that"

—he took the pot in both hands—"and you bring the sign in? Unless you wanted to paint it in the mudroom."

"Ah, no." I couldn't help but feel a little embarrassed. "Thanks. I'll bring it in. And I better bring some more firewood in as well. I brought some up from the woodpile. I was going to clean out the fire but thought I'm best leaving it until the day the guests arrive. We don't really need the wood fires, with the gas and all, but they really add to the feel and history of the house."

I was nervous-rambling. Like he even cared about the heating.

"I'll just put this in the kitchen. You bring the sign in and then you can show me where the firewood is in case I need to grab some and you're busy."

He didn't really give me time to argue. He was already walking off, but he reappeared a few seconds later empty-handed. He smiled at me, somewhat baffled. "The sign?"

Shit.

"Yep. Just doing that now." Instead of standing there staring at him, I went back into the mudroom and carefully lifted the sign. Jayden grabbed the drop cloth and followed me into the sitting room. He laid the sheet down and I gently placed the sign on top of it.

"Where's the paint?" he asked.

"Um. Still in the barn. I must have left it. I went to go back and get it but saw the pot. I get sidetracked."

Jayden pressed his lips together so his smile wasn't too big. "I get the impression that happens a bit, yeah?"

I shrugged, embarrassed. "Yeah. It's something I'm working on."

He put his hand on my arm, his smile kind, his eyes warm. "I didn't mean anything by it. You're trying to do fifty things at once. Come on, we'll get the paint and the firewood."

He led the way back to the mudroom, pulled his boots on, then helped himself to one of my coats hanging by the door. Not that I minded. It looked good on him.

Jayden was out the door while I was still pulling my boots on. I took my coat and slid it on as I followed him out. He was on the back deck, smiling up at the mountain that took up the entire view. A light snow was falling now, sunlight fading fast.

"Wow," he breathed. "You would never tire of that view, right?"

I looked up at the sheer side of the mountain. The peak was hidden by low clouds, the snow looked blue and grey over the trees, the occasional tree uncovered like a hole in a blanket.

It was beautiful.

It was also cold.

"No, I never tire of it. Some days I forget it's even there. Then other days it takes my breath away," I replied. "The colours don't just change by the season. They change by the hour and with every angle of the sun."

He pulled his coat a little tighter and pulled the hood over his head, still smiling up at the view. Then he looked at me, and his smile and the way his eyes shone like glittering snow was better than any display the view could put on.

I was beginning to think I was in a lot of trouble.

"I better get that paint," I mumbled, taking a step backward before bolting down the stairs and trudging through the snow to the barn. I found the paint and the brushes and quickly closed everything back up, heading back across the yard to the back veranda.

Jayden had found the woodpile at the end of the

veranda. It was covered with a tarp, which he had lifted up. "This end is the dry stuff, yeah?"

I liked the way he said yeah.

"Right."

"Just want me to grab what I can carry?"

"There's a bucket at the side. Makes it easier."

He dropped the tarp and found the bucket, loading a few logs into it. "And some kindling?"

"Yes, please."

It was so easy to just stand and watch him. I was also discerning how nice it was to have a guy helping me. Just to even have a man at my home, doing domestic stuff.

It shouldn't have felt this nice.

It made a distant place in my heart ache. A place I thought was long gone. A place that wanted companionship, a relationship. A place I never thought would see daylight again.

He walked back, carrying the bucket like it was some kind of trophy, and I caught a whiff of him . . . Nothing flashy. Just another man's deodorant and maybe a hint of the wood he was carrying.

It made my head spin.

I am in so much trouble.

It took a second for reality to kick in, that I was standing out on the back veranda in the cold, and I dashed back inside and closed the door behind me. Jayden already had his boots off but kept my coat on. I definitely needed to get the fire going.

It didn't take much. The hearth still had the remnants of last night's fire, which made for easy fire-making, and while I was concentrating, I hadn't really paid much attention to what Jayden was doing.

Until he sat on the floor next to me. He had his feet all

tucked up underneath him, a notebook in one hand, a pen in the other. He was still wearing my coat, but it was loose around his shoulders now. "Are you still cold?" I asked.

He smiled serenely. "Nope."

He looked incredibly comfortable, and for a fleeting second, I had visions of tackling him to the floor, making him laugh, and seeing how warm his body felt inside my coat, kissing him in front of the fire.

Jesus.

Yep. So much trouble.

"So," he began, oblivious to the scene that just played out in my head. "In your fridge you have fish, eggs, some beef, some vegetables, cheese. There's yoghurt—"

That made me smile. "Say that again."

He looked up then. "Say what?"

"Yoghurt."

He almost smiled. "Are you making fun of my accent?"

"No! Not making fun. I liked how it sounded."

"You have some plain yo-get in the fridge." He over-pronounced it in a very broad Australian accent. "Yo-get, and some mayo. A coupla jars o' jam, and some marg."

He sounded like Steve Irwin. It made me laugh.

"How was that?" he asked with a smile.

"That was both great and terrible. Who is marg and why is she in my fridge?"

He laughed. "Margarine. You have to abbreviate every-thing. That's the key to speaking Australian."

"All words?"

"No, just a select few in each sentence."

I put another log on the fire. "And the real trick is to know which ones, right?"

"Correct." He chuckled. "I've been here for so long, I'm sure if I went back, it'd be all foreign to me now."

"How long have you been here?" It seemed a natural question to ask.

"I came here when I was fifteen, so twelve years. When I speak to my parents on the phone, they tell me I sound more American every day."

"Do you miss it?"

He shook his head. "Nope. Miss my folks, of course. And I could move back if I wanted to, I guess. But this is my home. Well, not here. America is." He made a face. "I don't really have a home. Actually, everything I own is in my car. I'm not homeless. I finished up at my old job, moved out of my place, and drove here. Figured I'd keep going west when I finish up."

Oh.

"I thought I'd head toward Seattle or Portland," he added. "Get a place there and set up for a while."

"Have you always moved around?"

"Kinda. Even at school, with my dad's work, we moved a lot. I could just fit in and make friends anywhere." He frowned at his notepad. "It's weird though, because I'm over it; the whole moving on thing. When I was driving here today, on the highway, cruising along, I thought to myself I was done with it. I want to find somewhere permanent, somewhere where things become familiar, keep the same friends for more than a year, where people might remember me. I thought that'd be nice."

I studied him for a second. He didn't really seem like the drifter kind, though clearly he was. There was a resilience to him, yes. But also a vulnerability. He was kinda skinny, lean. He looked like he could gain a few pounds. But he didn't look scrawny or unkempt. His hair was shiny, his eyes were bright, his smile revealed perfect teeth. He looked after himself and was in good health, and every past employer I spoke to on the phone said he was the best worker, talented, honest, genuine.

It wasn't like he kept moving because he kept running into trouble.

Maybe he kept on moving because that was all he knew how to do. He said his dad's work had kept them moving. Maybe he didn't know any other way. The opposite of me . . . I came back to the very town I swore I'd never come back to.

Jayden held up the notebook. "Anyway, I wanted to know what you felt like for dinner. That was the point of my inventory of your fridge and pantry. Well, to see what I needed to get, but also to see what I could cook us for dinner."

"Oh. Dinner . . ."

"Yeah, if that's okay. I'm happy to have toast—"

"No, dinner's fine. It sounds great, actually. I don't cook dinner too often. Certainly haven't had it cooked for me in a long time." *Why did I say that?* "Nor have I cooked it for anyone else, I should add. I don't expect anyone to cook for me. I just meant that most nights, I finish late and it's just me so I'll sometimes make myself bacon and eggs for dinner. Or sometimes I'll even cook a batch of stuff and freeze portions for when I know I'll be busy."

His smile widened the more I talked. "Well, being prepared ahead is good."

"And I should just put this out there. I am not a good cook."

Now he laughed. "That's why you have me. How does beef ragú sound? If I can use the beef that's in the fridge?"

My mouth watered instantly. "It sounds amazing."

He seemed happy that I'd said yes, and he almost sprang to his feet. "I better get it started. Sauce takes a while. But you have a sign to paint, so you get busy with that and I'll get busy in the kitchen."

I watched him walk out and the crackle of the fire got my attention. It was well and truly alight now, so I went back over to the sign and propped it up in a stand so it would dry on both sides. I touched up a few places, which were now easier to see rather than in the more unforgiving light in the barn. *One more thing on my to-do list to fix.*

When the sign was done, I followed my nose into the kitchen. The smell was already amazing. Jayden was moving around my kitchen like it was his. He was adding something to the pot on the stove top.

"That smells really good," I said.

"Thanks."

"Are you sure you used ingredients from my kitchen? Because when I cook, it doesn't smell like that."

That earned me a smile.

"Can I ask you why you left your job? Because I spoke to your manager and he was sad to see you leave. He said you were great and everyone liked you."

"Ah . . ." His smile became rueful. He chewed on the inside of his lip for a second. "I was in a relationship with the boss of the kitchen, and that was fine."

I was not expecting that.

"Oh."

"And then he decided he'd prefer to sleep with our boss, and that guy was a dick. So it was kinda awkward and time for me to move on."

My stomach twisted; my heart galloped out of rhythm. My mouth was suddenly dry. "Oh."

Holy hell. He said *he*. He said he was sleeping with a *he*.

He. A man.

He was gay. Or bi, or pan, or whatever. I didn't know. But he liked men.

He stopped and his eyes met mine. "Is that okay?"

"Yes! Uh, yeah, sure. I don't care. I don't mind at all."

Jayden frowned and put his stirring spoon on the counter. He looked pissed but not surprised. "Are you sure you're okay with me being gay? Because you're looking a little pale and stunned. It's not information I have to share with you, and I'm happy to not bring it up again. I'll do my ten days and . . ."

He kept talking, still pissed off and probably rightly so. He was laying down some kind of rule about obligations and keeping to himself, but honestly, I didn't hear it all.

My blood was pounding in my ears, my heart was hammering against my ribs. I felt nauseous and nervous . . .

Say it, Cass.

Just freaking say it.

"Are you okay?" Jayden's hand was on my arm. "You're breathing funny and you look like you're about to swallow your tongue. Oh god, are you allergic to anything? Do you have an EpiPen?"

I shook my head and let out a laugh that sounded like a deranged five-year-old child. "I'm fine," I squeezed out.

"Are you sure?" He was not convinced, obviously. "Is this a panic attack? What can I do for you? Should we sit on the floor and do some deep breathing until it passes?"

I shook my head again and put my hand up and let out a deep breath. "No, I'm fine, honestly. I'm just going to say something that I've never told anyone. Well, anyone outside of my— God you know what? This is stupid. I'm gay. I've never said that out loud to anyone. Well, I told my wife. Now ex-wife. And I told my parents. Who still like to pretend I never said what I said. But I've never said it to anyone else. And I wasn't going to say it to you, my one and only employee who has been here for all of three hours, but you said *he*. You said you were in a relationship with a *he*. So it was now or never, and there it is. I said it. Out loud. To you."

Jayden's warm smile filled my vision. "How does it feel?"

I laughed, not sure if I wanted to cry or puke. "Really good."

He patted my arm, smiling proudly. "Thank you for telling me."

CHAPTER FIVE

JAYDEN

I THOUGHT Cass was going to pass out. Or vomit. As soon as I'd said I'd been involved with a guy, he began to react. First his eyes went wide. He paled. Then he went a strange colour and his breathing became irregular.

I thought he was going to freak out and tell me to pack my bags. My brain went to homophobia first because, well . . . because it was a knee-jerk reaction. I'd experienced my fair share of homophobic arseholes.

But then it wasn't anger.

It was panic.

Or nervousness at the very least.

He laughed, a strangled, tight sound, and then he said he was gay.

He also said he'd never told anyone, and there was a profound weight of responsibility being the recipient of that information. He was handing the weight of his secret to me —a burden I would gladly help him hold—until the weight and heaviness became relief.

There was a fine balance when someone had just revealed something profound. I wanted him to feel comfortable and give him a second to breathe. And the best way to do that was to carry on with some normality.

"Do you have a strainer?" I asked.

He blinked. "Uh, sh . . . sure." He looked through a cupboard or two and came up with the colander like a trophy.

I stirred the ragú sauce, then filled the big pot with water. "I cleaned all the cookware and I already made a bit of a start on tidying up your storeroom," I announced. "Hope you don't mind."

He was leaning against the kitchen counter, his hands shoved in his pockets, chewing on his bottom lip. "Oh no, I don't mind. I should apologise. I, uh, I've been meaning to get to that."

"I know. I found another to-do list in there. *Tidy the pantry* was on the list. I assume you went in there to start, found something else, and got sidetracked."

He smiled, kind of. "Uh, probably." Then he shrugged. "From memory, it was the vent in the ceiling. It needed to be cleaned, so I did that. Then I took the ladder back to the barn and decided the tool rack needed some work, and then once I took all the tools off, I realised I needed new angle grinder discs so I made a trip to town, and that's generally how things go for me."

I chuckled. "When we have dinner, we can make a list of the menu plan and all the things we need to get food-wise, and we can make a list of anything that needs doing before guests arrive. You said one client noted a low-cholesterol diet?"

"Yes. A Mr. Cantrell."

"That's easy. I can discuss a few options with him when he gets here."

He nodded, distractedly. "Yeah, that sounds good."

"I came out to my parents when I was fifteen," I said, adding a pinch of salt to the pot of water. "I told them I had a date and we were going to the movies and asked if my mum could pick my date up on the way. Of course she said yes. Out walked a guy and he got into the back of the car with me, kinda shy and nervous, and that was that. They absolutely knew beforehand, or so they told me afterwards." I opened the box of pasta. "I just didn't think I needed to make an announcement about it. If I had been dating a girl, I wouldn't have said, 'Hey, I'm straight,' and so it should be the same for us, right?"

Cass nodded slowly. "But it's not."

"No, it isn't. It should be, though. I was lucky, however. My parents were fine with everything that went on in my life." I smiled at him. "My decision to forego college and go to culinary school, and my decision to stay here when they went back to Australia."

I checked the water to find some bubbles on the bottom of the pot, so I tipped the pasta in.

"How about you? You said you'd never told anyone?"

He shook his head and shoved his hands back in his front pockets. "Nope. My wife and my parents."

I stopped what I was doing and walked over to stand in front of him, to look him right in the eye. "That can't have been easy."

"It was the hardest thing I've ever done," he said softly. He let out a long breath through puffed cheeks. "I knew I liked guys from when I was just a boy. High school was . . . well, high school was tough. I was the star quarterback on our high school football team, and I was dating Kendra, the prettiest girl in school. She was a cheerleader, of course, straight-A student, great family. We dated for years. There was pressure for us to get married right out of school. Hell, her dad wanted me to put a ring on her finger before we graduated." He shook his head and sighed. "I knew I liked guys. There were a few times in school, with other guys in the team, you know . . . in the showers."

I felt my eyes go wide. "Really?"

He laughed. "Oh yeah."

"I thought that was some urban legend or porn fantasy," I said. "It certainly never happened in my high school."

Cass's smile faded. "But being gay wasn't an option for me back then. I couldn't have done it. I wasn't brave enough. Ren was. He was out and proud, and his dad never treated him any different."

"Ren from the hardware store?"

He nodded. "A few of the fathers in town said some not-nice stuff about Ren at a football game once, and Ren's dad ripped right into them. And I knew then my dad would never have done what Ren's dad did. He'd never have defended me like that. And I heard my mom and dad talking about Ren one time and they acted like they didn't mind, but oh boy, were they ever so glad I was with Kendra."

I gave his arm a squeeze. "I'm sorry."

He was quiet for a second, maybe lost in some long-forgotten memory. "So I pretended. For years, I pretended, and I played the part everyone wanted me to play. We got married, we bought a house, we had two kids."

Well, shit.

"I was going to be the best husband and the best dad, and I was lying to myself every day."

I ran my hand up his arm and squeezed his shoulder. "You did what you needed to do."

"I shouldn't have lied to Kendra." He shook his head, this time glassy-eyed. "She was the best. She still is. She's a great mom, she's a wonderful woman. Strong and brave, and I will always love her. But I broke her heart, and that's on me. I hurt my kids, and I hurt my parents. That's on me too."

Fucking hell.

Okay, so I noticed two things at once. The first was, he didn't have anyone in his life he could tell all this to. And second, he really *needed* to tell someone.

"You can't blame yourself for that," I tried.

"Yes, I can. And it's fair. I did hurt them. I knew it would hurt them and I did it anyway."

"You'd have been miserable forever if you hadn't."

He met my eyes. "Whose misery is worse? Mine or theirs?"

"Theirs will ease, and so will yours."

He sighed. "Maybe one day."

I stirred the pasta and turned the sauce off. "Can you get out two bowls please?"

He did that, then grabbed the cutlery while I was serving up dinner, and we sat at the long dining table to eat.

"Well, this looks amazing," he said.

"I'd prefer to cook the sauce for hours and let the flavours really do their thing," I said, tasting my first forkful. It wasn't too bad.

Cass groaned as soon as he tasted it, the sound quite loud in the silence. Then he shovelled in another forkful and closed his eyes, clearly enjoying it. He chewed and swallowed, taking a sip of water. "Oh my god. Do you eat like this all the time?" he asked. "I mean, do you cook fancy food like this all the time?"

It was hardly fancy.

"I tend not to eat much when I'm working. Being around food all the time leaves me not too hungry." I swirled a ribbon of pasta around my fork. "And then when I'm off work, the last thing I want to do is cook. So I usually end up frying up some ramen with kimchi and egg, or some udon with a peanut sauce, or a quesadilla. Anything that takes five minutes."

Cass chewed thoughtfully. "Well, those sound fancy to me. The one thing I do miss about living in a bigger town is the variety of food options."

"What do you cook for dinner when it's just you?"

He made a face. "I'll cook a steak and boil up some potatoes and vegetables or make a soup. Sometimes, if it gets late and I've been busy, I'll just have some eggs on toast. Or soup."

"That doesn't sound too bad," I offered.

"Because I didn't tell you about the frozen pizza and frozen chicken tenders," he replied with a smile. "Or how sometimes when it's freezing cold outside and I get in late, sometimes I'll make a batch of creamy oatmeal and mix in some stewed apple."

I laughed. "Well, that sounds . . ." I made a face.

"It's good," he said. "Don't knock it until you try it. When you're frozen to the bone, a huge bowl of steaming hot oatmeal and stewed apple with cinnamon sugar will fix you right up."

"It actually doesn't sound too bad."

"My gramma used to make it when we were little. My cousins and I would be out playing in the snow most of the day and she'd bring us in, sit us by the fire to dry, and feed us that."

"Sounds like a nice memory," I said. "I love how we associate food to certain memories or people. My nan used to make a caramel tart that reminds me of summer barbeques in my parents' house back in Melbourne. I can feel the sun on my skin and smell the insect repellent."

Cass laughed. "Nice."

I chewed my mouthful and swallowed. "And even with her recipe, many have tried to make it, myself included, but it never tastes the same."

He smiled. "It never does."

"I kinda think she left something out of the recipe she wrote down on purpose, so no one could make it as good as her."

That made him smile, but we ate the rest of our dinner in amicable silence. "There's more if you want it," I offered.

He patted his belly. "I'm so full. But thank you. I think that was the best pasta I've ever eaten."

I went to take the plates but he stopped me, quickly getting to his feet. "I'll clean up. You cooked. It's only fair. And you can show me how to clean those pans."

Well, if he wanted to wash the dishes, I wasn't about to stop him. It was a good time to start the lists we needed to make. I grabbed the notepad I'd found in the pantry, and I watched Cass's back as he filled the sink with hot water.

He'd really been alone all this time. He came out of the closet by himself and hadn't had anyone to talk to about anything. He'd opened up to me, and at first I thought relaxing him into the conversation was a good idea. But maybe I needed to make a bigger deal of it.

The list could wait . . .

Standing beside him, I picked up a tea towel instead and dried as he washed. "And how are your folks now? Earlier, you said they just pretend you didn't say what you said?"

He made a so-so gesture. "I think they were shocked, and

they were concerned about Kendra and the kids, which is fair enough. I think in the beginning they thought we'd end up back together, or it was just a phase." He ran his hand through his hair and laughed, embarrassed. "It's not like I've been seeing anyone or brought any guys around to meet them. So they've never seen me be gay, if that makes sense."

I nodded. "It does."

"Now when I see them or if they come here, our conversation is usually about the kids or about what needs to be done at the house. Dad helped me with some fencing last summer and I thought for sure he was going to ask me something totally embarrassing." He shrugged. "But nope, not a word. So they're not against it, per se. But they're not baking rainbow cookies or organising any local pride parades, if that's what you mean."

"So your mom didn't enter you in America's Gay Bachelor?"

He snorted. "Uh, no."

"Well," I said, taking the soapy plate from him before he could put it in the rack. "I'm assuming you didn't have to sit through the mortifying parental attempt at the safe gay sex talk when you were a teen."

He turned wide-eyed, aghast. "God no. Did you . . . have to sit through that?"

"Yep. My dad floundered for a solid ten minutes, beet-red, and began talking about respecting my body."

Cass grimaced. "Oh, he didn't?"

"He absolutely did. Then he sputtered about how the male body was different to the female body."

Cass's mouth fell open. "He did not."

I laughed. "He did! And before he could give himself a brain aneurism, I told him I knew all about it; there was nothing he could tell me that the internet already hadn't.

He threw a box of condoms on my desk and bailed, and that was then, and remains to this day, the most excruciatingly painful day of my life."

He laughed. "Wow."

"I was fifteen. I hadn't even so much as kissed a boy by then, let alone done anything the internet had shown me."

He laughed again, a deep, rumbly sound. "I never looked on the internet for anything gay when I was at school. I was always too scared someone would see my search history or find out somehow. I did when I was older, of course." He mumbled the last part, as if watching porn was a bad thing.

"Oh, believe me, I watched all there was to watch between the ages of fifteen and eighteen. I'm surprised my dick didn't fall off with all that tugging."

He laughed so hard he had to lean on the sink. But then he said, "High school was the most guy action I've had. Well, the most consistent, anyway. That's kinda sad, isn't it?"

"Not at all. There's no quota for a gay qualifier." Then something clicked. "Wait . . . you in high school, fooling around in the showers. Was that with Ren from the hardware store?"

He blushed like a tomato. "I do not kiss and tell."

I laughed. "You don't have to. Your face says it all."

He chuckled and put a soapy spoon in the drying rack. "It wasn't just him. There were a few of us. We just used to joke around that it meant nothing. A hand was just a hand, right? Someone else's was better than your own."

"Did it mean anything?"

He shook his head slowly. "Nah, not really. It was just fooling around. But I knew I liked it way more than anything I did with Kendra. It felt better, more natural to me. Not that I told anyone that."

"Well, we might have just discovered why Hamish isn't your number one fan. You were getting action with his man long before he was."

Cass shook his head but didn't smile like I was aiming for. "We were just kids, and it was a long time ago."

I wasn't sure if that was the whole truth, but I decided to let it go.

"So, has there been anyone since you came out?"

His cheeks tinted pink. "No one permanent. Just casual stuff."

"Hook-ups? Like from Grindr or something? In this town?"

He scoffed. "Uh, definitely not in Hartbridge. If I go to Billings, then yeah, hook-up apps come in handy. But that hasn't happened much. Like maybe three or four times in two years. Which is kinda lame, right?"

"No. Not at all."

He shot me a look that told me he didn't agree. "Kinda feel like I'm doing the whole gay thing wrong."

I reached out and patted his arm. "You're doing it perfectly. There's no right or wrong way, and you need to go at your pace. All that gay shit you see on Instagram is fake and unrealistic, and don't even get me started on porn. But equating gayness to the frequency of sex isn't fair."

He baulked. "Oh no, I just mean . . . I just meant that I finally came out after years of torturing myself, and I ripped my whole life apart—and the lives of everyone in my life—so I could be the real me, and I haven't . . . nothing's changed." He shrugged. "Except now I'm living apart from my kids, I made my ex-wife a single mom, and I'm still not seeing anyone or making any effort, I guess. I don't know."

Oh man.

Now I put both hands on his shoulders, turned him to face me, and waited for him to look me in the eye. "Everyone's story is their own. You're not doing anything wrong. If you want to put yourself out there, then that's great. Not sure where the closest town is, but maybe we could look online for a LGBTQ+ support group, or a rainbow club, or whatever they have. And if you can't find anything, then maybe you could start something."

He looked horrified. "Me?"

"Sure. Why not?"

"I don't know how to do anything like that."

"Um . . . Cass? You run a B&B. You know exactly how to host people. Well, I hope you do. Because you have people turning up in three days."

He laughed. "I guess."

"You don't have to do it here, though you certainly could. Host a lunch and a coffee afternoon for any LGBTQ+ folks. Once a month or something. They could stay the night, drum up some business. You could hold gay movie nights and get a projector screen for the rec room and play foreign gay films and everyone could sit in bean bags and eat fresh-made popcorn."

He blinked with a little shake of his head, as if the idea blew his mind. "I never thought of doing anything like that."

"It's food for thought, anyway. Something you could consider." I gave him a smile. "Have you got many booked in after the holidays?"

"A few. In January. I don't expect things to pick up until spring, to be honest. Winter's always the quietest. Hartbridge isn't a ski town. Fishing and hunting is big in the warmer weather."

I'd worked in enough hotel kitchens to know how that worked. "Oh, sure."

We finished in the kitchen, then Cass went to check on the fire, so I followed him with my notepad and perched up on the couch while he stoked the embers and added a piece of wood.

"Okay," I began. "So, Christmas menu." I tapped the pen to the paper. "What were you thinking?"

Cass's plan or ideas for the Christmas menu were actually pretty good. He'd at least had the foresight and initiative to order in meats and a supply of fruit and veg and different breads from the market. There was still quite a list of grocery items we needed to get, but the main things had been ordered in advance. After a bit of back and forth, and him wanting my input on most of it because I was the one cooking it, we had a meal plan, a menu, and a whopping grocery list.

He was a bit of a paradox because on one hand, he was super organised and very efficient. And on the other hand, there were things left half-done or not done at all.

"I think you have all the equipment I need," I said.

"I can't take the credit for any of that. It was mostly all my great-aunt's. My mom told me it might be worth something."

I gasped. "Well, you can thank your mom. Most of it's worth a fortune."

He smiled and fell into the recliner with a tired groan. "What else you got there on your list?"

I held the list to my chest. "I love lists. Not unlike your to-do lists, but ones we will actually finish."

"Ouch."

I chuckled. "I admire your tenacity in writing as many as you did. I think I've encountered three half-done lists in my afternoon here. In various locations all over your house, including the barn."

One corner of his mouth pulled upward. "I have no problem in starting 'em. It's just finishing 'em that's the problem. And you see, there's some jobs I start but I think 'that's an inside job, I can do that at night or if the weather's bad.' So I leave those jobs and get the outside jobs done while the sun's out. Then the inside jobs get left out or completely forgotten because ten other things needed to be done."

I got up, notepad in hand. "Come on, we'll do a walk-through of all the rooms and note the things that need doing. That way we can get anything we need when we go into town."

Cass looked up at me from the recliner like I'd lost my mind, so I walked over and held my hand out. "Come on. Get up. We've got stuff to do."

He smiled at me and took my hand.

CHAPTER SIX

CASS

JAYDEN'S HAND fit in mine like no one else's ever had. It was warm and a little rough, and the weirdest thing occurred to me.

I'd never held hands with a man before.

I'd done all kinds of things in bed, sure. But held hands? Never.

It made my heart hurt a little.

"You okay?" he asked. He'd pulled me to my feet and I must have been standing there for a beat too long.

"Oh sure, I just . . ." I shook my head. "You know, never mind."

He cocked his head. His eyes were kind and encouraging. "Tell me."

I was certain my whole face was bright red. "I realised just now that I've never held hands with a man before."

Jayden stared at me in utter disbelief. "You . . . never . . . ?"

I shook my head and laughed it off. "I've never dated a guy. And the guys I hooked up with weren't the hand-holding type, if you know what I mean."

It was weird and probably way too much information, telling him all these things about my private life. But I'd never had anyone I could talk to about this kind of stuff. Once I started, I couldn't seem to stop.

I could be gay in front of him. I could talk about guys, about hooking up, and first gay experiences, about how it all felt, and I'd never been able to really talk about that with anyone. It was invigorating and enlightening.

And Jayden didn't seem to mind one bit.

He grinned and snatched up my hand again, twining our fingers, and pulled me toward the hall. "First room first," he said, opening the door. "Let's have a look."

This was crazy.

He could have been leading me to go look at a rotting animal carcass and I'd have gladly gone with him.

Because him holding my hand was quite possibly the best feeling in the world.

I was light-headed, giddy even. Which was stupid. It felt like my first ever kiss, or my first time having sex with a guy. Maybe it was even better than that. There was no fumbling and awkwardness. Jayden held my hand with certainty and purpose.

I was nervous and . . . happy.

Like I said, crazy.

Don't think too much of it, Cass. Just enjoy it for what it is.

"Okay, so this room looks fine," Jayden announced. "Actually, it looks great. Did you furnish all these yourself?"

The room was one of my favourites. It had white and pale lemon colours, a white iron bedframe, gorgeous framed citrus pictures on the wall.

"I call this the lemon room," I said. "And yes. I did this. I did all of them."

He turned to look at me. "You did? Cass, this is beautiful."

"Thank you."

He took my hand again and pulled me across the hall and opened the door. "The library." But we didn't stop at the door; he walked us in. "Okay, so it's beautiful. But the cabinet in the corner needs to be finished."

He dropped my hand and wrote down things on his notepad.

My hand felt oddly empty and cold. I rubbed my thumb into the palm, but the feeling of his hand was gone.

"Anything else in here you want to get done?" he asked.

"No, just the cabinet. The door wouldn't latch and one of the hinges wasn't much good. The door doesn't shut well, but it's an easy fix, and I have the parts in the barn."

"But let me guess," he said with a smile. "You went to the barn to get what you needed and found something else that needed fixing first."

He didn't even give me time to roll my eyes. He simply took my hand again and led me to the next room, and the next, which was the room I hadn't finished.

He seemed to be doing some math in his head. "How many bedrooms do you have available to guests?" he asked.

"Six, but you're in one, so that leaves five."

"And you've got five couples coming?"

He wrote something down, then opened the next door and looked around. And I was glad he was doing this, helping me get organised.

But I just wanted to hold his hand.

He gestured to the wall. "Cass, people are gonna be sleeping in here in three days."

He was referring to the wall with the window. "It's just that section," I explained. "The other walls are done. I had to repair the window, which meant repairing the architraves, and so then I had to patch up the drywall. It's not a big job." I shrugged. "I will need to wash all the linens before I make the bed though. And hang the blinds."

"We can do this first thing tomorrow," he said. "Actually, we could probably give it one coat tonight. We probably should."

I'm not sure where he got this *we* business from. "You don't have to do that," I replied. "I didn't bring you here to help me with the finishing touches. I just got a bit behind, but it's only small stuff. I can knock all this over in a day."

"But tomorrow you have to finish the road sign, which I'd imagine is gonna take some time. We need to go to the grocery store tomorrow as well, which I'll need your help with, so if you help me, I can help you and we'll get it done faster. Plus, to be honest, I think you're gonna need me to help you to get it all done. As long as my kitchen's organised and I have all the food, I'm free to help. I can start on prep tomorrow and get a good head start."

Prep?

"I'm sorry, some what? You want to start on PrEP?"

He blinked, then laughed when he realised what I meant. "No! I mean, yes, I've taken PrEP before, but that's not what I'm talking about. I meant prep, as in preparation, which is doing all the stuff that can be done days in advance. Pharmaceutical PrEP is a different conversation."

I could feel my cheeks heat. "I thought our conversation had taken a bit of a leap there. Sorry, I didn't mean to just blurt it out like that."

Jayden laughed. "Don't be sorry. I have no qualms in you asking or answering any questions about that kind of stuff. Did you want to ask me anything?"

Boy, that was a loaded question, and one I was not

prepared for. I didn't need a mirror to know my face had gone nuclear red. "Uh, I can't think of anything off the top of my head."

He smiled widely but thankfully took some mercy on me. He nudged me with his shoulder. "Don't be embarrassed. Come on, let's go take a look at the next room."

We checked the other rooms and noted anything that needed attention. "Oh, I do love this one," he said, taking in the dark berry colour scheme. "It could have been overdone but you've got it just right. Not that I'm an expert, but this is so well done." He shot me a bewildered look. "And you decorated all these rooms by yourself? How?"

I put my hand to my chest. "Well, firstly, I'm gay."

That made him laugh, and it felt *so* good to just say that so flippantly.

"And secondly, I'm also one of the design executives for the Eurythmic Press Magazine line." Eurythmic was the umbrella media company that produced several leading national magazines.

He stopped, and he stared. "You are not."

I chuckled. "I am."

"And you never mentioned that before now? I've been prattling on about colour schemes like I would have the first clue, and you let me!" He playfully shoved my shoulder. "How do you fit that in with all the work you do here?"

"At the moment, I have two weeks' leave. But I also work remotely. Have done so for years now. I have to go into the regional head office a few times a year." Which would coincide with my random hook-ups if he wanted to connect the dots. "And having flexibility means I work when it suits me. And most of the work I've done inside the house I did at night, usually. Maybe do some urgent stuff if it comes up, if no one else can do it. And there are always deadlines, but mostly now I just oversee all the hard work. And I can get a lot done in three days, uninterrupted."

He let out a low breath. "Well, it explains your impeccable taste in décor. And how you knew what food and produce to order, and your menu plan was fairly solid, not gonna lie."

"We've run a lot of dinner party plans and holiday cooking specials in all our magazines over the years."

He was smiling, but he shook his head. "I cannot believe it. That's amazing."

"My work has given me the freedom and the financial backing to get this place right. I want to do it right from the start."

"Well, I think you're well on the way." He held up his notes of odds and ends that needed to get done. "But this here is all the more reason for me to help you get stuff done. I can't build anything and I wouldn't like my chances on fixing a door hinge or making a road sign, but I can do other stuff to help out. Like I said, I'm good at organising and cleaning. And at the end of the day, you're paying me to work."

"I'm paying you to cook and prepare food, not help me around the house."

Jayden shrugged. "Well, that's up to you. If you want to work sunup till midnight every day while I sit there twiddling my thumbs waiting for jellies to set or a roast to cook, you can. You're paying me either way. But . . ." He looked me in the eye. "When you have hired help offering to help, maybe let them."

He had a very good point. "I'm not very good at delegating . . ."

He smiled. "So you're a control freak, is that what you're saying? Because that's what I'm hearing."

I found myself smiling back at him. "Maybe. A little."

He rolled his eyes. "Look. You're the boss. I'll do as you want, but I *am* offering to help. I will tell you if something is beyond my capabilities, but if two sets of hands get the work done twice as fast, then why not utilise that while you have it?"

"Okay, okay," I relented. "Normally people don't argue to have more work, just so you know."

He grinned. "Well, I'm not most people."

I can tell that already.

He shivered and rubbed his hand on his arm. "It is cold down this end of the house."

"Did you turn the heater on in your room?" I asked. "I should have told you, it's probably best to turn it on early because it does get colder at this end of the house."

"No, I didn't. I should do that now. I don't sleep too well if I'm cold."

We crossed the hall and he opened the door to his room. His suitcase was now under the bed. I assumed his clothes were in the closet and drawers. A jacket was thrown on the bed. Some shoes were neatly toeing the wall.

He was very tidy and organised.

He pointed the remote control at the heating unit and it came to life, but then he picked up the notepad again and smiled at me. "Okay, now we can go through the other end of the house and see what needs doing."

But that wasn't all.

He held out his hand for me to take. "Did you like holding hands?"

I looked at my feet before I found the courage to meet his eyes. I ignored the fact my face felt like it was on fire and how I was sure some butterflies had exploded to life in my belly. "I did, yes. It was . . . nice."

His smile broke into a grin. "I never would have thought you were the blushing kind."

I groaned and tried to turn away, but he quickly grabbed my arm and laughed. His hand slid down my arm until our fingers entwined. It sent a trail of sparks through me, but he just laughed as he pulled me out into the hall.

"Holding hands *is* nice," he said as we walked hand in hand.

Was it weird? A bit.

Was it better than nice?

Yes.

"So underrated," he added. "How quick we move on from holding hands and sitting close. As soon as . . . other things enter the chat, the basics are forgotten. And that's a shame."

"Enter the chat?"

"Yeah, you know . . . when other things are introduced."

"I thought that's what you meant, but I wasn't sure. Is that an Australian thing?"

"No, that's a twenty-something-year-old thing."

I stopped walking. "Are you calling me old?"

He laughed, a free and happy sound. "No."

"But you're right, holding hands is . . . well, it's better than nice. It's a comfort, a connection, I guess."

"Yes, a simple but understated connection," he repeated happily. "Come on, let's get through this list so I can go to bed. It's been a long day and I want to start early tomorrow."

I'd forgotten he drove here this morning, that he'd packed up his car and left his old life behind.

"Yeah, shoot. Sorry."

He made notes of all the things that needed tending to in the formal sitting room and in the rec room, and his list was getting longer and longer. But he shuddered. "Ugh, it's a bit cool in here. I can see why you block it off when it's just you here. It's a lot of house to keep warm."

"It is. The furnace works well to take the chill off but I'll still have to bring in wood for all the separate fireplaces tomorrow. It just brings a cosier heat."

"I'll add it to the list," he joked, but he wrote it down.

"Let's go back to the family room and the fire."

"Good idea."

I closed the doors off behind us and Jayden went and sat on a couch by the fire, his feet curled up underneath him. "Want some hot chocolate?" I asked. I don't know why I asked him that, but his face lit up.

"Oh my god, yes. Thank you!"

I set about making us hot chocolate, which didn't take too long, and when I brought his out to him, he had an odd look on his face. "Cass?" he asked.

"Yeah?"

"I've been trying to figure out what was missing or what was amiss, and I couldn't put my finger on it until now."

I looked around the room. "What is it?"

"Well, it's Christmas. And you have people coming to stay *for* Christmas. We have a Christmas menu planned and you said you want it to be festive. And I know Christmas is a few days away, but . . ."

"Uh . . . but what?"

"But you don't have one decoration. Not one. I don't mean to be rude, but where is your Christmas tree?"

CHAPTER SEVEN

JAYDEN

I DON'T KNOW why I hadn't noticed it before. It wasn't until we'd done a walk-through of all the little things that needed doing that I realised . . .

There wasn't one Christmas decoration.

He was opening his business for the first time *for* Christmas. He'd planned a menu, ordered food, all centred around a traditional Christmas, so it was hard to believe that he was opposed to decorating for it.

"Oh, there are boxes of decorations I brought over from the barn," he started, walking over to behind the couches. "I was going to put them up last night, but Kendra asked if I could take the kids the day after tomorrow and I thought they might like to help. I have three trees being delivered, and I wanted them to help . . ." He sighed and opened the flap on the first box only to let it fall closed again. "Last Christmas was our first as a . . . separated family. I didn't make it a great one. I mean, I tried, but I could have done a bit better; made it more about them. I want to do it better this year, involve the kids more."

Oh man.

"Tell me about them," I said. "Your kids, that is."

"Wyatt is eight and Charlotte is six." He smiled but it was tinged with sadness. "Wyatt loves any sport that involves a ball, a puck, or running or jumping. Before I laid the flooring in the rec room, he would practice hockey on the floorboards, and he thought having an indoor rink was the best thing ever. He was so disappointed when the new floors went in. Charlotte loves everything from unicorns to Transformers and baking and makeup and tractors and mud pies."

He clearly loved them and missed them very much.

"Wyatt looks like me but he's competitive like Kendra, and Charlotte's the spitting image of her but she's laid back like me. They're good kids."

My heart hurt for him. I didn't pretend to know the first thing about his relationship with his kids, or his ex-wife, but I could see he was hurting. I went to him and peered into the box that seemed to be full of wreaths. I put my hand on his arm and gave it a squeeze. "Well, then you need to make this Christmas decorating day with the kids the best ever. Just means we need to get everything done tomorrow so you have the whole day with them."

He smiled at me, and we were close enough that it felt a little personal.

"Thank you."

I sipped my hot chocolate so I didn't have to make eye contact. My heart was playing staccato as it was. "This is good hot chocolate."

Cass touched my upper arm and trailed his hand down to my elbow before he walked over to the fire. My skin burned in the wake of his touch, and he said something about adding more wood to the fire. My brain was scrambling to make sense of why he touched me like that.

It wasn't a reassuring squeeze. It didn't feel like a friendly gesture. It felt . . . intimate.

This was stupid.

"Jayden?"

I spun at the sound of his voice. He was now standing by the fire. "Everything okay?"

"Oh yeah, sure," I replied quickly. "Just more tired than I realised."

"You've had a long day."

I nodded. "I should go to bed."

He came over and took my empty cup, his fingers brushing mine, his body far too close and nowhere near close enough. His voice was low and lovely. "See you in the morning. Sleep well."

I met his gaze and regretted it immediately. His blue-grey eyes were a storm that I wanted to get lost in. I somehow managed to speak. "Night." Then I somehow managed to make my legs work and I walked, albeit light-headed, down the long hall to my room.

Turning the heater on had been a great suggestion. My room was toasty and warm. I brushed my teeth, washed my face, and climbed into bed.

I checked the time in Melbourne and called my mum. She answered the call with, "Oh, I was just wondering about you?"

"Hey," I replied.

"Did you get to your new place okay? You're staying there, yes?"

"Yep."

"So, what's it like?"

"It's probably the prettiest town I've ever seen. You know in the movies with those little country towns with the pretty shopfronts and lamp posts? Well, it looks like that."

"Oh, a small town sounds nice, Jay."

"Nice for a change, yeah." I wasn't sure if I could live in a town with a population of two hundred people. Not that I'd ever tried.

"And what's your boss like?"

I smiled at the ceiling. "He's kinda great."

There was a silence, and then a very suggestive, "Oh?"

I laughed again. "Mum, it's not like that." Even if I wished it was. "I'm not staying on here. I'm leaving two days after Christmas."

We chatted a little more but she could tell I was tired. "You get some sleep," she said.

"I will. I'll call you in a few days. I think I'll be busy for the most part, but I'll try."

"Okay, love. Speak soon."

I clicked off the call and put my phone on the bedside table. I was tired, that wasn't a lie. But I also needed to put some distance between me and Cass. He had eyes I could melt into, his hands were big and calloused in all the right places, and his smile did pleasant things to my insides. He was well built and a little bit older and possibly the sexiest man I'd ever seen.

He also had no hesitation in talking about his vulnerabilities and inexperience, and he spoke candidly about his marriage and kids. He really did seem like a 'what you see is what you get' kind of guy, even with some surprises at every turn.

He was genuinely a nice guy, and someone I'd like to get into bed, if I was being honest.

But this was a work relationship, and he had a lot riding on this. It was his grand opening, and the launch of his new Bed and Breakfast business. He needed to focus and not get involved with the only hired help he had.

This couldn't be some temporary sex thing; I needed to look at it from Cass's perspective.

Unless his perspective was that this was only temporary, and by his own admission of not hooking up often enough it might make it tempting for him to want to have some fun with me while I was here.

I certainly wouldn't mind if he wanted to use me for sexual gratification while he had the chance. A week of orgasms wasn't a bad thing. And maybe I'd be doing him a favour, giving him that gay experience he was so sure he'd missed out on . . .

I rolled over, pulled the covers up, and hugged the pillow. I could feel sleep creeping up on me, and my last thoughts were wondering if Cass would be interested in exploring his sexual freedom for the duration of my stay.

I WOKE up in a strange bed with strange light coming through the window and it took me a second to remember where I was.

Then I remembered the long to-do list of things that had to get done today, so I rolled out of bed and hit the shower. My morning wood seemed a little persistent, so I gave myself a few long strokes . . .

Then I remembered Cass and his steely blue eyes and breathtaking smile, and it made jerking off a lot more visual. Imagining his hands on me, his erection pressed against my arse . . . and then I remembered my revelation last night and wondering if Cass would be up for some fun when the work was done and the sun went down.

I hoped he was a top. He seemed like a top. In my head he was; in my fantasy he was. In my shower fantasy, he pushed me against the tiles and rammed his cock into me, filling me with his come.

I came so hard the room spun and my knees went weak. I was actually so spent and so weary and boneless, I considered going back to bed to sleep it off. As it was, it took me a few moments to pull myself together, but I dressed for the day and headed back to the kitchen.

There was no sign of Cass yet, and I wasn't sure if he wanted me to try and salvage the fire, so I didn't. I opted to cook us some breakfast and set about scrambling eggs and frying bacon. I couldn't find the toaster, but I managed some coffee. And I don't know if it was the smell of food that lured him downstairs, but he shuffled in just as I was serving it up.

"Morning," I said brightly.

He was showered, though he still looked half-asleep. He wore dark jeans and a grey sweater, and his socks were striped black and grey. He looked good.

Really good.

"Morning," he mumbled, one eye squinting a little.

"I couldn't find the toaster," I said, handing him a plate. "But the coffee's fresh."

He looked at the plate he was holding. "You cooked this for me?"

I chuckled. "Yes. We have a lot to do today."

We ate our breakfast and Cass was finally starting to wake up a bit by the time he'd finished his coffee. "Did you sleep okay?" he asked.

"Like a baby. The bed's comfy, the room was warm."

"Good."

"Did you?"

He was taken aback by my asking. "Uh, yeah. I just didn't get to sleep till late." I was about to ask him why when he volunteered, "I got the sign painted, though, which was good. Just need to add the writing this morning."

"I'll finish in the pantry while you do that," I said. "Then we can head into town for supplies. Did you need to see Ren?"

Cass nodded and drained his coffee. "Yeah. Thank you for breakfast. I wasn't expecting you to do that, honestly."

"You're welcome. I actually like cooking for people. I like feeding people." I took his plate and stopped. "That sounded weird. I don't like feeding them, I like seeing them fed. I like providing food. It's not a fetish."

God, why did I have to make it weird?

He snorted out a laugh. "Well, I don't judge anyone for what floats their boat."

Weirdness aside, I wasn't sure if now was a good time to bring up the possible-sex option, or even now in the light of day, if it was a good idea to bring it up at all.

"Well, that's good, about the no judging people." I stood there like an idiot with the plates in my hands. "Not that I have any reason for anyone to judge me. No fetishes to judge, at least. Unless judging me for not having fetishes is a possibility. I guess it is. I just like average sex. I mean, not average. I prefer great sex. And all sex is great, but some is really great. By average, I meant that I just like normal—normal's not the right word. Whose definition is normal anyway? What I meant to say was I wouldn't call my sexual preferences vanilla. Not at all. Variety and exploration can be a lot of fun, only if everyone's willing, of course—"

Cass was watching on in comedic horror as I kept speaking. "You okay?"

I turned six shades of mortified and went to the sink. "Yeah, yeah, I'm fine. Sorry. I didn't mean to say all that. I actually didn't mean to say *any* of that, so if we could just pretend it never happened, that'd be great."

I turned the tap on and squirted detergent into the water and began collecting the dirty kitchenware. Cass leaned against the kitchen counter, his arms crossed, but he was trying not to smile, clearly amused. "So," he hedged. "When you said not vanilla . . ."

"Ugh." With my hands on the edge of the sink, I hung my head. "I was trying not to make this weird, but it's safe to assume that's not working out too well for me."

Cass laughed. "Well, it probably wasn't a conversation I was expecting to have at breakfast."

"Yeah, sorry." I shut the water off and began washing up. "I . . . sorry."

He was quiet for a while, drying as I washed. "You seem nervous. Like you want to say something but you don't know how, or if you should—"

"Did you want to pretend with me?"

Shit.

Cass stared, his smile gone. "Pretend what?"

"Pretend to be . . . you know, gay."

His eyes narrowed. "I'm not pretending—"

"That's not what I meant. Sorry. I'm getting this spectacularly wrong. Let me try again . . ." I took a breath and tried to regroup. There was no backing out now. "Yesterday you said that you felt you were doing the whole gay thing wrong. You wondered if you were being true to yourself because you hadn't dated anyone or been with anyone, apart from a few randoms. Which is fine, and you're definitely not doing anything wrong, but I wondered if you wanted to practice with me. While I'm here. No questions, no strings. You're an adult, I'm an adult, no complications. I'm here for nine more days, that's all."

He was now staring at me as if I'd lost my mind.

"It doesn't have to be sex," I added. "It can just be holding hands. You liked that last night, and I did too. Happy to do more of that, if you want. We can watch movies and be all cuddly on the couch, if you want. It doesn't have to be crazy. Just experience dating a guy without the pressure or the hassle of meeting anyone, or getting to the dating stage. And it's totally okay if you don't want to. I won't be offended at all. It was probably out of line for me to ask, considering you're technically my boss, but I just thought . . ."

He still wasn't smiling, and he didn't appear to be considering my offer. He actually looked offended.

I turned back to the sink and began scrubbing the frying pan. "Sorry. Forget I said anything. It was just one of those stupid ideas that pop into your brain at 2am and they sound like the best idea ever until you say it out loud and you realise it wasn't."

He was silent and watched as I tried to scrub the coating off the pan.

"Jayden, I . . ."

Fuck.

"It's fine. I'm not offended and I respect your right to say no." I gave him the best smile I could manage. "It was just a stupid idea and I should have thought it through some more before just blurting it out like that."

"It's not a no. I mean, I wish it wasn't a no. I wish I could . . ." He ran his hand through his hair and sighed out a laugh. "Under any other circumstance it would be a very quick yes."

"But?"

"But work complicates things, and if something happens or goes wrong and you decide to leave, then I have a house full of customers and no chef. Or if things become awkward or if lines get blurred . . . I can't afford for this week to go wrong. It's launch week and I need it to go well." He frowned. "Sorry. I wish it were different."

I sighed. "I get it. I really do. I should have considered your position, and I'm sorry." I turned to face him, resting my hip against the sink, deciding to play it off with humour instead of awkwardness. "So can we just pretend this is not awkward at all, and actually, let's take it as a compliment, from me to you. Because honestly, who doesn't like to hear that you're totally bangable and sexy as hell? So please, accept the compliment and we can act like nothing happened."

He laughed. "Totally bangable?"

I rolled my eyes. "You're one hundred percent totally bangable and sexy as hell, and once you get this business up and running and put yourself on the official dating market, you'll have a line-up a mile long."

He blushed a warm pink that bloomed over his cheeks and ran down his neck, disappearing under his collar. "Oh well, I don't know about that."

"Well, I do." I took the tea towel from him. "You should go and finish making your sign, and I'll finish up in here. We have a long to-do list to get through. And we should probably get started on that room that needs some painting this morning before we have to head into town."

He smiled but it was weird. I'd made it weird, and the best thing I could do now was to forget the whole embarrassment. It was barely 7am and we did have a lot to do today. Not to mention the fact we also had nine more days of working together.

God, I was so stupid for propositioning him.

"Jayden." Cass's voice was deep and warm even from

across the room. I met his gaze, my hands wringing the tea towel. He chewed on the inside of his lip for a second, nervous. "Thank you for the compliment. And for what it's worth, I really do wish I didn't have to say no."

There was such sincerity in his voice, in his eyes, and I knew he meant it. He walked out and I turned back to the sink. My heart was thumping, my blood running hot in my veins.

He really did wish he could say yes.

I smiled.

WHEN THE STOREROOM off the kitchen was suitably organised, I went in search of Cass. I found him on the front veranda, holding the sign up against the wall. I could see then that there was also a huge plaque on the wall by the door with the name of the house on it. The writing on the plaque and the sign was a perfect match. He'd obviously made both.

"You're very clever."

He straightened when he saw me and smiled. "I wanted to be sure I did them the same."

It was white and had black writing, clear and precise. It looked professionally done.

Arabella Manor. Four miles.

"Does the name Arabella hold any significance?" I asked.

"It was a family name, somewhere back in the ages," he said. "The man who built it, my great-uncle, or third cousin four times removed, or whatever relation to me he was. He named it."

"It's a beautiful name. It suits this place."

Cass nodded. "It does."

"Both signs are great, by the way. You really do have graphic design experience."

That made him laugh. "Uh, yeah. What I do these days is all online, but drawing and signwriting is fun. I did the sign on the house last year. I wanted this new signwriting to match."

"It's perfect." I rubbed my arms. I'd been nice and warm inside and the air outside was cold. Even if the sun was out. And, I realised, stupidly, that despite the cool air, the sun was warming my face. It felt divine. And the view . . .

"Wow."

Cass followed my line of sight to the absolute vista of snow and trees and river, and the mountains across from us.

"It's pretty, isn't it?"

"It's the prettiest view I think I've ever seen."

He laughed again. "Well, considering you've travelled the world some, I'll take that as a compliment."

"I am just full of compliments this morning."

Aaaand I just had to bring up our earlier conversation. *Nothing like keeping things awkward, Jayden.*

"How about we finish off that bedroom?" I said. "The painting and the cutting in, or whatever it was you said needed doing. No time to rest today."

With a nod, he opened the door. "And you came outside without a coat or boots, so yeah, we should head inside."

"I didn't know where you were," I explained as he followed me in. "If you were in the barn, I'd have dressed appropriately."

"Sorry. I'm not used to having anyone here or anyone who might need to know where I am. If I'm going to the barn, I'll be sure to let you know."

"Do you like living here by yourself? I mean, when your kids aren't here."

"I do. It felt like a home the second I walked into it. Yes, she's old and she creaks and groans a bit when the weather changes, but I think this house was built as a labour of love and that sentiment is in her bones." He chuckled. "That probably sounds stupid."

"Not at all." I was dead serious. "You ever eaten food that was made with love, with ingredients that are cared for, and you can tell the difference. Nothing compares to something made from the heart."

Cass stared at me, holding my gaze, and nodded. "Exactly."

"I get it. And I can feel that in this house too." I clapped my hand on his upper arm. "Come on, we need to finish that bedroom. Then we can go into town."

He followed me down the hall and into the bedroom that still needed making up. "Are you always so bossy?"

I grinned at him. "Yes."

But we got busy without any fuss. Cass spread out the drop cloth, prepped all the brushes and paints, and produced a ladder from somewhere. I pulled out all the bedding and got it into the washing machine, then went back in to help Cass. And by help, I mean that I stood holding the ladder and passed him everything he needed as he cut in around the top of the window frame. The room, when finished, would have light cream tones with soft brown and white furnishings. "Can we call this the caramel room?"

He chuckled. "You can call it whatever you want."

I grinned. I got to name it! "The caramel room it is."

"You don't have to stand around and watch," he said. "I'm sure you have something else you'd rather be doing."

"I don't mind. I've finished the pantry. It didn't take too long. And anyway, the view here is great."

He looked down and out the window of the back of the house toward the barn. It really wasn't that great a view . . .

"Oh, I'm not talking about that view," I said, giving his legs a good up and down. "I'm talking about *this* view."

He rolled his eyes and half-heartedly tried to nudge me with his foot, but he wobbled on the ladder and I was quick to grab on. To the ladder, not to him.

He stepped down and I was quick to apologise. "Sorry, that was . . . out of line. That's twice in as many hours that I've been . . . inappropriate. It was just funnier in my head."

Cass smirked and handed me the paintbrush. "Payback. Get busy."

"You want me to paint?" I gawped at him. "Where people will see it?"

Now he laughed, but he poured more paint onto the roller tray and pointed it toward the ladder. "Up you go."

He began painting the part of the wall that needed painting, looking ever professional like he'd done this all his life. I climbed gingerly up the ladder, holding on for dear life with one hand and the little brush in my other. "What did you need me to do?"

Cass paused, roller on the wall, and he looked me up and down, then grinned up at me. "Oh, nothing. I just wanted to enjoy the view. You were right. It's really good."

Oh my god.

A sense of humour?

I pretended to be mad, waving the brush at him. "If I fall, tell the coroner my last words were 'That's actually funny and I probably deserved that.'"

He laughed as he held the ladder for me. "You did deserve that."

I pointed the brush at him and opened my mouth to tell him off when the washing machine beeped down the hall.

He grinned. "Oh, saved by the bell."

I faked a growl, shoved the brush out toward him, making him laugh as he took it. "Yes, you were."

I went to the laundry, smiling to myself as I put the sheets into the dryer and put the bed cover into the machine. I liked that Cass was more relaxed around me and that he could joke with me.

There was no awkwardness between us at all, and that made me very happy. And so relieved.

When I got back to the bedroom, Cass was almost finished painting, so I cleaned up around him and in no time, we were done.

A job that took less than one hour that he'd been putting off for weeks.

Well, it was done now.

"So, next thing on the list." I read over the things we needed to do. "Which would you prefer to do first? A trip to town to get all those groceries, or should we fix the cabinet in the reading room and unpack those few boxes?"

Cass didn't hesitate. "Town first. I need to get that sign up ASAP. I can fix the cabinet and unpack boxes at night."

"Okay, then town it is."

I found a coat and pulled on my boots, and when I found Cass again, he had his phone to his ear.

"Are you sure that's no problem? ... Okay, that'd be great. See you then."

He ended the call and smiled at me. "I just wanted to check with Ren if he could still help. He can come by later." His eyes widened. "Oh, that reminds me. I have a propane cylinder that needs a refill."

"Oh, okay."

He was still smiling at me.

"What?"

"You're wearing my coat again."

I tightened it around me. "It's warmer than mine. Want me to change it?" He had four hanging in the mudroom.

"No. Looks good on you."

His eyes did that cut-right-through-me thing. *Damn.*

"Got your food supply list?"

Relieved to break eye contact, I patted my coat pocket. "Sure do."

He locked up the house and I followed him out to his truck, trying to forget what that little exchange between us had been about while he grabbed the empty propane cylinder, and we drove into town. His truck was a few years old but very clean inside. It was bouncy but warm, and sitting up next to Cass was kinda fun.

I could see more too, being higher up but also not driving, and it was all somehow prettier than it had been the day before.

"Oh, look at that," I said, pointing off the side of the road. "Is that the river down there?"

Cass nodded. "It's a bit of a gorge. Some steep rocky inclines. It used to be all open up here when I was a kid. Anyone could go down there, and we'd jump off the highest part into the water. But then some kids went wandering in the dark, through the trees, and took a forty-foot dive. They closed it off after that. They still have access points to the river by the bridge if you want me to show you. It's really pretty down there and super busy in the summer."

"Super busy for Hartbridge. Which is probably twenty people."

He laughed. "Hey! We have more than twenty people."

I chuckled. "I'm just kidding. It's honestly one of the

prettiest towns I've ever seen. Well, what I saw of it yesterday. Which was all of the main street and the hardware store."

"Well, prepare yourself. You're about to experience the huge shopping complex known as Home Market. World renowned for its vast size and complex range of products."

I laughed, but then we drove into the town and along the main street. "Oh my god," I said. The town was pretty, yes. But it was getting a Christmas makeover. There were people on ladders adding more decorations, more signs, more tinsel and baubles to lamp posts, and potted Christmas trees decorated and gorgeous. I tried not to be too excited, but it was hard to rein it in. "This is the best thing ever!"

Cass laughed as he turned off Main Street onto Bridge Street. There were a few more shops this way. A hairdresser, an electronics store, a women's clothing store and a men's. And the huge shopping complex known as Home Market.

When Cass said huge and shopping complex, he meant a tiny convenience store. Or a Thrift Away. It was still cute though. It was an old building with an old-fashioned awning like it was the 1950s.

Wait . . . were those . . . "Are those automatic sliding doors? Very fancy."

Cass laughed and shut off the engine. "Got an upgrade a few years ago. They had an official opening day with a ribbon, and the mayor cut it and all the kids got free ice cream. It was quite a day for Hartbridge."

I couldn't help but laugh. "Did the mayor have those really big scissors?"

"Just normal size, I believe."

I sighed. "Such a missed opportunity."

Cass laughed and opened his door. "Come on. Much to do today, apparently."

Inside the store was more modern than I was expecting. Considering I was expecting to walk into the set of *The Waltons*, based on how it looked from the outside, it was way more twenty-first century inside. Cass laughed at my expression and I followed him up to the service counter.

"Hiya, Cass," the woman behind the counter said with a bright smile. She wore a denim shirt with the store logo on it and had her brown hair pulled up into a bun. "Got your order for ya, all ready to go."

"Thanks, Rosie."

She took a clipboard from under the counter, took out a piece of paper, and handed it to him. It was an itemised receipt, which he then handed to me. "This is what I've ordered. Wanna check it against your list?"

I gave a nod and took the receipt.

"Rosie," Cass said. "This is Jayden. He's running my kitchen these holidays. Anything he needs can just go on my account."

"Sure thing," she replied. "Nice to meet you, Jayden."

"Likewise." I looked at Cass and patted down my pocket. "Uh . . ." Reading me completely, Rosie held out a pen. I grinned at her. "Thank you."

What Cass had ordered was fairly extensive. He'd done a pretty good job. I crossed off on my list everything he had ordered, and there wasn't much left for us to grab in store. Once the clients arrived and our needs changed, I probably would need to come into town to grab a few things every day anyway.

But there were a few things I took the liberty of grabbing: two bags of super cheap onions that were on sale and some dry yeast and bread flour. "French onion soup and fresh bread," I explained.

Cass stared. "Can you just make that? Like, from scratch?"

I laughed. "I sure can." I walked around the fresh produce section. "Is there anything you would like me to cook? For you, maybe for dinner tonight? And what am I feeding your kids for lunch tomorrow? Will they be staying for dinner?"

"I don't expect you to cook for my kids. That's not your responsibility . . . I mean, you don't have to worry about that."

"Of course I do. It's what I do." I wasn't offended or hurt, because he obviously didn't want me to be inconvenienced. "I'm not sure what kids eat, to be honest. Do they like sausages and mash potato? Or dinosaur nuggets? Lasagne and salad? I can make homemade nuggets, which will be a lot healthier . . . well, it's real chicken at least."

"What about lasagne for our dinner tonight and the kids can have leftovers for lunch tomorrow. Is that okay?"

"That's easy. What else would you like?"

"Oh, that's . . . that's enough, surely."

I laughed. "You're really not used to having your own personal chef, are you?"

He snorted. "Uh, no."

I grinned at him. "Well, you're paying me. Use me to your full advantage." Then I realised how that sounded, and by the way his eyes widened, clearly Cass did too. "Okay, so that sounded wrong. Even though I offered that before too, but not because you're paying me. That makes me sound like a—" I leaned in and whispered. "—hooker."

He snorted.

"Which I'm obviously not. Because I couldn't even

proposition you properly, so trust me, I'm a much better chef than I could ever be a hooker."

Cass chuckled but he looked around to see if anyone could have heard. No one was even close, but he still blushed. "You did just fine. It was me who said no. And I still can't believe I said that, just so you know."

Okay, so we were talking about this now. In the middle of the produce section of Home Mart. "You're a man of strong convictions and will. I can admire that."

"I'm an idiot, that's what I am."

I laughed. "No, you're not. You made the right choice. You mentioned all the bad things that could happen, but also what if we did . . . do what I suggest, and it was so good that we don't surface for days because we can't stop? Or if we break furniture and your guests hear us?" Then I stepped closer to make sure no one could ever hear the next part. "Or what if you can't help yourself and bend me over the kitchen counter and someone walks in?"

His pupils blew out and he took a stuttered breath, but words failed him.

"That wouldn't be good for business," I said, pushing the cart over to the dairy aisle. "So it's probably just as well you said no."

I looked back to see Cass standing where I'd left him, glued to the floor, apparently. He put his hand to his forehead and shot me a disbelieving look.

I laughed and took out the list. "Did you order yoghurt? Pretty sure I saw it on your receipt."

He came over and took the papers out of my hands. "Yes, I ordered yoghurt. You can't just say something like that to me in the middle of the grocery store."

I met his eyes and smiled. "Where else would I ask you about ordering yoghurt?"

He sighed and handed me back the list. "You're terrible."

I snorted out a laugh. "Sorry. But you're not an idiot. You're a very responsible business owner who made the conscientious and sensible decision to put professional needs before personal. Even if it could have been mind-blowing—"

"Hi, Mrs Littlejohns," Cass said to an elderly lady pushing her cart past us. "All ready for the holidays?"

"Oh, yes," she said, stopping for a chat about the weather and Cass's parents.

I took it as my cue to leave and go check out the Christmas decoration aisle, which was where Cass found me five minutes later. "This is cute," I said, holding up a Santa doll. It was basically just all hat with dangly red legs and black boots and was meant to sit on a mantel or a hall stand. "Do you need any more decorations? This little tree is cute too."

"I have a lot of decorations," he replied.

I held up the tree. "But do you have a ten-inch miniature white tree with orange and black baubles, which was clearly left-over stock from Halloween? I'm all for repurposing and reusing, but this is next level."

Cass looked from me to the tree I was holding. "It's hideous."

I gasped. "I beg your pardon. It's amazing and would totally be the best." I checked the price tag. "Jesus . . . the best $12.99 you've ever spent."

He laughed, took the tree, and tossed it back onto the shelf. "What else do we need? Did you need to grab anything personal while we're here? Deodorant? Toothpaste?"

"Are you saying I smell and have bad teeth?"

He froze, horrified. "No, that's not what I meant. I just meant personal toiletries, if you needed to get them . . ." He shrugged and murmured, "You smell good, actually, and your teeth are perfect."

"I wore braces for two years in my awkward teen years. Worth the pain and the money." I gave him a toothy grin. "And no, I don't need any personal items. I have a decent supply of condoms and lube, so I'm all good."

He scrubbed his hand over his face. "That's . . . that's not what I meant either."

I laughed. "Maybe not, but now you know. If you change your mind about my offer."

He closed his eyes and sighed again. "Are you trying to wear me down?"

"Not at all. I respect your no." Which was true. I wasn't trying to coerce him. I mean, if he changed his mind at any point under his own volition, I wouldn't complain. "I thought we were just at the joking-about-it stage, you know, to stave off the embarrassment of the whole exchange."

He rolled his eyes and chuckled. "Do all gay men just talk about sex and condoms in the grocery store? Is this something I should have been prepared for?"

I laughed. "No, I don't think so. I'm just being facetious." I double checked my list. "I need to get lasagne sheets. I prefer the fresh ones and if I had time, I'd make them but the box ones are fine. And some ricotta, if you didn't order any. Once the guests arrive and we get a feel for demand, I can come back into town whenever we need. It's no big deal."

Cass smiled, but it didn't exactly sit right. He nodded, and when he spoke again, his voice was much quieter. "Sure."

After all the shit-talking I'd done since we got here,

something crossed the line. "I'm sorry, did I say something wrong? I don't have to come in every day. If I do, you can give me a budget, or I can work out a cheaper menu if you'd prefer. You said you got wholesale prices, yeah?"

He shook his head and laughed it off. "No, it's not the money."

"Then what is it?"

He made a face. "You just say *we* a lot. As in, you and me. When we get a feel for demand, whenever we need, what we do."

Well, shit.

"I'm sorry. I didn't realise that was offensive at all. I know it's your business—"

He snorted and shook his head. "No, Jayden. It's not about that."

I was confused.

"I like it," he added softly. "I like how it sounds, and I like how it feels."

Oh.

"Cass," Rosie called out from the end of the aisle. "Your order's ready to go."

He gave her a polite smile. "Perfect, thank you." He turned in my general direction but didn't look at me. "We should get going."

WE LOADED ALL the boxes into the back of Cass's truck and went to the servo . . . sorry, gas station, to get a new propane cylinder.

"You know, some things will always be Australian to me," I said, when it was clear Cass wasn't up for talking. "Like, this is a servo. I still don't think gas station in my head, even after all this time. Not even service station. And that there," I pointed to the next store over. "Is a bottle-o."

"A what-o?"

"A bottle-o. Short for bottle shop, or a liquor store, as you'd say here."

"Do you abbreviate everything?"

"Mostly. Like afternoon is arvo, and a liquor store we call a bottle-o, which is short for bottle shop."

"So you'd call Home Market a marko?"

"Definitely not. We call them a supermarket. Or we just shorten the name. Like Woolworths is Woollies."

He made a confused face. "You still have Woolworths?"

"Yep. It's a grocery chain."

He seemed to consider this for a second. "What predetermines which words get abbreviated? What is the deciding factor?"

"Not entirely sure but I think the frequency in which it is used is key." I shrugged. "There's no rhyme or reason. Like McDonald's is Macca's, and I still think of it as Macca's, even after all this time. But there are some things I think of in American now. Like server or sidewalk. Sometimes it surprises me that I think of that instead of waiter and footpath but it's how I know I'm becoming more Americanised. It's not just what I say but it's how I think. Maybe that's because I never really learned or said the word waiter before I moved here, so I never really learned it in Australia. I dunno. Accents in our heads are weird."

"You think in American?"

I snorted. "Yep. I'm beginning to."

He pointed out the front of his truck. "What's that?"

"A windscreen."

"You mean the windshield?"

"Yep. Windscreen."

"I actually meant the gas station. What did you call it?"

"A servo."

He laughed. "That's funny. I'm just going into the *servo*. Won't be long."

"Very funny."

He took the propane tank with him and he was back four minutes later with another one. He was smiling and he grinned when he saw me watching him. He lifted the cylinder into the back of the truck and climbed in behind the wheel, a cold burst of air coming with him.

"What's so funny?"

"Nothing. You ready to go home?"

Home . . .

"Yep."

Cass chuckled as he started the engine. "Ren's gonna be there soon. Said Hamish wanted to come out and see how you were settling in."

"Oh?"

Cass shrugged. "I didn't ask him to elaborate."

I wondered if that was weird or if it was a small-town thing. Like a welcoming thing, or maybe just because we were both Australian and gay. Or maybe I thought it was a little weird because I'd spent all my time in bigger cities where almost everyone had an ulterior motive and now I was cynical to think someone couldn't just drop by to say hello.

We unloaded the boxes from the truck, across the yard, through the mudroom, and into the kitchen. After the third trip, and with six rather large boxes spread out over the kitchen, I had to stretch my lower back. It seemed like a lot of food, but considering we were feeding five couples for five or six days, it really wasn't.

"Right, first box," Cass said, opening it.

"Ah!" I said, smacking his hand. "I'm doing this. I need to catalogue and double-check the list. I want to inventory and date whatever goes into the freezer, and I need to write on everything when we received it."

He stared.

"Do you have a Sharpie? I need to write the date on anything that we freeze."

"Um . . . yeah . . . somewhere." He disappeared, and by the time he came back with the Sharpie, I had three piles of neatly organised papers. He seemed scared.

"Stock receipts from today," I said, indicating to the first pile. "Stocktake of what items and produce you already have" was the second pile. "And this will be my daily quota sheet. How much I used, how much it cost, so at the end of every day you know I'm within budget and so we can see what needs to be reordered at a glance."

Cass was now staring at the papers. "You do all that?"

"Of course. All commercial kitchens do. Well, all good ones. Especially at hotels where there are many levels of management. Any chef or manager can walk in and know exactly what's going on, what needs to be ordered, what's been wasted."

He handed me the Sharpie. "I didn't even think of that kind of thing. I was . . . well, after the holidays, when things are a bit quieter, it was just going to be me doing all the cooking. Guess I didn't put enough thought into how to manage the inventory."

"You're doing just fine. We all learn on the job, and no one knows everything when they start."

"Well, I'm grateful."

The sound of an approaching car interrupted us. "That must be Ren and Hamish."

Sure enough, a truck pulled around the back of the

house. I followed Cass out through the mudroom onto the back deck just as Ren and Hamish were getting out.

"Hey, thanks so much," Cass said, walking out to greet them. I stayed on the deck, and after a quick hello to Cass, Hamish came my way. He was carrying a container.

"Hello again," he said brightly. He kicked the snow off his boots on the step, then gave me a wide smile. "I thought I'd come say hello while they go build a sign."

He sounded as interested in the sign hanging as me. "Come on in," I said, holding the door for him.

He held up the container. "These are for you."

"Oh."

"Don't get too excited," he said with a laugh. "It's just a little welcome gift; something to have with a coffee."

We took our boots off in the mudroom and I led the way out to the kitchen.

"My god," Hamish muttered. "How gorgeous is this place?"

"I know, right?" I replied. "He's done so much work."

"And it's huge. I had no idea until we drove up to it."

I walked into the kitchen first. "I had the same reaction when I got here and when he gave me a tour. There's a reading room the size of a local library, and a rec room the size of an average house." I gestured to the boxes from the grocery store. "Don't mind the mess. I have to get all this inventoried and put away."

Hamish put the container down on the kitchen counter and pulled the lid off. "I brought you some welcome cookies. Now, I know you're a chef and you're probably horrified, but it's a Christmas tradition Ren and I have. We bake Christmas cookies, and of course there's a hundred too many so I thought I'd bring you some."

Inside the container were some candy cane cookies,

some pinwheels, some Santas, and some stars. "They look great. I'll start the coffee machine. I not long ago turned it off so it won't take long."

He sighed. "I bought an electric kettle. I couldn't stand not having one. Ren hated it at first, but now he uses it all the time."

I laughed and stacked all the cold items into the fridge, marking each one off as I went. "How've you found Hartbridge?" I asked. "It's such a quaint little town."

"Isn't it gorgeous? I just love it here. My sister lives down in Mossley, which is like an hour's drive from here."

"Oh nice. I didn't know you had family here."

He nodded. "How about you?"

"Nah, my parents moved back to Australia."

"And you found yourself here," he said with a smile. "You might want to look out. Hartbridge has a way of collecting Australian men."

I put two mugs on the counter. "I'm only here for nine more days."

"And I wasn't supposed to be here at all. But I crashed my car and a very convenient blizzard found me stuck at a gorgeous man's house for the holidays."

"Sounds like a Hallmark movie."

Hamish laughed. "That's what I said! Complete with the gorgeous town, the gorgeous hardware store owner . . ." He smirked. "Kinda like the gorgeous B&B owner and the chef. Sounds a bit Hallmark-ish too, no?"

I laughed and poured two coffees. I handed him his. "Well, I might have propositioned him, put it on offer, if you know what I mean."

His whole face lit up. "And?"

"And he said no."

Hamish put his cup down slowly, his eyes wide. "Is he

insane? You're gorgeous! And you offered and he turned you down?"

I waved him off and sipped my coffee. "It's his business's opening week and I'm his one and only employee. He made the right decision."

Hamish took a cookie, and though he didn't say anything, his face said it all. He very clearly didn't agree, but he relented. "When you put it like that."

I took a candy cane cookie and bit into it. "This is good."

"Thanks. I don't think I'll ever understand the American tradition with Christmas cookies, but I don't complain because . . . well, cookies."

I smiled and washed down my mouthful with a sip of coffee. I didn't know if I should ask this, or if Hamish was the right person to ask, but something had been playing on my mind. "Tell me," I said. "What's the story with Cass? I mean, he's sweet and kind, but I feel like I'm missing something. He seems kind of . . . isolated. I don't know if that's the right word. Sure, he's been really busy here, working non-stop. But I think he really craves interaction with other gay people and he hasn't had any. Not by choice, I don't think. Just that he feels he can't? I don't know. I think he carries a lot of guilt for ending his marriage and breaking up his family. Maybe that's stopping him, I don't know." I was probably talking way out of school here, but I had to know. "Did something happen that I don't know about? Because he's told me a lot about himself, but I feel like there's something missing. I don't know why I care, to be honest, because I'm not staying in Hartbridge, but Cass just seems on the outer and a bit lost. And you and Ren seem like a great couple, but I get the feeling you don't like Cass and I just wanted to know why."

CHAPTER EIGHT

CASS

WORKING WITH REN FELT . . . nice. It just felt really good to be working alongside someone. We didn't talk a great deal. We didn't need to. We just got busy doing what needed to be done.

We'd driven to the corner where the sign would go and parked up off the road. I shovelled the snow away while Ren backed his truck in closer to the post so we could use the bed as a platform. And it wasn't until I began to attach the metal bracket while Ren held the cross-post arm in place that we had time to even speak.

"Are your ears burning?" Ren asked me. He craned his neck to rub his ear on his shoulder. "Mine are on fire, and I reckon Hamish and Jayden are the reason."

I laughed. "You think they're talking about us?"

"One hundred per cent." Ren laughed. "Well, Hamish definitely. He's probably telling Jayden I made the cookies wrong."

I snorted. "My ears feel okay at the moment . . ." I tilted my head. "No, wait. There it is. They're definitely talking about us."

Ren grinned. "So, how's Jayden finding his time here? I know it's only been, what? A day?"

"Good so far, I think. He's only here until after Christmas, then he's heading on to Oregon or Washington, or so he said."

I felt Ren's eyes on me but I pretended not to notice.

"He's gay, right?"

I looked at Ren then. "Ah, yeah."

"You don't think—"

"I turned him down."

Ren stared.

"He asked me if I was interested in fooling around for as long as he was staying, and I said no."

Ren was quiet for a few awkward seconds. "Why? I mean, if you don't mind me asking . . ."

"Because I'm his boss. Because it's my grand opening, and I didn't want it to complicate things. What if it all goes wrong and he decides to leave? I have ten people staying for a week. I need a chef. I can't—"

"Yeah, sorry. I get it. I didn't think of that."

"I wish I could. I told him I wished I could. He's cute as hell and funny, and he's kind. We can talk for ages and I'm out of practice with the whole 'getting to know each other' thing, but it's so easy with him."

"And he landed on your doorstep like some Christmas miracle?" Ren smiled at me. "Sounds familiar."

I sighed, long and loud. "I just don't know. Seems kinda cruel that he does land on my doorstep and I can't go *there* with him. Especially when he offered."

Ren grimaced. "Yep, that's cruel. How are the clamps?"

"Good." I tightened the last bolt. "Now we just need to drill them, fix the chain, then drill the U bolt. No one's stealing this sign."

Ren laughed, but he fixed the chain and the U bolt while I did more drilling.

"I should have gotten this done in the summer," I grumbled at my poor time management. "I really do appreciate your help. I couldn't have done it by myself and I know you're busy with the store."

"It's good to get out for a bit. Lunch times are always quiet, and Mrs Barton yells at me if I think she can't handle it."

That made me laugh. "She's worked there forever."

Forever was a stretch, but I remember her being there when we were in school. Ren and I never really talked about our high school days, considering what we did together. I certainly wasn't about to bring it up now.

"She sure has."

We fixed the hooks into the cross post and hung the sign. It was heavy but the hooks and chain should hold it. It looked really good.

The bolts might need to be fixed come springtime or summer, but for now it was a job well done. We packed everything up and got back into the warmth of the truck. The wind was starting to bite.

We headed back to my place, and after about a mile of silence, Ren scrubbed his hand over his face and sighed. "Can I offer some advice?"

I had a feeling he was going to offer it whether I wanted him to or not.

"Sure."

"You're in Hartbridge for good, right? No plans to move on? With your business and all . . ."

Not what I expected, but okay. "No plans to move for the next forty years at least."

He nodded. "Same. This place is my home."

"Same."

"So the chances of meeting someone are pretty slim, right?"

"I'd say non-existent. Unless they crash their car in front of your house."

He chuckled. "Or unless they answer a job posting and are staying in your house with you."

I groaned. "He's not staying for good, though. He's not even staying for long."

"So maybe just enjoy it for what it is," he said gently. "If you both know what you're getting yourselves into. I know it's not that simple. But an opportunity to be with someone doesn't come around too often in this town."

He slowed the truck and pulled into my drive, and drove up toward the house. "I know. I wish it were different. I told him I had no experience in dating a man. I didn't even know where to start, and he suggested we just do the basics like hold hands and cuddle on the couch." God, I couldn't believe I was admitting this to him. Ren, of all people. "Sounds stupid."

"No it doesn't. Sounds nice, actually." We drove around the back of the house and pulled to a stop. "It sounds to me like he's into you. And he did offer, so clearly he wants to." He shut off the engine. "Is that all there is to it?"

I chewed on the inside of my mouth and stared at the back of the house. "When he leaves, I'll know what I'm missing. Right now, I can guess. I can wish, and I can long for it. But I don't know what it's like, how it feels, or how much I want it. And if he shows me . . . when he leaves, I'll know then what I won't have again. I'll know what I'm missing." I shook my head, not really believing I just admitted that out loud. "Not sure I could handle that."

Ren was quiet. I'd made it awkward.

"Sorry, I shouldn't have just dumped all that on you." I undid my seatbelt and he reached out his hand to stop me.

"Take the chance. If it lasts a night or a week or a life-time, take the chance on happiness whenever you can. And if he does leave, then at least you had something good, no matter how long it lasts." He shook his head. "I dunno. I don't mean to tell you how to live your life, but I wasn't going to take a chance on Hamish. He was set to leave too. He was only staying for a few days. But look how it turned out? Taking a chance on him, on just a few days of fun, well, it turned out to be the best thing that ever happened to me."

I nodded woodenly. Our circumstances were different, but the sentiment was the same.

Ren offered me a grin. "Come on. We better go check what mischief these two are up to. Any guesses?"

"Well, I hope for Hamish's sake he didn't try to help Jayden in the kitchen because I tried that and he smacked my hand and told me to stop."

Ren chuckled. "Sure you're not married already?"

I couldn't help but smile at that. Jayden and I were familiar around each other, even after such a short time. There was no awkwardness or timidness. That was for sure.

We got our gear packed away and went inside to find the kitchen empty, though all the groceries had been put away. "Jayden?" I called out.

"In here," came his voice. "In the library."

"This way," I said, and Ren followed me. I had a fair idea what Jayden was doing in the reading room, and I assumed Hamish was with him. And I was right. Jayden was sitting on the floor beside one of the boxes with books pulled out, sorting them by the looks of it.

"I finished sorting the kitchen," he said.

"I wasn't allowed to help," Hamish added.

"Then I took the bed cover out of the dryer and made the bed in the caramel room," Jayden said.

Hamish nodded. "I helped with that."

"We still need to hang the blinds though," Jayden added. "I wasn't sure what you wanted done with the rolls of linoleum in the rec room, so we left that. I did unpack the two boxes of old board games and stuff, and we stacked them in the bookcase on the far wall. If that's not where you wanted them, I can move them. And then we started in here. I didn't touch the cabinet door," Jayden went on, making a face. "Because I am not handy like that at all, but I can sort and organise books."

"You didn't need to do any of that," I said. "But thank you. Both of you. I really appreciate it."

"It was fun," Hamish said. "This is a beautiful house."

I wasn't expecting a compliment from him, but it was very welcome. "Thank you. It's been a labour of love for sure. Almost done . . . well, I think there will always be something that needs work, but for now, it's almost done."

"This room is fantastic," Ren said, walking over to the chess set. He grinned at Hamish. "I should make us a chess board with different pieces."

"Did you get the sign up?" Jayden asked as he stood up and dusted his hands off.

"Yep, all done," I replied.

"Looks good too," Ren added.

"You two must be hungry," Jayden said, smiling at me. "Want me to fix you something to eat?"

"Ah, we can't stay," Ren said. "I have to get back to the store. But thank you for the offer."

"Another time," Hamish added.

I wasn't sure if he was being nice because he and Jayden were new friends, if it was because he was in my house, or if

I had imagined his hostility toward me over the last three years? But he seemed very amicable now.

"Oh, let me grab your container for you," Jayden said. "And thank you for the cookies. They were great."

We walked back to the kitchen where Jayden found the container and handed it to Hamish, but Ren was smiling as he took in the rooms. "Wow," he breathed. "It somehow hasn't changed one bit, but it's all brand new."

That made me so happy. "That is exactly what I was aiming for. Thank you."

"I can see where all the gear you bought from the store went, anyway. Man, you've done some work here."

I nodded, and it was hard not to feel a little proud. "You remember it?"

"I remember being here when I was about five," he said. "There was a huge playroom with a pool table and a wooden racing car track."

I laughed. "I remember that race car track. Come through here." I led him through the double doors into the family room and on to the rec room. "Here it is."

"Oh my god," Ren said. "Carter, this is . . . I remember this. But the floor was old boards."

I tapped my foot on the floor. "Still there, but too cold and too much work. If I wanted to keep the old floorboards, I was going to have to pull them up, re-insulate the under-floor, and re-lay the boards, and that was if they didn't sustain damage getting lifted. And once you start doing that kind of work, new building codes come into play and the list gets longer and a lot more expensive. It was just easier in the long run to lay new flooring over the top."

"Ah," Ren nodded knowingly. "Makes sense."

I'm sure Ren and I could talk renovations and home repairs all day long. He was the hardware guy, after all. But

I'd taken up enough of his time. "I better let you go or Mrs Barton will give me the stern brow next time she sees me."

Ren laughed. "The stern brow. I know it well. But yes, I should get back there."

We walked them out, thanked them again, and waved them off. Jayden and Hamish clearly got along well and I liked that they did . . . but Hamish was definitely nicer toward me and I wanted to know why.

"You must be starving," Jayden said as we walked back inside. "I'll make us some sandwiches and coffee. Hamish brought some Christmas cookies over." He shook his head. "It's some tradition he and Ren have, apparently."

He made himself busy in the kitchen and it got the better of me. I had to ask. "Did you say something to Hamish about me?"

He shot me a look, the buttered bread momentarily forgotten. "Why?"

"Because he was nice to me. He even smiled at me and spoke to me. Which is probably a first in three years."

Jayden layered on some turkey, some kind of relish, some green leafy thing, some cheese. "I might have said something—actually, I might have asked him something. And you were a topic of brief discussion, but it was nothing bad or anything like that, so please don't be mad."

I could hardly be mad when Ren and I had talked about him.

"I'm not mad. I just wondered, that's all."

"I asked him why he didn't seem to like you. I told him it was weird because you were so nice and lovely, and the other people in town I'd met seemed to like you, so I wondered why there was a chill factor when it came to Hamish."

"And what did he say?"

"He said it was nothing you'd done to him at all, and it wasn't anything personal. He said you'd once said something to Ren that was a bit off, but it wasn't really his place to say. That was all."

My heart sank.

I knew what he was talking about.

Goddammit.

Jayden shrugged. "But Ren certainly doesn't mind. He likes you just fine. So maybe Hamish was just being a bit overprotective of his man. Maybe he's the type to hold a grudge forever, I dunno."

"But he was nice to me," I said, my mouth a little dry. "So something changed, I guess."

"Well . . ." he said, cringing. "When I asked him what his issue with you was, I said I wondered why you seemed to be on the outer. I said, here you were, newly single, newly out of the closet, and Hamish—one of the only other gay people in town—treated you like you weren't in the cool club. Know what I mean? I wondered if you'd done something terrible and what I'd got myself into by working here," he said with a bit of a laugh. But then his smile faltered. "I told him you seemed lonely and isolated and a bit lost being newly gay and in a small town and all alone. Maybe that was out of line, sorry. But it's the truth. I mean, just because there are three out and proud gay guys in town doesn't mean you need to form a friendship circle or a gay committee club that meets over rainbow cocktails and episodes of *Drag Race*. But I just expected some empathy and compassion, that's all."

So that was a bit to unpack. I wasn't sure where to begin. "Oh."

"So yeah, I wondered if you'd done something so terrible that it warranted Hamish's attitude. But he said what he said about it not being his place to say, and I respected that. But he obviously thought about what I said some, because after we'd made the bed in the caramel room, he said he didn't realise your perspective. He said he should have realised you were a newborn gayby and he should have been more welcoming and inclusive. He said he hated the thought that he'd made you feel unwelcome in the gay community."

"Hartbridge has a gay community?"

"Well, it's you, Ren, and Hamish, that he knows of." He held up three fingers. "I said you don't have to become besties, but a little understanding might go a long way."

Okay, wow. I ran my hand through my hair, not sure what to say.

Jayden handed me a plate with a sandwich on it. "I'm sorry if I overstepped. I didn't mean to, but we were just talking and he seemed genuinely sorry. He was nicer to you when you got back, so hopefully something sank in." He frowned. "If you want me to call him and tell him to please forget what I said—"

"No, it's just . . . I don't know. I don't know if I like how much you told him about me, but you also defended me and no one's ever done that, so thank you? I think?"

He handed me a cup of coffee before sliding a plate of cookies in front of me. "He made us cookies. I'm really sorry if I spoke out of turn. I didn't mean to make you mad or upset with me. But honestly, you're a great guy and he could at least try being a little nicer to you. I just reminded him that it's not easy coming out and living your truth at any age, and you're here doing it all by yourself when the least Hamish could do is smile and ask how you're getting on."

I smiled at that, but the truth was a dark cloud overshadowing me.

"What I said to Ren, that Hamish didn't like . . ." I put my sandwich down, my appetite suddenly gone. "I have never told anyone this and I'm embarrassed to say it now. It was years ago, before Hamish moved here. I was still married but I was struggling with it, you know? Anyway, we came back here for my great-aunt's funeral. Me, Kendra, and the kids. I called into the hardware store for something . . . I can't even remember now. Something for my parents' place. Anyway, it was good to see him." I shook my head. "Not in any kind of affectionate way, just that he was someone who knew . . . he was someone I'd fooled around with when we were younger. He knew I liked guys, even if he never said anything, and he was out and proud, living a life I wanted so bad. It was stupid and wrong, but I went back just before he closed up and I asked him . . . I asked him if he would be interested in hooking up."

Jayden stood, listening intently.

"I was so confused and messed up. My marriage felt like a lie, and I was desperate to feel . . . right. Being with a guy would feel right, just for a few hours." I let out a sigh. "Ren said no, of course. I was married and it was wrong. He was so nice about it, and he told me if I wanted to talk to him about coming out, then he would happily help with that. But he wasn't about to help me cheat on Kendra."

"Oh, Cass."

"Maybe it was coming home, maybe it was staying at my parents' house, sleeping in my old room where I spent my entire teenage years staring at the ceiling wishing to god I wasn't gay. Maybe it was the funeral and the reminder that life is too damn short. But I went home and Kendra knew something was wrong. I sat her down and told her . . . everything."

I rubbed my eyes, not expecting to relive this whole ordeal today. Especially to Jayden, a guy I'd known for a matter of days. When I looked up, he was in front of me, his eyes full of concern, and he put his hand on my arm. "I'm sorry."

"So I'm guessing that's what Hamish took issue with. And fair enough. To him, I was married and looking to drag Ren into an affair. And I probably wouldn't like me much for that either."

Then Jayden put his hand to my hair, my face, my shoulder. "He doesn't know the truth. Don't be so hard on yourself, Cass. Like you said, you were struggling, and living a lie is pure torture. The road to finding yourself isn't always paved perfectly."

God, his touch was so warm, so welcome.

I sighed again, so mad at myself for saying no to him, wishing I could give in. Ren's words echoed in my mind.

"What's wrong?" he asked quietly.

I met his gaze. "I wish I could take you up on your offer. I wish I . . ."

"Do you need a hug?" It was a serious question, even though his eyes held some humour. "Because I'm sure that doesn't cross any boundaries. People hug all the time. And hugs are the best thing ever. I think you need a hug. Just a hug, nothing more."

He held his arms out a little, and so god help me . . . my whole chest ached with the need of it.

I tried to roll my eyes, as though this was stupid and I was placating him, but I opened my arms and he drew in like a magnet. Fast and wholly complete. His arms went around me and I almost sagged with the relief of it.

I slid my arms around him, and we were close. Our fronts were touching, melded against the other, all the grooves and angles fitting like puzzle pieces. I closed my eyes and inhaled deeply, drinking it all in. Him, his touch, being held.

I had no idea I needed it that much.

I didn't want to let go. I wanted to remember this moment, store it away in my mind, what it felt like, what he smelled like.

"You okay?" he murmured next to my ear.

Reluctantly, I pulled back, missing that contact immediately. "Yeah, I'm fine. I . . . guess I needed that more than I realised." I took a step back and let out a laugh. "You know, I'm not usually such a mess. I dunno what it is about you. I never talk about emotional stuff and yet, with you it just pours out of me. I'm sorry."

He put his hand to my face. "Don't be sorry. I like that you talk to me about that stuff."

I leaned into his touch and sighed. "God."

"Cass . . ."

"I talked about you to Ren today," I blurted out to stop him. I panicked, but it sounded like he was about to say something I wouldn't be able to turn down.

Jayden slowly took back his hand. "You did?"

I nodded. "You talked about me to Hamish, so I guess we're kind of even."

He seemed amused by this. "And what did you say?"

"I told him about your offer." I cringed, because that sounded bad. "That you offered to help me . . . not only in the kitchen."

He smiled. "Oh? And what did he say?"

"I'm pretty sure he thinks I'm an idiot for saying no."

That earned me a laugh. "Hamish said something like that."

"Oh good, so they both know." I laughed because this was all a huge mess. "Ren told me to take a chance."

"He did, huh?"

I nodded, and I could tell from the look in his eye, how he smirked, how he inched closer, what he thought I was about to say. "So I'd like to put in a counteroffer? If that's okay?"

Jayden snorted. "A counteroffer . . ."

"Yes. That maybe we could explore your offer after Christmas Day. Once the main event is over and the main dinner, you know. When there's less pressure and when, if you did decide you made a mistake and I woke up to find you gone, it wouldn't leave me without a chef on the biggest day of the year."

He drew his bottom lip in between his teeth to stop from smiling. "Your counteroffer sounds fair. Not that I would leave you without a chef. I'm not the kind to renege on my word. Or on our contract, for that matter. But I respect your position, trying to do the right thing by your business."

I nodded and laughed. This was ridiculous. "So . . . is that a yes? To maybe after Christmas . . . you're here for two days after Christmas. And that's not long, and I realise this is all my demands and not yours, which isn't fair, so feel free to tell me to shove it."

Jayden put his hand on my chest this time and slowly drove it up to my jaw. It was incredibly intimate, and I wondered if he could feel my heart knocking in my chest. "I could make a dozen jokes about telling you to shove something up my somewhere, but I'll refrain." He grinned.

"Until after Christmas, that is. Then all cards are off the table."

Needing a second and a little less intimacy, I reached up and took his hand, holding it, threading our fingers. "So that's a yes?"

"Yes. I'll accept your offer, Cass."

"I know things could change between now and then, and you can definitely pull out of this agreement at any time."

His grin widened. The gleam in his eye was wicked. "Oh, believe me, there'll be no pulling out."

Oh god.

It was suddenly very hot in the kitchen and he was very close. Too close, yet not close enough. His lips were right there, his body. I could feel the ghost of his hug, the warmth and strength of his arms . . .

His voice was low and gruff. "You keep looking at my mouth and I might think you want to kiss me."

I felt drunk. Had I even breathed at all in the last few minutes? I was beginning to think I hadn't . . .

I could so easily just kiss him right now. Push him up against the counter and press against him. I wanted to . . . I wanted to know what that was like. I wanted to know what he tasted like, how sweet his tongue was . . . "I want to," I breathed, ready to throw all plans of waiting out the window.

Then his phone rang in his pocket.

The buzzing sound cut the air, cut the tension between us, like reality snapped its fingers in our ears.

I took a dazed step back, and he groaned, taking his phone out. I saw the word Mum on the screen and he groaned again, more frustrated this time.

I took a bigger step. "You should take that. I'm going

to . . ." I looked out the kitchen window. "I'm going to lie in the snow for a bit. Or hang some blinds, or take the rolls of linoleum out to the barn."

Till my blood reduced from a boil to a simmer, at least.

As I made my escape, I heard him laugh and then a bright and cheery, "Mum, you have the worst timing ever!"

I think my breathing was back to normal by the time I got into the barn, even if my head was still full of Jayden's lips and his sparkling brown eyes.

I would remember how he hugged me for a long time.

But I'd asked him to maybe reconsider his offer when the Christmas rush was over. Why it had come out like a police hostage negotiation, I wasn't sure. Adding a formal tone seemed to make it easier to get it out. Less personal that way.

But he'd said yes.

And that made me all stupidly giddy inside. Thinking about how we almost kissed turned my insides into a hot, bubbly mess. Not to mention how my dick was suddenly awake.

I had to put it all out of my mind for five days. Surely, I could do that . . .

He felt so good against me. I wanted to taste his mouth, press my body to his.

Nope. Gawd. Back out into the snow I went. I cleared the linoleum from the rec room like he'd reminded me, then I moved a few things that didn't need to be moved, I stacked firewood that didn't need to be stacked, and I checked on the treads and risers on all the steps that didn't need to be checked.

It worked.

Because I went back inside some stupid amount of time later and could barely feel my fingers. Not my brightest idea, but at least I wasn't about to grab Jayden and kiss him so deep his knees buckled.

I figured my time was better spent hanging the blinds in the caramel room, and when that was done, I went upstairs to my office where I could do some work that actually needed attention. I checked and answered emails, made phone calls that needed to be made, and I got a surprising amount done. Which worked as a great distraction until I lost track of time. When I looked up, I realised the sunlight was fading.

Shoot.

I raced downstairs and the delicious smell told me Jayden was in the kitchen, and the happy whistling did too. I knelt in front of the fire, smiling as I stacked some kindling, listening to Jayden whistle and hum to himself, oblivious to my being in the next room. "Is that a Britney song?" I called out.

He laughed. "It's Britney, bitch."

I chuckled as the fire took hold and I followed my nose into the kitchen. "Something smells amazing," I said, walking in. "Sorry, I lost track of time. I just got the fire started."

"Oh, I didn't even notice. I got busy," he explained. And that was clearly true. He had containers all laid out, each with different things: peeled carrots, chopped onions, diced onion, sliced peppers, and a huge container of peeled potatoes covered with water. "Do you have any more clipboards?" he asked. "I need one more."

"I think I might," I replied. "In my office upstairs. What is that smell?"

He grinned. "Lasagne. That was the plan, yeah?"

"Oh, yeah. I just . . ." I clutched my belly. "I didn't realise how hungry I was."

"It'll be ready in five minutes. Which would be just enough time for you to maybe go and find me that clipboard?"

I chuckled. "Message received and understood."

He grinned. "Salad okay with dinner?"

I really was not used to having my meals prepared for me. "Oh, perfect."

"Is there anything you don't eat? Allergies?"

I shook my head. "I'm good with anything."

He raised an eyebrow and smirked. "Good to know."

I took a deep breath and turned on my heel, not needing to revisit the snow to cool off. I went back upstairs and found an old clipboard I'd never really used and took it down to him. Figuring it was best to try and steer the conversation away from anything sexual, physical. It didn't help that when I walked back into the kitchen, he was bending over to get the lasagne out of the oven.

Christ.

I held up the clipboard like a shield to ward off the imagination. "Found it," I said.

"Oh cool, thanks. I need it for my lists." He slid the still-bubbling dish on top of Ernace the Furnace. If it smelled good before, it smelled amazing now. My mouth watered.

"Oh, yes. Your lists," I said, watching him collect two plates with salad on them. "Want me to do something?"

"Set the table?"

"Want to sit on the couch in front of the fire?" I wasn't sure if that was too casual, or . . . "It'll be cosier."

He grinned. "Perfect. Then cutlery and two glasses of water, please."

We sat, like I'd suggested, on the couch by the fire, eating the best lasagne I'd ever tasted in my life. It was steaming hot and I tried not to shovel it in. "This is so good."

He smiled warmly. "I'm glad you like it."

"How do we use the same ingredients, more or less, and yours tastes amazing and mine doesn't?"

He smiled around his mouthful of food. "Same goes for your sign writing. Same tools, same paint and brushes, but I can assure you, yours is so perfect it looks like a computer did it. Mine would look like art and craft day at the local kindergarten."

I smiled and sipped my water. "So, what did your mom call you for? Is everything okay back home, or was it just for a chat?"

He waved his fork and rolled his eyes. "She's getting a new car for Christmas. She forgot to tell me the other day. I told her she has the worst possible timing."

"I heard."

"How was the snow? Did you lay in it, or was that a metaphor for something else?"

I snorted. "I considered lying down but didn't actually do it. I got some stuff done outside, though, until I nearly froze to death. Then I opted for the warmth in my office and decided to check some emails and whatnot, and I lost track of time."

"I got a lot of prep done. Most of the veggies are peeled and ready. I bagged everything, froze some stuff, stored the rest. It was good, actually."

Should I mention the almost-kiss?

Was that something we should talk about, or would it make things awkward?

He beat me to it.

"So, of course, after telling my mother that she has the worst possible timing ever, I had to explain why. I told her the sexiest man alive was just about to kiss me and her phone call ruined the perfect moment."

I snorted at how ridiculous this was. At how embarrassed I was. "World's sexiest man?"

He nodded earnestly. "Well, I don't know about *the* sexiest, but you'd have to be close. They have those polls every year, but I don't know if I can trust those. I'd need to see the qualifying criteria before I cast my vote or put any credence into their nomination system."

"That's very responsible of you."

He chuckled. "Thanks. I take my civic duty seriously."

"Obviously."

He put his empty plate on the side table. "Everyone's great back home. Getting ready for Christmas. Mum said the heat was terrible this year, which is hard to imagine now with how cold it is here. I used to love hot summers. Now it wouldn't be Christmas without snow and wood fires and warmed apple cider."

I screwed my nose up. "Do you like spiced apple cider?"

"Yep. You don't?"

I shook my head. "Not since the Christmas I turned twenty-one. First and last time ever drinking that. I was so drunk, and oh boy, was I ever sick."

"Do you like eggnog?"

"Nope. It's gross."

"Oh, thank god. I don't understand what it's even supposed to be."

That made me laugh. "The only hot drink I have in winter is hot chocolate. Which is kinda lame, but I don't like hot cider and my days of downing Flaming Lamborghinis are well and truly behind me."

"Hot chocolates are so underrated. They're like a hug in a cup. And they're not just for kids? Who made that rule?"

"Someone who doesn't like a hug in a cup."

Jayden laughed and stood up, taking his plate. He put his hand out for mine. "I'll clean up."

"But you cooked," I tried. "So I should clean up."

He chuckled as he walked into the kitchen. "Well, normally I would say that's correct. But I have to put all the prep away and tidy up. Why don't you go fix the cabinet in the reading room and I'll bring us in a hot chocolate when I'm done here."

I considered that for a second. "Are you . . . are you low-key bossing me around? Telling me what to do?"

He shot me a look and quickly saw I was joking. He smiled, but there was a seriousness in his tone. "There's nothing low key about it. I am bossy. We have a list of stuff to get done, and tomorrow you're busy all day—Christmas trees are being delivered after breakfast and then your kids arrive for the day—so the cabinet needs fixing tonight." He shooed me out. "Out of my kitchen, my Sexiest Man Alive. I have work to do and won't be distracted by how cute you are."

I laughed as he all but pushed me out of the kitchen. "Okay, okay. I'm going. One fixed cabinet, coming up."

I found myself smiling as I mended the cabinet door. Having Jayden here, being around him, joking or having a serious conversation, just felt so natural.

Maybe I'd just missed the company. Maybe I'd been alone too long.

But when he brought in a tray with two mugs of hot chocolate and a plate of Christmas cookies, I had to wonder if it was more than that.

My heart skipped a beat or two and my stomach swooped when he smiled.

Was it loneliness speaking? Or my heart?

CHAPTER NINE

JAYDEN

I WAS nervous when I made us an early breakfast the next morning. Nothing more had happened last night between Cass and me, not since the almost-kiss anyway. I made us some hot chocolates after dinner and I emptied the last box and organised some books, and by the time he had the cabinet door fixed, it was bedtime.

We'd said goodnight and each gone to our own rooms. There was no awkwardness and no other almost-kiss moments, which was a little disappointing if I was being honest.

So why was I nervous?

I would be meeting his kids today, and possibly his ex-wife.

Cass clearly had some guilt issues over how that had all ended, and I could understand that. But I had to wonder how much anger and guilt-stoking had come from his ex-wife.

That was pure assumption on my part. And I could also understand why she'd aim that residual anger at Cass. But I couldn't even pretend to understand the dynamics and complexities of a marriage between two people I didn't know. I knew, a little, of who Cass was now, but I didn't know him as a married man with two kids.

I was going to see a different side of Cass today.

I guess I was nervous to maybe find out that this idyllic, dreamy guy wasn't so dreamy. Would I like how he was with his kids? Was he a kind father? Would I like how he treated his ex or how she treated him?

It wasn't any of my business, really. I wasn't staying in Hartbridge. I wasn't in any kind of relationship with Cass that these things should be an issue . . .

I didn't know why they mattered to me.

But I made an omelette for breakfast with thick-cut toast and fresh coffee, which Cass all but inhaled in between moans and utterances of thanks and gratitude.

"This is so good," he said, finishing the last bite.

I did my best to ignore the groans. "Glad you like it."

"Please let me clean up. It's the least I can do. I really don't expect you to cook for me."

"I like cooking for people," I replied, but just then the sound of a truck arriving made Cass panic. He looked at my plate, which still had egg and toast on it, and my barely touched coffee. I laughed at his expression. "Go. You don't need to clean up here. Go get your Christmas trees. I need to start the bread maker anyway."

He wasn't kidding about getting three trees either. One rather large one, one medium size, and one smaller. The old guy who delivered them helped Cass get them inside, thankfully, because I wasn't sure if I would be much help up the back deck steps and manoeuvring through the mudroom.

But I got to see Cass's biceps in action through his

sweater, which I would consider payment for cleaning up after breakfast.

The man who delivered the trees looked exactly as you might expect a Christmas tree delivery guy to look like. A bit like Santa but in overalls and a flannel shirt and with a thick country boy accent. His name was Cliff, and he might have been about sixty-something but he was the size of an ox, and as strong as one. I said a quick hello but Cliff didn't seem too concerned about me. He was honest to god looking around in wonder.

"Oh, Carter, I really like what you've done with the place," Cliff said. "I remember thinking you must've gone 'n lost your mind when you bought this place, but wowzers. You've done a mighty fine job."

"Thank you, Cliff."

"My dad used to play tennis here as a boy," Cliff said. "Back when it was a country club. He'd sure love to see what you've done with the place."

"Bring him over any time," Cass said. "After Christmas. I'd love to hear his stories."

Cliff said he just might do that, shook his hand, and left with a huge smile.

Carter seemed pleased with the whole transaction and the trees. He gestured toward them. "Well, what do you think?"

"I think they're the Goldilocks of trees. You've got a papa tree, a momma tree, and a baby tree."

He grinned. "Papa goes in here, momma in the family room, and the baby tree in the rec room for the kids. I mean, they're all trussed up right now, but they'll look okay once we cut the ropes and they settle, right?"

They were very green, very healthy-looking Christmas

trees. "I think they'll look amazing. They smell incredible already."

"I need to get them set up and settled before the kids get here," he said.

"I'll help. Tell me what you need me to do."

He stared at me for a beat too long and I thought he was going to say it wasn't necessary for me to help, but he gave a nod and a smile. "I'll get the stands."

The 'stands' as it turned out, were hidden in the three wicker-basket-looking things that had been on the back deck. We carried the trees to their allocated rooms, and I was thankful the papa bear tree wasn't going far.

Cass did all the lifting and the adjustments and whatever else needed doing while I basically watched and held onto things or handed him things as requested. But it was fun, and I'd never really been involved in a real Christmas tree preparation.

Each tree looked incredible, but the biggest tree was a showstopper.

"Wow," I murmured. "I know I'm extremely gay so this shouldn't surprise you, but the papa bear tree is definitely my favourite."

Cass laughed as he came to stand next to me so he could get a proper look. "Is it centred in the window okay?"

"It's perfect." I inhaled deeply. "I cannot get over the smell. It's amazing. Is it a special kind of tree?" I really had no idea.

"It's a noble fir." I could feel his eyes on me so I turned to find him studying me. "Did you not have trees at Christmas?"

I shook my head. "Growing up in Australia, we had an artificial tree, and the few years my parents lived here, Christmas was always kinda low-key. Since then, I always worked over the holiday period. It's the busiest time of the year in hospitality. I'd work all hours and get home late, so I never really bothered with a tree. And I lived in a shared place, or in a dingy place. It just never happened. The only Christmas trees I ever saw were in stores, or on the street."

Cass frowned. "That's kind of sad. I'm sorry."

I shrugged it off. "Just means this will be my first with a proper tree, and you have three, so that kinda makes up for it."

He didn't smile. "And now I'm making you work another Christmas. I'm sorry . . ."

"If I wasn't working here, I'd be working somewhere else. It's what I do. I'm in between permanent work and finding somewhere to live, so this is actually a great place to spend the holidays. And you promised me mind-blowing sex as a Christmas present, so who really wins here?"

Cass stared at me, blinked, then snorted out a laugh. "Mind-blowing might be a stretch," he said, his cheeks red. "Please remember it's been a while for me, and your expectations will likely far exceed my capabilities."

I clapped his shoulder and laughed. "Practice makes perfect." Then I stopped. "Uh, you didn't expressly say it was a once-only thing, right? Just that after Christmas Day we could have at it, so if it's like five times in one night, that's fine?"

His eyes went wide. "Five times? Your expectations far, far exceed my capabilities."

I grinned at him. "Okay, so three times in one night. Even twice. And I'm here for two days after Christmas, so that's a respectable amount of dicking."

He stared at me and swallowed hard. "You don't make it easy to wait."

I raised an eyebrow. "I don't mean to entice you. I

respect your decision to wait. But if you change your mind . . ." I licked my lips. "I could take the edge off for you."

His steely eyes darkened and his nostrils flared. His gaze went to my mouth, then back to my eyes. When he spoke, his voice was low and gruff. "I think I need to go stand out in the snow for a bit."

I laughed but put my hand on his arm. "I'm kidding. I mean, I'm not. I totally would go to my knees for you right now. But I shouldn't play you like that. I'm sorry. It's not fair."

He scoffed out a laugh and took a step back. "Yep. Snow. Gonna need to lie down in it for sure this time. Face down, even."

I cracked up laughing. "Sorry."

Just then we heard the sound of tyres on snow. "Oh shit. That's Kendra and the kids," Cass said, readjusting his crotch. "I really am gonna have to go stand in the snow."

He dashed for the mudroom and I went back to the kitchen. My nerves were back, and a little anxiety. I liked Cass. I did. There was no point in denying it, and I didn't know what to expect from meeting them.

Would he be different around them? Would he not want me near his kids? Would that be fair or unfair? He was their dad; he had to think of them first, naturally. I wouldn't expect anything different. Actually, if he didn't put them first, that would be a hundred times worse.

Ugh. I was so out of my depth.

I'd never been with a guy who had kids or an ex-wife. Not that Cass and I were 'together' . . .

Jeez, Jayden. Get a grip.

I watched from the kitchen window as a black SUV pulled up and Cass went down the back steps. The back car doors opened and a fair-haired boy jumped out and ran straight into Cass's arms. He crouched down and hugged his boy so hard, and when a little blonde girl ran around the back of the car, Cass opened his arms and collected her too.

It made my heart ache.

I had to swallow the lump in my throat.

I immediately felt bad for ever thinking for one second that this was about me.

Then a woman, who I assumed was Kendra, got out of the car, smiling widely. She wore jeans and a coat, a beanie over the top of her long brown hair. She opened the back of her SUV and collected a bag, and when she walked over to Cass, he stood up and gave her half a hug before they turned for the deck and made their way inside.

My insides were doing all sorts of bubbly acrobatics.

There was chatter in the mudroom before the sound of little feet ran into the house, and I quickly made myself very busy in the kitchen. Was it too late to go hide in my room?

"Mom, look at the tree!" the boy called out. "It's the biggest tree ever."

I smiled as I took the flour out of the dry storeroom. Cass wanted his kids to be excited about the trees and it certainly sounded like they were.

"Wow," Kendra said. "It sure is . . . big."

I almost laughed, but I put the flour cannister on the counter just as she walked in.

And stopped.

"Oh."

Shit.

"Uh, hi," I said.

Cass followed her in and she turned to him questioningly, then she smiled. Suggestively, even. "Oh?"

Cass put his hand up and shook his head. "No. Uh, no.

This is . . . um, Jayden. Jayden, this is Kendra." His cheeks were a rosy red.

She studied Cass for a second before she turned back to me, killer smile and her hand out. "Nice to meet you," she said.

I shook her hand. "Likewise."

Her eyes were warm, her face was just so lovely. She seemed . . . nice.

"Jayden's the chef," Cass explained. "So the guests don't have to eat my cooking for Christmas."

Kendra almost laughed. "That's probably a good thing." Cass rolled his eyes and Kendra smiled at me. "So how long are you staying for?"

"I'm just here for the week," I replied.

Before anyone could say anything else, the two kids, cute as hell, ran into the kitchen. The boy, Wyatt, was so excited. "Mom, there's more Christmas trees. Come and have a look!"

Charlotte took Kendra's hand. "Mommy, come and see."

"Okay, okay," she said, being led out, smiling over her shoulder at Cass.

He waited a few seconds after they'd gone, glanced at me, smiled awkwardly, then followed them out.

They really did seem like the perfect family. And for the life of me, I couldn't remember why I'd assumed his ex-wife would be horrible.

I'd heard horror stories of break-ups, especially if it was because one person came out. The remaining partner would be hurt and angry . . . and maybe Kendra had been in the beginning, but I'd met her for all of two seconds and already liked her.

You know how some people exuded bad energy, and

how some people radiated positive energy? Well, she was all positive energy. She had an honest smile and kind eyes, and when she'd assumed that maybe I was in Cass's kitchen for a different reason—her questioning 'oh?' had been suggestive—it was only meant with friendly curiosity. Like she'd be happy for Cass if I was there for other reasons than to be his hired help.

I wasn't expecting to like her.

Maybe that was why Cass's guilt had troubled him so much.

Anyway, I couldn't possibly pretend to know these people, so I put it out of my mind and began to worry about making the gingerbread cake instead. I was going to steam it, so it would probably be best to make some smaller test ones first.

I began mixing the ground ginger, cloves, and nutmeg, the smell immediately taking me back to every Christmas I'd worked.

I heard their voices getting closer and Charlotte appeared first, followed by her brother. They both stopped when they saw me; it probably didn't help that I was holding a knife. I quickly put it down and offered them a smile instead.

"Morning!"

"Who are you?" Charlotte demanded.

"Dad?" the boy yelled. "There's a man in your kitchen."

Had they not even seen me when they ran in here before?

"Um, hi," I tried. "I'm, um—"

Thankfully Cass appeared. He put a hand on each of their shoulders. "This is Jayden," he announced. "He's a chef. He's staying here to cook for all the people staying over the holidays." He smiled at me. *Was he nervous?* "Jayden, this is Wyatt and Charlotte."

I really wasn't sure what to say to kids. I'd never spent much time with them. "Hello," I tried. "You guys gonna help your dad decorate those trees today?"

Charlotte's whole face lit up. "Yes! And Daddy said he bought new decorations."

She was honestly the cutest kid I think I'd ever seen.

Wyatt side-eyed the bowl. "What's that? It smells funny."

Kendra made an apologetic face. "Wyatt, we don't say that to people about their food."

I laughed. "It's okay. It does smell kinda funny. It has spices in it. I'm making a special cake for lunch on Christmas Eve."

Wyatt looked at the fruit and was more horrified. "Spicy cake?"

"Not spicy. Ginger, nutmeg and cinnamon. It has a strong smell. I was going to make some special little chocolate lava cakes that you might like." I had no idea if they were allowed to eat chocolate or cake or if I should have even said that?

I should have asked Cass about all this before. I could have made a list . . .

"Just for Christmas though," I added. "Only if your mom and dad say it's okay?" I looked at Cass for help. "Sorry."

He appeared amused. "That sounds nice."

"It sure does," Kendra added. "I better get going. I have a lot to do, and my sister is expecting me." She turned to Cass. "Thanks again for today."

"Anytime. Anytime at all."

He walked her out and Wyatt and Charlotte ran out to

open the new Christmas decorations. I watched through the window as Cass opened Kendra's door and waved as she drove away.

I got that weird, longing ache in my chest again.

I don't know what I was longing for . . . The way he looked at her? The way she smiled at him? What they had, what they still have?

Cass came back in and I could hear him sort his kids out a bit: helping with the boxes, giving them instructions, and then they disappeared to the rec room to decorate the kids' tree first.

Cass came in a short while later. The fruit was soaking in brandy and I was washing up. "Hey," he said quietly. "How's everything going in here?"

"Great." I dried my hands on a tea towel. "How is the tree decorating going?"

"Good, for now. The wheels are likely to fall off soon when one of them wants it done a different way, but there's no tears yet."

That made me smile. "Cass, they are the cutest kids I've ever seen. And I'm not surprised, considering their dad is, well, you. And their mum is as pretty as a picture."

Cass smiled. "Thanks."

"But the important part," I began.

He gave me a wary, guarded look. "Yes?"

God, what did he think I was going to say?

"I need to know what they can and can't eat. For snacks. I offered them chocolate cake without asking! That could have been a disaster. Do they have allergies? I washed the board and the knife before and I haven't opened any packets of nuts, and I was certain to keep everything separated. There was no cross contamination. I promise." I grabbed one of the clipboards. "I can make a list. And things I should and shouldn't say."

Cass pulled his bottom lip between his teeth as if he was trying not to smile. "Jayden, you don't need a list. They're not allergic to anything. I would have told you before now if they were." He gave my arm a squeeze. "How you were before, with them, was perfect. Just be yourself."

"I don't really have experience in dealing with children. If you haven't guessed that already."

"I might have, yes."

"But they're both adorable, and you're right. Wyatt looks just like you. And Kendra seems really nice. I can see why you fell in love with her. They're just all adorable."

Was that out of line? That was probably out of line . . .

A flash of different emotions crossed his face: hurt, happiness, truth, regret. He opened his mouth but closed it again and settled on a nod. "Thank you."

I had the feeling that was not what he wanted to say. I hated seeing him so sad. He wore his guilt like an overcoat.

"So," I said, trying to brighten the mood, which I had been the one to sully. "Leftover lasagne for lunch still okay? Should I make a salad, or am I wasting my time? Oh, I guess I can make a salad for you and me. If your kids eat it, then it's a bonus. How about some fresh baked bread to go with it? I'll have the oven on. It's not like it's hard to make. You have a bread machine on the bottom shelf of the storage room."

"It was a wedding gift. I got it in the divorce. Never been used."

"Is it okay if I use it while I'm here?"

"Sure. You okay? You're nervous."

I shot him a look. "I was out of line for mentioning your family, sorry. I made you uncomfortable."

He smiled sadly. "You can read me well."

His expression was like a neon billboard, but okay.

He stared out the window for a long moment. "I spent years hiding how I felt. I thought I was better at it."

There was so much I wanted to say right now, but it wasn't the time. It probably also wasn't my place to say it, but I really wanted to try and ease his pain.

"You were right," Cass said, still looking out the window. "I did love Kendra. I still do. She's a wonderful person, an amazing mom. But I didn't love her like I should have."

I shook my head. "No, you didn't *not* love her like you should have. You couldn't love her like she needed. Like you needed. You're not to blame for that. You tried, and you struggled with it for years. If you'd have stayed, it would have killed you, or you'd have resented her. In the end it would have been so much worse." I sighed and took a mixing bowl from the cupboard. "I'm sorry. I've already said too much. I just hate seeing you blame yourself."

When I turned to face him, he was staring at me. This time I couldn't quite gauge the emotions. Was he mad? Sorry? Thankful?

I didn't know.

It looked like he was trying to figure something out, and again, he opened his mouth to say something, but Charlotte called out from the rec room. "Dad! Wyatt won't let me use the beads."

I smiled. "You better go save the tree."

He nodded and disappeared through the door. He said something to the kids and put an end to their bickering.

I shook off the heavy feeling in my heart, the wish that Cass could let himself be happy. Yes, he'd ended his marriage, and that must have been horrible and extremely difficult. Truly awful, for everyone.

But isolating himself and never allowing himself to be happy, as some kind of exchange rate, just made me sad for him.

He deserved better.

I tried to put it all out of my mind, reminding myself that I was not staying in Hartbridge. This was not a permanent position. And with that, I was reminded why I was here and that Christmas guests would be arriving tomorrow, and I needed to get busy with the cakes in the steamer. The gingerbread cake would taste the same, of course, but it would be dense, very moist, and the sauce would soak into it.

Oh, and the bread I mentioned to Cass . . .

I checked the bread through the little window on top of the maker. It smelled amazing but had a little while to go. So, using Cass's great-aunt's pudding steamer, I set the cake on the stove top in a pot of simmering water, sent up a prayer to the cooking gods, and put the lid on.

I really loved all the old trays, pots and pans she'd had all those years ago. That pudding steamer was as old as this house and still as good as the day it was made. Though the new bread maker was great as well, there was something about using generations-old kitchenware.

It made my little chef heart happy.

By the time I got everything cleaned up, the bread was almost done. I reheated the lasagne and when I set the dining table, I could hear them in the formal lounge decorating the middle-sized tree. They didn't seem as enthusiastic now. But one of them would laugh every so often, and it squeezed my heart every time.

"Lunch is ready," I called out.

"Yes," Wyatt said, and he came running. Charlotte had to finish putting on the bauble she was holding, and Cass waited for her to be done. He took one look at the table, at the plates of lasagne, a bowl of salad in the middle of the table next to a still-steaming loaf of fresh bread. I had to admit, it smelled pretty damn good.

His eyes went to mine. "You made this?"

I nodded. "Bon appétit."

Then Cass did a double take, counting the plates. "There's only three . . . are you not eating with us?"

I shook my head. "No, you guys enjoy. I have to watch the steamer."

So that wasn't true, at all. I had a plate put aside in the kitchen where I'd eat mine. Cass should enjoy this time with his kids without a tag-along. Plus, I'd made a bit of a mess that I needed to tackle before my afternoon of more prep and more cooking.

I was here to work, after all. And I had a lot to do.

A little while later, both Wyatt and Charlotte carried their very empty plates into the kitchen, put them in the sink, and turned to me. "Thank you," they said in unison.

Cass stood at the door, smiling proudly. He'd clearly told them to do it, but it was sweet, nonetheless.

"You are very welcome!" I told them.

"The bread was deeee-licious," Wyatt said.

Charlotte nodded and patted her belly. "Daddy said I could have two pieces. He said you made it."

"I sure did." Then I gestured to the bread machine. "Well, I had some help."

"Can we make some more?" Wyatt asked. "To take home for mom?"

"Oh," Cass began, about to say it would be a bother.

I laughed. "Of course we can. What time are you getting picked up?"

"Five o'clock." Cass checked his watch.

"It takes a while in the bread maker, so how about you guys come in at two, and we can make some. It'll be ready when your mom gets here."

Charlotte turned to her dad. "Can we, Daddy?"

Cass smiled at me. "Sure can."

I put my finger up. "Only if you both help though. I'll need you both to help me. Is that a deal?"

They excitedly agreed and ran back to the tree decorating. Cass stood there a moment, still leaning against the doorway, half a smile on his face. "Thank you."

His gentle tone, the softness in his eyes, and how he looked at me made my heart skip a beat.

"You're welcome."

WHEN WYATT and Charlotte began to bicker one too many times over the finishing touches on the second tree, Cass suggested they put their boots and coats on and head outside.

I watched through the kitchen window as they walked to the barn like a family of ducks. It was so cute.

But I got a lot done in the afternoon after lunch. Every day would be busy from here on in, with guests and three meals a day and, of course, Christmas Day. But I'd done as much as I could do for now.

I'd heard them all come back inside. The sound of small feet and small voices and Cass's deep voice gave them away, and it sounded as if they were bringing in some wood for the fire.

But soon two excited little faces appeared in the kitchen. "It's two o'clock," Wyatt said.

"Can we make the bread?" Charlotte asked. "Daddy said we had to ask."

"Of course you can," I said, putting two bowls on the counter. I'd brought in an old apple box from the dry storeroom for Charlotte to stand on. "But first we need to wash our hands."

Cass stood to the side, smiling, while I had them both mix equal parts of the dry ingredients in their bowls—which wasn't really necessary with a bread maker, but I figured kids liked to mix stuff with spatulas. But while the bread maker made it very easy, it also made it a little anticlimactic.

Making bread, or any kind of baking should be about kneading and getting your hands into it. But making bread by hand with two little kids was probably not a good idea, and I didn't think they'd appreciate a good old Aussie damper. So I went with something better. "Okay, now it's cookie making time."

Making a quick cookie dough took no time, and both Charlotte and Wyatt loved measuring everything out and helping. But Cass was still just standing there . . . he was smiling, even laughed a few times, but he wasn't involved.

I nodded to him. "Daddy needs to wash his hands too," I said. "He can help."

Once he stepped in, I stepped back and let him enjoy this time with his kids.

They helped each other, they laughed, they all took turns in mixing and rolling out the dough. Wyatt chose chocolate chips and Charlotte chose sprinkles.

Cass's smile was something special.

We didn't have cookie cutters, so I suggested using the rim of a drinking glass. It wasn't perfect, but using it made

Charlotte and Wyatt happy and they took turns. And Cass was the happiest I'd seen him.

Once the cookies were in the oven baking, Cass took both kids to wash their hands properly in the bathroom while I began to tidy up the kitchen. I had no idea kids could make so much mess.

I heard the TV go on and a second later, Cass appeared at the kitchen door. "Kids are hungry. I'll make them a snack, if that's okay?"

I laughed. "Of course it's okay. This is your house, it's their house." I checked the oven. "Cookies will be done in a few minutes. How about you put some milk on the stove for hot chocolates?"

He nodded woodenly, as if he was nervous. "Look, I . . . I just wanted to say thank you. For today."

What on earth was he thanking me for?

He seemed to read my face. "For letting me spend as much time with them as possible. For making their day fun and special."

"Cass," I said gently, "any day they spend with you is fun and special."

He smiled to the floor between us, his cheeks pink. "I'm just really grateful."

"Well, you're very welcome." I wanted to touch him, his arm, his shoulder, his neck . . . but I didn't. Even though he was now looking at me with those steely eyes that cut right through me. "Now, about those hot chocolates."

He seemed to snap out of whatever it was between us. "Right. Yes."

I continued to pack things away until the oven timer told us it was cookie o'clock. Cass made the hot chocolates, and while the cookies were still warm, the kids enjoyed afternoon tea as they watched Christmas cartoons on the

TV. Cass fixed the fire, and I had to admit, it made me a little sad.

I'd never considered having kids.

Not once, not ever. It was something that was off the table for me. Not that I ever didn't want it. It was just something I never thought possible.

I never realised it was possible.

I never realised I might want that.

I wasn't stupid enough to think baking cookies with kids was any indication of what parenthood really was. But seeing Cass with his kids, seeing him fix the fire while they laughed at cartoons as a light dusting of snow fell outside . . .

Well, it made my heart ache.

The bread maker beeped to signal it was done, so I took it out to cool when I heard someone driving up to the back of the house. Kendra's car appeared out the kitchen window, and she dashed up the back steps to get out of the snow.

"Mommy!" Charlotte cried. "Come see what we made."

Poor Kendra was dragged into the kitchen without even a second to say hello. "Cookies and yummy bread. We made it," Wyatt told her.

"I thought something smelled wonderful," Kendra said, giving me a smile. "Hello again. Sorry if they were under your feet today."

"Oh no, it was my idea," I replied quickly. "I helped with the bread, but Cass made the cookies with them."

"Well, the cookies were Jayden's idea," Cass replied. "But I did help."

Oh shoot.

I gave Kendra a grimace-smile. "Oh yeah, sorry. Bread and cookies is a lot of white flour and sugar. Sorry about that."

Kendra just laughed. "It's fine."

"The bread is for you, Momma," Charlotte said. "We ate it at lunchtime and it was so good we wanted you to have some."

"Really? For me?"

I nodded. "They asked if they could make some for you. It was fun. I'll wrap it in a tea towel for you. It's still warm."

Cass put his hand on Wyatt's shoulder. "Hey, buddy, how about you run and grab your backpack?"

"Mom needs to see the trees first," he said, and Charlotte heartily agreed. I think she might have forgotten about decorating them. But then they dragged poor Kendra out of the kitchen to the rec room.

Cass smiled at me before following them.

I finished wrapping the bread and put the cookies in a container for them to take home. Kendra was most thankful, and I didn't want to intrude when Cass walked them out.

I'd barely stepped foot out of the kitchen all day, and I hadn't paid the big Christmas tree much attention. I noticed it had a few decorations on it but it wasn't finished. I assumed a third tree in one day was too much for two little kids.

There was a box full of gold and white decorations by the tree, so I picked up a gold bauble from the box and popped it on. Then another, and another, and one more, until Cass cleared his throat behind me.

"Oh," I said. "I was just . . ."

Cass wore an odd expression. Was it determination? He strode over to me in quick, long strides and pulled me in for a crushing hug.

Oh.

Okay then.

I was so stunned, it took me a second to realise I wasn't

hugging him back. I put my arms around his lower back, not entirely sure what this hug was for or what it meant.

But he felt good. Warm and strong, and he smelled like Christmas tree, fire smoke, and cookies. He held me tight and sighed.

"You okay?" I didn't want this hug to end but I had to ask.

He pulled back and I could see his cheeks were pink, but that determination was still there. "Yeah, I'm sorry. I just wanted to say thank you. For today. Everything you did was perfect, and it allowed me to spend every second with them. When they're here, I worry I'm not feeding them enough, and then there's the cleaning up . . ." He glanced toward the kitchen. "God, I should clean up the kitchen."

I grabbed his arm. "It's done. You don't need to worry about that."

He met my gaze and shook his head. "Jayden . . ."

"It's no big deal. I'm trained to clean as I go and to clean every station after I use it. It's ingrained in me."

"I really appreciate everything you did. The kids think you're the coolest."

"Well, they're not wrong," I said with a laugh. "Though I don't know what you want for dinner. There's some pork. I could make us something with rice. Korean or Japanese? What do you feel like?"

"I don't expect you to do that," he amended.

"Cass, you're paying me to cook."

He shook his head. "Tonight's your last night before you'll be cooking non-stop. Let me take you out for dinner."

"Out?"

"Yep."

"Where in Hartbridge is there to go for dinner. We'll

need to be back relatively early because this tree isn't finished . . ."

"Where is there to go?" He grinned. "Just the finest dining experience of your life."

Oh dear.

Fine dining? In Hartbridge?

"Is there a fine dining experience in Hartbridge?"

Cass laughed. "The finest."

CHAPTER TEN

CASS

CARL'S DINER was an icon in Hartbridge. Carl had opened his diner back in the seventies, and he'd raised his family here. Now his grandkids lived here. And his food was real Montanan comfort food.

He was famous for his cheesy macaroni and his roast beef. He also made his own pastries, and everything on his menu filled your belly and made you smile.

And the truth was, I wanted to take Jayden out of the house. The first guests were due to arrive tomorrow afternoon, which meant he'd be flat out every day for the next week.

I wanted to spend time with him where he didn't feel obligated to work for me.

"Is there a dress code for this restaurant?" he'd asked, a little horrified. He'd changed out of his flour-splattered shirt and put on clean jeans and a fresh sweater. "This is about the best I've got. The rest is packed in my car."

It made me laugh. "What you're wearing is perfect."

We put on our coats, gloves, and beanies and climbed into my truck. "I'm excited," he said. "But when you say

Hartbridge's finest dining experience, what did you mean exactly?"

"It's a surprise."

Well, he was surprised, that was for sure.

"The diner?"

I laughed. "Yep. Just wait till you try it."

We got out of the truck and made it to the sidewalk when he grabbed my arm. "Oh my god, Cass. Look!"

He was staring at the window display, the small Christmas trees, a snowman decoration, and all the Christmas lights that were . . . well, everywhere. Main Street looked amazing this time of year.

"Looks good, huh?"

"Is this even for real?" he asked. "Who does this?"

I shrugged. "Everyone. The town council, mostly. But all the store owners do their bit too."

"It's like a movie set." His face was lit by the string of fairy lights on the awning, glowing gold, making his brown hair glitter, and he turned that heart-stopping smile toward me. "Cass, it's magical."

"It sure is," I whispered.

He stared at me and I knew he knew I wasn't talking about the decorations.

I couldn't bring myself to care.

I was feeling things for him that weren't strictly professional. Especially after today. He'd done everything he could to make my day with the kids the best day, and dinner was the very least I could do.

I held the door open for him. "After you."

He walked in and stopped. "Oh wow."

I chuckled and pulled off my beanie and my gloves. When I said Carl opened this diner in the 1970s, the décor hadn't changed. There were a few other people at tables and two at the counter, not paying any attention to us.

"Evening, Carter," Christa called out.

"Hi. We okay to take a booth?"

"Course, love. I'll be out in a few."

Christa had worked at the diner for maybe twenty years. She knew everyone in town by their full name, how they took their coffee, and what they were likely to choose off the menu. She was a stout woman with a penchant for coral coloured lipstick who had worn her hair in a French twist every day since I'd known her.

She was one of my favourite people in town.

"Oh my goodness," Jayden said as we took a booth. "This place is awesome. It looks like those old-fashioned milk bars you see in old movies." He nodded to one of the empty tables. "I think my grandmother had a table like that. Very retro."

"Well, some would call it retro. Some would call it original. You'll be pleased to hear the kitchen got a redo in the last decade though."

Smiling, he pulled his beanie off and tried to tame his hair. "The Christmas decorations in here are amazing. I love it."

This wasn't *just* decorated. It looked like the North Pole. "Some might say it's a touch overdone."

He looked around happily. "Not me." Then he tilted his head and shrugged. "Well, I mean, it's clearly been done by someone on the heterosexual side of the Kinsey scale, but it's a valiant effort."

I laughed. "I think it was Christa."

Jayden looked over to her where she was ringing someone's order up. "She's so cute, I could just put her in my pocket."

"She's lovely. She was very kind to me when I came back to town, freshly single and the new owner of the old manor out of town. She told me to keep my chin up and to ignore the rumour mill. She made sure I stayed fed in the beginning, which was nice."

"Was the rumour mill bad when you came back?"

I leaned in. "This town's power supply is run on the rumour mill. Those wheels keep churning to keep the whole place going, like a hydroelectric plant."

"Ow. That must have sucked."

"Wasn't so bad. While they were talking about me, they were leaving some other poor soul alone." I smiled at him. "Honestly, it wasn't terrible. People were bound to talk, and I wasn't about to deny it. Both mine and Kendra's parents are still in town, though, so it wasn't much fun for them. But like all rumour mills, a few days later, it was somebody else's turn and it all died down."

"What was the talking point? You being gay, you and Kendra separating, or you buying the old manor house?"

"It was a trifecta, for sure. All three."

Christa appeared at our booth. "Carter, how are your plans for Christmas coming along? All ready by now?"

"Uh, yes. Just about all done. First guests arrive tomorrow."

"Ooh, how exciting." Then she smiled at Jayden and tapped her name badge. "Name's Christa."

"Sorry," I said quickly. "Forgot my manners. Christa, this is Jayden Turner. He's helping me out this week. He's a chef."

I noticed then a few of the others in the diner were watching us now, listening. They seemed to be waiting to hear who Jayden was and what he was doing with me. Like they thought we were on a date or something.

Oh god. They thought I was on a date with a man . . .

"What can I get for you boys?" Christa asked.

Jayden looked at me for help. We hadn't even opened the menus. "What's the special today?" I asked.

"Carl's sticky pork brisket with cheesy mashed potatoes, and it's gooooood."

"How does that sound?" I asked Jayden.

"Sounds great, actually."

I held up two fingers. "Two of those, please. And two Cokes." I checked with Jayden. "Is Coke okay?"

"Perfect."

She went on her way and it suddenly felt like every set of eyes were on us. They weren't . . . when I looked. But it felt like it.

"Everything okay?"

"Mm." I tried to smile and I spoke low enough so only he could hear. "I just realised that people in here probably think we're on a date or something."

Jayden's eyes went wide. "Should we act straight? Should we talk really loud about football or something? Hockey? I'm not entirely up to code on het-speak."

I rolled my eyes. "No. I don't want to pretend . . . Not like that. I just haven't done this . . ."

"Oh." His eyes flashed with a second recognition. That I'd never been on a date with a man and certainly not in public. "Shit. I'm sorry."

I shook my head. "No, it's fine. I . . . I need to get used to it, I guess. If I ever start dating. God, this is embarrassing."

Jayden fidgeted his hands on the table as if he wanted to reach out and touch but had to stop himself. "It's nothing to be embarrassed about."

"Does it always feel like everyone's watching?"

He chuckled. "No. It did in the beginning for me too.

You're wondering if someone's going to be a jerk about it. But after a while, I stopped noticing them." He shrugged. "What you're feeling, that nervousness and a little anxiety? That's completely normal."

I let out a long breath and nodded. "Well, good. I suppose."

He leaned in. "It's totally fine with me if you want to pretend this is an actual date."

An actual date? I was kind of thinking maybe this already was?

"I mean," he continued. "My last proposal was for you to experience 'dating.'" He finger quoted the air. "So this is no different, really. Actually, it's kinda fun. Hit me with your first date questions."

I stared at him. "Um. The last first date I went on was with Kendra and we started dating when we were sixteen, so . . ."

"Okay, wow. Look, honestly, I'm not really an expert. Most of my first dates were a quick cover of all the bases just to get to the home run, if you know what I mean. Sometimes we skipped all the bases." He made a face. "Which sounds terrible. I only did that a few times. The other times I ended up seeing people I worked with, so we knew a bit about each other already and we just fell into that casual friends-with-benefits type of thing. So actually, the art of dating might not be my strongest suit."

I found myself smiling at him but figured if it was question time . . . "Why are you moving to Oregon or Washington?"

He blinked, not prepared for the change of subject. "Uh, because . . . well, because I don't know. I was coming through here for this job, and the road keeps going west. I figured it was as good a place as any."

"Do you like moving around so much?"

He shook his head. "No, not really. I could have stayed in Missoula, but something told me to move on. Chefs tend to follow work a lot, move around. I'd like to find something permanent. Maybe start my own business one day. I dunno."

"A place like this?" I gestured around to the diner. "Your own diner or restaurant?"

He shrugged. "Maybe. It's a lot of work and I don't have the capital for that. I can run someone else's kitchen though. Like at the hotel I was at."

"I've seen how organised you are."

Jayden chuckled. "Can I ask you something?"

"Sure."

"Why do people call you Cass? Some call you Cass, some call you Carter. Is Cass short for Carter somehow?"

Just then, Christa brought our dinner, sliding our plates onto the table, then our drinks. "Enjoy, boys. Lemme know if I can get you anything else."

On each plate was a mountain of pulled pork, mashed potatoes, and a side of green beans. Jayden tasted his first. "Oh my god," he murmured. Then he shoved another forkful in and moaned. "This is so good."

I laughed as I took my first bite. "Everything on the menu is this good. He makes these bear claws but you need to be early because they sell out."

He shook his head, savouring the taste. "This is . . . I want to marry this meal."

I chuckled, pleased that he was enjoying it. I'd worried for a hot minute that as a chef, he might be overly critical. But I should have known better. Jayden was too nice for that.

He was just nice; a down to earth, generous, humble

guy. He was also gorgeous, and his eyes shone like sapphires when he smiled. His pink lips were tantalizingly kissable . . .

Head in the game, Carter.

"I've been called Cass since I was a little kid," I said, answering his earlier question. "I had snow-white hair, if you could believe that. And my family called me Casper, which was shortened to Cass. So those who know my family tend to call me Cass. I'm Carter to everyone else. But most people here in town know my family, so . . ."

"That's cute," he said, taking a sip of his drink, smiling. "I noticed your kids have blond hair, but you and Kendra both have brown."

"They weren't as blond as me, but their hair's already getting darker."

Jayden pointed to his own hair. "See this? Same shade of brown since the day I was born."

I laughed and pointed to the hair above my ears. "Mine's changing again. Silver, this time."

He leaned across the table and whispered. "And it's sexy as fucking hell. Just so you know."

I thought my face might catch fire.

He leaned back, smiled, mighty pleased with himself. "So is the blush."

I ducked my head and let out a rush of breath. "Jesus."

He laughed and patted his belly. "I'm so full."

He changed subjects so fast it took me a second to catch up. "You ready to go home?"

"Does Hartbridge have any kind of nightlife at all?"

"Uh, no."

"Then home it is." He chuckled. "I don't go out much anyway. I'm usually working nights and weekends. Then during the day, it's usually only cafés or restaurants that are decent. They're more my style anyway."

"I'm not a big drinker," I admitted. "I don't like drinking alone at home. It's not a good habit to get into. And when I have dinner at my parents' place, I have to drive home." My life sounded so lame, even to me. My days of wild parties or drunken benders were long behind me, but there wasn't even a mention of friends or weekend cookouts.

Those days seemed behind me too.

"I've been so busy with the house," I added flatly.

Jayden reached across the table and gave my hand a squeeze. "It's okay, Cass. Your entire life got a reboot. It's perfectly normal to take some time to find your feet."

"My whole life got turned on its head."

"No, it got set right. This is the life you were supposed to live."

My gaze went to his and I couldn't look away. Everything he said was something I needed to hear. How did he know that? I wish I'd known him when I began on this path. Maybe I wouldn't have been so hard on myself . . .

"Jayden," I began, not sure what I was trying to say.

"Ah, Carter," Carl said, walking toward us. "Good to see you, son. Christa said you were in." He was shuffling a little. No doubt the end of a long day would do that to a man of his age. He got to the table and held his hand out, which I shook. Then he turned to Jayden. "And who is this young man?"

"Carl, this is Jayden. He's the chef who's helping me over the holidays."

"Ah, a chef?" Carl said. "Ah, if I'd have known you were a chef . . ."

"Please don't change a thing," Jayden said. "Honestly, one of the best meals I've had in a very long time. And I've eaten a lot of those fancy meals at those big-name places, but your pork was perfection."

"It's true," I added. "He wanted to marry it after just one bite."

Carl's loud laughter was contagious. "I'm glad. Been cooking it the same for fifty years."

"That's why it's so good," Jayden said. "I was just thinking today, I made a steamed gingerbread cake with caramel sauce in one of Cass's great-aunt's old steamers. It must be almost a hundred years old, and that cake turned out near perfect."

"A steamed pudding?" Carl put his hand to his chest. "A man after my own heart. My grandmother would cook a pudding with a thrippence coin in it when I was a boy. I haven't had that in many years. And gingerbread cake?" He looked up at the wall and gave a nod. "I should make one."

Jayden smiled. "I'll make you a small one, and Cass can drop it in for you."

Carl clapped my shoulder. "You be careful, or he'll steal my heart. Making me sweets, don't you let my wife hear."

We all laughed and he went on his way. I didn't get the chance to tell him, to clarify, that Jayden and I weren't a thing. If he stole someone's heart, it was no concern of mine.

Unless he stole mine . . .

"You okay?" Jayden asked.

"Oh yeah. I think he thought we were together."

Jayden studied me for a second. "And how does that feel? That you could be in here on a date and no one would care. In fact, they'd be happy for you."

I couldn't help but smile. "It feels good."

His smile became a grin. "Good." He picked up his beanie. "And I'm totally going to make him a tiny little gingerbread cake. We can bring it in . . . *oh*, we can bring it in when that Christmas festival thing is on."

I'd forgotten about that.

"Oh, you wanted to go to that?"

He nodded. "Absolutely."

"I think Kendra is taking the kids."

He clapped his hands. "Perfect."

"And my parents."

He blinked. "Ohhh-kay." Then he frowned. "Did you not want me to . . . I can go by myself."

"Oh no, it's not like that. I'd like to go with you." That stupid blush gave me away every time. I ignored how hot my face felt. "I just wasn't sure it was something you'd want to do."

"Ren said it was all about snow, Christmas decorations, and festival food. I'm sorry, but those are three of my favourite things." He shrugged. "I'll just make sure everyone at the house is fed, and I'll come into town."

"Well, chances are all the guests will be at the festival." I frowned. "More than likely. It's kind of a big deal for Hartbridge." I took a nervous breath and thought, what the hell . . . "And, if it's okay with you, we could go together."

CHAPTER ELEVEN

JAYDEN

I COULDN'T BE SURE, but I had a sneaking suspicion Cass had asked me on a date. Asking me to the Christmas light festival might have been nothing special, considering it had already been mentioned, but he was so nervous. And his eyes were doing that steely thing again, and when I said I'd go with him, he was so happy, so relieved, I was certain it wasn't some off-the-cuff suggestion that we go together.

We were going *together*.

Cass paid the bill and we drove home . . . well, back to his house. He could call it home, but it sounded weird when I said it. We passed his new sign, which looked amazing, even at night. He never said much on the drive, but he smiled at me a few times.

It was sweet, but there was something between us now. A nervousness or awkwardness. It wasn't weird or off-putting. It was just . . . there. I wasn't quite sure what to call it.

Like something needed to be addressed, but neither of us were brave enough to try. I didn't even know where to start. Was it the maybe-date that changed us?

Or was it the acknowledgment that maybe he and I were a little more interested in each other than we cared to admit?

As soon as we walked in, Cass went to stoke the fire and I went into the kitchen. "Want a hot drink before we tackle the tree?"

"Uh, no thanks. I couldn't fit one more thing in." There was a brief pause and he appeared at the kitchen door. "What do you mean tackle the tree?"

"The big Christmas tree. The papa bear tree. It needs to be decorated. People are arriving tomorrow, and I'll be busy all day, and you'll no doubt have things to do in the morning. I thought we'd do it tonight."

Why was I suddenly aware that we were standing just a few feet apart? That he and I were in the kitchen alone together. In the whole house alone, together. Just us. Alone, and so close I could touch him.

My pulse quickened and my heart thumped in my chest. The air seemed to buzz, such an electric thrill.

"You don't need to help me," he said. Was his voice lower? Was I imagining things? He ran his hand through his hair and cleared his throat. It seemed to break the current between us. "I mean, I can do it. It's no big deal."

"I'd like to help, if that's okay?" I shrugged one shoulder. "I haven't really decorated a tree in years, so . . ."

Cass's smile slowly widened. "Then you should absolutely help me."

"First, I need to go turn the heater on in my room, and if you don't mind, I need to take these jeans off."

He blinked. "Uh . . ."

I snorted. "No. I didn't mean it like that. I just meant I ate too much at dinner and now need something with an elastic waist. Like pyjamas."

He laughed and his cheeks flushed dark pink. "Oh, sure. I wasn't sure what you meant."

I raised an eyebrow and said, half-joking, half-not, "If you want me to take 'em off, you only—"

He put his hand up to stop me. "I'll go start unpacking the box of Christmas tree decorations."

"And maybe find something Christmassy on the TV. The cheesier the better," I called out as he walked off. I chuckled as I went down to my room. I quickly changed into my pj's and hoped he wouldn't mind the old tracksuit pants and crew-neck, long-sleeved shirt I wore to bed. "Don't worry," I said when I went back out. "None of the guests will see me in my pj's."

Cass was lifting a tray of baubles out of the box and he stopped when he saw me. "You're cute."

Um . . . "Pardon?"

He looked positively stricken. "I mean your pyjamas are cute. Not you." He waved his hand at me. "I . . . oh god, that's not . . . what I meant . . . yes, you are cute too, but I misspoke; I meant to say your pyjamas are cute. That's what I meant to say."

I laughed. "Well, thank you. I take compliments for me *and* my pyjamas. I don't discriminate."

His shoulders sagged. "I'm sorry."

I took the box of gold baubles from him. "Don't apologise." Then I noticed the TV was on and *Home Alone* was playing. "Ah, this movie is a classic."

"There's some *Home Alone* marathon on," he said. He still seemed embarrassed and awkward. "Wyatt and Charlotte love these movies. If you want to look for something else . . ."

"No, this is perfect." I looked in the box of decorations. "Okay, so what do we do first, the ornaments or the tinsel?"

❄

DECORATING a Christmas tree took way longer than I thought it would. Cass and I worked well together, sometimes talking, sometimes not. Sometimes watching the TV, sometimes laughing. But there was no more awkwardness, no more weirdness. After a crazy amount of gold ornaments, tinsel, and lights, it looked amazing. It was worthy of a magazine cover.

It was just a really lovely night. But it was late by the time we said goodnight, and I crawled into bed. And I lay there, thinking back over the day we'd had. It had been wonderful with Cass's kids, meeting Kendra, and learning that Cass really was just a charming, decent guy. Then there was our 'date' and the amazing dinner . . .

And as I curled onto my side, ready for sleep to settle over me, I realised that maybe the awkwardness and tension between Cass and me was sexual tension.

I felt like an idiot for not realising what it was earlier.

He definitely liked me. He definitely wanted something to happen. We'd agreed on exploring a physical and sexual thing after the busy period was over.

I had to wonder what his hands would feel like on my skin. I bet those rough, calloused hands felt like heaven. I just knew he kissed like his life depended on it.

I wondered what he tasted like.

I wondered how long I could hold out for. How long he could hold out for? Was the day after Christmas too far away? And I was leaving after that. Would such a brief encounter be enough?

I wondered . . .

❄

I WAS up before Cass and handed his not-a-morning-person self a cup of coffee as he walked into the kitchen. "Morning," I said with a smile.

Grumpy-sleepy Cass was adorable. "Hmm."

"You're not a morning person, are you?"

He squinted, scrunching his whole face as if trying to wake himself up. "Not really. Takes me a bit to wake up." He sipped his coffee. "Thank you for this."

I chuckled. "You're welcome." I put some bread into the toaster. "Toast okay for breakfast? I have a bit to get done this morning."

"I can get it," he said. "Let me make it today."

I began pulling the cannisters I'd needed from the pantry and set them on the counter. "What time do the first guests arrive?"

The toast popped up so he buttered it, and I slid the peanut butter in front of him and put on the perfect amount. "Two o'clock. The Nicholsons and the Baileys. Two couples."

"Nice."

"The other three arrive tomorrow. I think one said they'll be here before lunch, but the others are due around two."

"I'll make some sandwiches and leave them in the fridge in case they haven't had lunch by the time they get here. And if they don't eat them, then you and I are having sandwiches for dinner."

Cass smiled at me. "That's really thoughtful, thank you."

I raised my coffee cup to him. "To your first official day. May they be the first of many customers."

He clinked his cup to mine. "Let's hope so. And thank you for saying that."

I held up two fingers and smiled. "Okay, so two things. One, I'm going to need more toast. And two, after you've made us some more toast, I'm going to need you to get out of my kitchen."

He chuckled. "Your kitchen, huh?"

"For as long as I'm employed here, yes. If you get under my feet while we have a house full of people, I'll put you on dish duty."

He nodded, smiling behind his coffee. "Understood."

"So, the toast?"

"Right, right." He finally got himself into first gear and popped some more bread into the toaster. "You don't mind being bossy, do you?"

I laughed. "Not at all." I poured us a refill of coffee. "I've never had a problem in asking for what I want."

He shot me an exasperated look. "I know. You just come right out and ask for all kinds of things."

I put the eggs on the counter and shrugged. "Toast. Holding hands. Sex. All the good things in life. I haven't asked you to kiss me yet, and I bet you know how to kiss. And I mean *really* know how to kiss."

Cass leaned both hands on the counter and dropped his head and sighed. I thought I might have said too much, pushed the joke too far, but then he spun around. "Ask me how strong my self-control is. Go on, ask."

I tried not to smile. "How's your self-control holding up there, Cass? By a thread?"

"By a tiny thread. A single strand of thread. That's it. Just one."

"Is it gonna last until after Christmas?" I asked. "Because I was lying in bed last night wondering if Christmas was just too far away. You know, for both of us."

His nostrils flared and he raised a finger. "Jayden."

The toast popped and he jumped, making me laugh. He grumbled as he buttered it and I tried not to smile too big when he handed me a slice. "Thank you."

"Enjoy it," he said, now gripping the edge of the kitchen counter as if he was stopping himself from touching me. "I . . . I think I'm gonna need to go lie in the snow for a bit."

I chuckled as I chewed my toast. "Sorry. But you know where I am if you need me. And honestly, that's gotta be so much better than the equivalent of a cold shower."

"Oh, so I'll be allowed in your kitchen for . . . that. I thought I had to get out."

"There are two exceptions for you to be in here. Dish duty and dick duty."

He stared at me for a long second, then burst out laughing. "Right. This is not how I imagined our morning conversation going."

I waited for him to leave, but he didn't. He just stood there, his chest rising rapidly, his knuckles white as he gripped the counter.

Holy shit.

Was he considering it?

My body was all for this, was ready for this. My dick was certainly ready for some action, thickening in anticipation. Without thinking, I readjusted myself. His eyes followed my hand, and he swallowed.

But then he shook his head quickly. "Nope. Nope." And then, with the worst or best timing ever, his phone buzzed in his pocket. He answered it, glaring at me. "Carter Campion speaking. Oh yes, Mrs Bailey . . ."

His customer arriving today. For a sinking moment, I thought she might be calling to cancel.

"That's no problem at all," Cass said, smiling at me. "Any time is fine. See you soon."

He clicked off the call. "They'll be here before lunch."

"Excellent. Then I better do something more than just sandwiches."

Cass leaned against the counter and stuck his thumb and forefinger into his eyes, and I felt bad for adding to his stress.

I picked up the wooden spoon. "Sorry about before. I shouldn't have played you like that. Let me know if there's anything you need me to do."

I glanced over at him just in time for him to grip my shoulder, push me back against the kitchen counter, and kiss me.

And I mean *kiss*.

His full body against mine, anything but gentle. His rough hand on my jaw, his mouth open, his tongue tasting mine.

My knees turned to jelly, my head spun, but he pinned me against the cupboard and held my face, kissing me for all he was worth.

Holy shit, he knew how to kiss.

Before I could even think to put my arms around him, to hold him tight and keep him right where he was, he grunted in my mouth and pulled back.

With his weight suddenly gone, I almost fell or slithered to the floor. I don't think I'd even drawn a breath the entire time. I tried to speak and made an obscure squeaking sound, and he smirked.

That fucker smirked because he knew . . . He knew what his kisses could do.

"Hm," he groaned, smug and sexy as hell. He licked his bottom lip. "We have work to do."

And he just turned and walked out.

Like his legs still worked and his brain was functioning.

Mine were not.

I had to lean on the counter and squeeze some air into my lungs. I was pretty sure I heard him laugh from somewhere in the house. And when he came back into the kitchen a few minutes later with his arms full of kindling, he laughed.

I was still standing there, holding a wooden spoon in my hand, dazed. I felt drunk.

"You okay?" His grin did stupid things to my heart.

"No. I think . . . I think the brandied fruit is making me drunk."

Cass laughed. "Mm-hmm. Sure. The brandied fruit. With the lid still on."

I pointed the wooden spoon at him. "Warn a guy next time."

He grinned. "I don't think I will."

I snorted. "What?"

He was still holding a whole forest of twigs and kindling. That couldn't have been easy, but he managed it just fine. Actually, I appreciated the effort his biceps were making. "You said you shouldn't have played me. Earlier, you said, 'Sorry, I shouldn't have played you,' because the game was fun when you were in charge. And you were right. I really wanted to kiss you. I've wanted to kiss you since you got here, pretty much. So I took charge."

I found myself smiling at him. "And how does that feel?"

"Really good."

I laughed. "Well, you can take charge all you like, because holy shit, that was one helluva kiss."

"That wasn't even a decent kiss. That was just to shut you up."

I scoffed, stunned that this was the same Cass. "Did you just wake up today and decide to take me up on my offer?"

He shook his head. "No. Your offer is still subject to my terms and conditions. We'll get through Christmas Day, then see if we're still interested."

"Oh, will we?"

"Yep. Unless you decide you don't want to. I thought you liked how I kissed you."

I snarled at him and pointed the wooden spoon at him again. "You know damn well I liked that."

He hummed and fought a smile. "This game is so much more fun now that I'm winning."

I rolled my eyes. "Out of my kitchen. Unless you're here for dish duty or dick duty. Clearly you're not here for either, so out with you." I shooed him. "I have things to do."

He went willingly. Smugly.

"And just so you know," I called out after him. "You're not winning."

There was no reply but I could picture him smiling. And this *game* was fun, and this side of him was very cute and playful, and that kiss damn near curled my toes.

But . . .

But now I wasn't sure it was even a game. Because somewhere in the last few days, I'd begun to like him. My heart had noticed the kindness in his, the sweetness, and the honesty. And if this was just a game, I doubted there'd be a winner at the end of my time here.

If both teams lost, why bother playing at all?

Enough of that, Jayden. Just do your job.

Making little individual steamed gingerbread cakes, as I told Carl I would, was a great distraction. They wouldn't take long in the steamer at all, but it gave me enough time to throw a hearty vegetable soup together. It wasn't long until the Bailey's arrived. I tried not to eavesdrop, but it was hard not to hear. They were a couple in their fifties, at a guess, who had come to spend Christmas with their cousin and aunt, whom Cass knew. Of course he did. He knew everyone.

Cass gave them a tour, and after showing them the family room and the rec room, he brought them into the kitchen through the dining-room door, which I wasn't expecting. "This is Jayden. He's the culinary wizard," Cass said. "Please be thankful I'm not cooking for you."

"Morning," I said brightly, hiding my surprise. I wiped my hand on my apron nervously. "Excuse the civilian clothes. I usually wear a uniform."

Cass raised an eyebrow. I ignored it.

"Well, we're early," Mrs Bailey said, smiling sweetly. "Something in here smells delicious."

"I made a pot of soup for lunch to have with some sandwiches," I said.

"How wonderful," Mrs Bailey said.

Cass led them on for the rest of the tour, taking them into the reading room. They were clearly enamoured with the house, and Cass was so proud. And happy. He was so happy he could burst, and after he left them in their room to rest and freshen up, he ducked into the kitchen. Where I pretended I hadn't just spied on them.

He let out a long breath, smiling but nervous. "How did you think it went?"

"I couldn't hear all of it, but I think you did great. They seem lovely too."

He nodded. "Cousins to the Bailey's on Juniper Road. Nice family."

I put my hand on his arm. "Take a breath, Cass. You did

great. Your first guests are here. The last two years of hard work are done. You're officially open for business."

He nodded quickly and got a little teary but shook it off. "Okay, wow. I wasn't expecting that."

I chuckled. "And I wasn't expecting you to bring them in here. Look at how I'm dressed."

"You look more than fine to me."

I nudged him with my elbow. "I do have a chef's uniform. I'll wear it tomorrow. Looks more professional. The shirt, at least."

"Hm. I shall look forward to seeing you in that shirt. The ones with all the funny buttons down the front?"

"Yes. Makes it easy to rip off."

Both his eyebrows shot up. "Sounds fun."

I rolled my eyes. "In case something spills on me, like boiling fat or fire."

"Oh." He made a face. "The version in my head was more fun."

I smiled at him. "Feeling a bit better?"

Cass nodded. "I am. Thank you. You have a knack for that."

"For what?"

"For saying the right thing. Whatever it is I need to hear."

"And you have a knack for kissing me when I least expect it. So we're even." I bumped his hip with mine. "Want some soup?"

"Yes, please."

CHAPTER TWELVE

CASS

THE REST of the afternoon flew. The Nicholsons arrived at a little after two, and Jayden offered coffee, cookies, and leftover sandwiches for an afternoon snack.

Then it was dinnertime, and he served grilled chicken with some divine chutney sauce and a type of vegetable pasta. It was amazing.

He was amazing.

I didn't dare get in his way. He was so well-organised and had everything timed down to the minute. By the end of the night, the Baileys were settled in by the fire in the sitting room and the Nicholsons were in the family room and I'd helped Jayden clean up.

"The boring D-duty," he said when we'd finished washing up and cleaning down all the surfaces.

"The what?"

"D-duty," he explained. "Dishes or dick. The only two reasons you're allowed in here, and you chose the boring one."

"Get much of the fun one at your old job?"

He snatched the dishtowel off me. "Some. Are you jealous?"

"No."

He grinned. "You absolutely are." Then he shrugged. "Could be getting some of the fun D-duty here too, but you said no. Well, we could have *before* the guests arrived. Now the chances are nil. Which is fine. Guess we'll just have to wait until after Christmas Day. Unless you want to kiss me again. You said it wasn't even a proper kiss. Would you care to explain?"

"Not really."

"It felt like a proper kiss to me. So now I'll just have to lie in bed and imagine what a proper kiss from you entails." He took a breath in and moaned on the exhale. "It will involve my hand and lube, just so you know. Probably both hands, actually."

I snorted quietly, trying very hard not to picture that.

Too late. Way too late . . .

Jayden laughed. "You're picturing it right now, aren't you?"

I sighed, long and loud. "No."

"You're a terrible liar."

"I know."

He smiled and hung the dish towel over the edge of the sink. "Well, on that note, I'm off to bed. Bigger day tomorrow, and I need my beauty sleep." He held his hand up and winked. "And I have a date with my hand."

I laughed. "I'd say goodnight, but it appears you already have that under control."

"I do. Well, I will have in about ten minutes."

This was an absurd conversation to be having so casually. "Well, good luck with it."

"Thanks."

He turned to walk out but there was something I wanted to say. "Jayden?"

He stopped. "Yeah?"

"Thank you for today, and for everything you've done for me. Your food tonight was exceptional, and I just wanted you to know that I really appreciate it."

He smiled. "Thank you. It's really no problem, but I do appreciate you saying that."

He left with a nod and a smile, and I stood in his kitchen, looking around at everything so meticulously organised, his lists on clipboards hanging from the shelf in the storeroom, things labelled and dated in the fridge.

The truth was, I'd have been lost trying to do this without him.

Without someone's help, anyway. But any other chef wouldn't have helped and supported me like Jayden had.

His words of encouragement really helped me these last few days. The way he thought to congratulate me on my first day, on being officially open for business.

How was I going to do this when he wasn't here?

The thought of him leaving sat like a stone in my belly.

You'll cope, Carter. You'll manage just fine. You'll find a way, you always do.

Not even my internal monologue sounded convincing.

I turned the kitchen light off and opened my laptop on the dining room table instead of going upstairs to my quarters in case any guests needed me.

I managed to get some things done, all while definitely not thinking about what Jayden was probably doing in his room. Thankfully the Baileys and the Nicholsons both called it a night relatively early, so I fixed the fires for the night and made sure the house was locked up before heading upstairs.

My first day, my first official day, as Jayden had called it, was officially done.

I'd long wondered if this day would ever happen. Everything I'd done, everything I'd sacrificed, built and mended, organised and put together in making Arabella B&B what it was, all came down to today.

And I went to sleep knowing I'd done the best I could. And it was good enough.

The new part of my life had begun.

So why did it feel like something was missing?

I didn't want to put a name to it because that would make it real.

Why did I have to kiss him?

Now that empty space had a name and a face and cute-as-hell smile.

He tasted like coffee and peanut butter and . . . exactly like what was missing in my life.

THE NEXT MORNING, I walked into the kitchen and stopped.

Jayden was wearing a black chef's shirt with black pants and black pull-on boots. The shirt was the kind with the two rows of buttons, and it was . . .

How was a chef's uniform hot?

"Morning," he said brightly. He was always so chipper in the mornings. He grinned at me. "See something you like?"

"You weren't kidding about the uniform."

"No. Why would I be?" He pressed his shirt down, then pulled at the hem a little. "Looks more professional, yes? Especially if the guests will be seeing me."

I nodded because that was very true. "It looks great."

"So you do like it?"

I rolled my eyes.

"Enough to kiss me again?"

I groaned.

He laughed, but thankfully, or maybe disappointingly, he let it go. He clapped his hands together. "Okay, first up, coffee for you and me. That's your job. I've already put the cereal out on the dining table, if anyone wants to help themselves. Breakfast menu is a choice of eggs cooked however the guest prefers, bacon, fried tomato, toast."

I barely had the brain function to operate the coffee machine. "How are you so organised first thing in the morning?"

He chuckled. "Today's breakfast is easy. There are two couples and us two. That's nothing. Tomorrow will be different." He was busy pulling stuff out of the fridge and the cupboard, doing ten things at once. "What time does everyone arrive today?"

"One couple's arriving before lunch, the last two between two and three o'clock." I handed him a steaming cup of coffee. "What did you need me to do?"

He sipped his coffee and smiled. "The answer of 'I need you to do me' is not what you're looking for, is it?"

I smiled into my coffee. "Not exactly."

"Shame."

"It is."

"Then the D-duty rule applies, I'm afraid," he said. "Dick or dishes, and there's no dishes to be done."

"I really love the smell of temptation in the morning."

He laughed. "Do you want me to cook you something before the guests want theirs?"

What I really wanted was to kiss him again.

"How do you like your eggs?"

I walked over to him, took the frying pan out of his hand, and slid it onto the counter. He was surprised at first, but then he smiled until I cupped his jaw and he realised I was going to kiss him again. His smile faded, stars appeared in his eyes, and when I thumbed his bottom lip, he chased it with the tip of his tongue.

I tilted his face up and slowly brought his lips to mine. Where our first kiss had been hard and rough, this was soft and tender. I was gentle, and when our tongues finally touched, his knees almost buckled.

He sighed and fell into me, his hand finding its way to my neck and into the hair at the nape of my neck, holding onto me.

He was strong and hard planes of muscle and bulges in all the right places.

It felt divine.

He kissed me back this time, deep and very thoroughly.

I could just imagine what getting naked with him would be like. Making him come, making love . . .

I broke the kiss to breathe, and I smiled at his dreamy expression. "Was that a proper kiss?" he murmured.

"Hm, I can still do better. Maybe next time."

He groaned out a laugh. "Tease."

But there was no chance for a next time for the rest of the day. We got busy and didn't stop. Even after dinner with a full house, I was busy with guests and he was busier in the kitchen. I was beginning to think the next day was out too. I'd hoped to catch him in the kitchen before any guests came down for breakfast, but I found him already talking to Mr Cantrell, an older man who liked to rise early.

He also liked to talk, apparently.

Jayden grinned when he saw me. "Oh look, here's the boss. I better get back to work."

Which left me with Mr Cantrell, telling me how great it was to see such a house so lovingly restored.

For thirty minutes, without drawing a breath.

He was just getting to the part about the library he used to go to as a small boy when, thankfully, Mrs Cantrell arrived. "Dear, let the poor boy go do his job," she said, giving me an apologetic smile as they sat down for coffee, which gave me a chance to escape. I headed straight for the kitchen.

"Oh my god," I mumbled.

Jayden laughed. "I went to fill the coffee," he whispered. "And he latched on. Likes a yarn, apparently."

He'd already made the coffee and he handed me one. "Thank you."

"Sleep okay? Must make you a bit nervous having all these people in your house. Is that weird for you?"

I put my finger to his chin and lifted his face, kissing him softly. It was just a brief, gentle kiss, the kind that made my heart knock against my ribs. "I wanted to do that all day yesterday."

His grin was something remarkable. "You know which room is mine, right? The one at the end of the hall? If you wanted to kiss me so bad, you knew where to find me."

I laughed and sipped my coffee. "I believe you're talking about more than just a kiss in the kitchen."

"I do believe so, yes." He leaned against the counter. "So, is you kissing me in the kitchen a thing now?"

"I do believe so, yes."

He chuckled. "I'll have to amend the D-duty list to include that."

I met his gaze and we stood there, not looking away,

both of us smiling. My heart was thrumming and I had butterflies, which was ridiculous and lovely. It made me laugh, and of course my cheeks got all hot.

Jayden groaned. "That's so hot. You might wanna go back out and lay in the snow again, in case you burst into flames."

"Shut up."

He laughed. "Okay, but for real, unless you're in here to help, you're gonna have to ship out. I have a lot to do today, and I'm going to need to make a trip into town to the store before the Christmas light festival thing. I'm looking forward to that. The weather's supposed to be perfect. Maybe even a light snow tonight."

Oh, the festival. I'd almost forgotten about it.

"I asked everyone yesterday and they all said they were going, so I don't need to worry about dinner tonight. But they'll all be here for lunch so I was going to make stew and sandwiches. That should tide them over before the festival, but I will restock a few things before tomorrow."

"I can go for you. Just give me a list."

"I was going to take the mini cake in for Carl. I was supposed to take it yesterday, but we got busy and I could take it tonight, but then he'll be flat out."

"I can take it for you." I shrugged. "I know you're busy all day. Yesterday you didn't stop once."

"Neither did you."

"But I'm supposed to be busy. I didn't expect it to be so much work for you." It really just reminded me that I was embarrassingly unprepared to be doing this on my own.

He waved his hand, brushing off any concern. "This is easy. I just assumed one of us should be here as long as there are guests still here. I wouldn't be comfortable leaving some strangers in your house without one of us. Not the first time. I guess it gets easier." Then he made a face. "Oh. Did you want me to go? I guess I'm just as much a stranger . . ."

"You're not a stranger." So I'd known him for no more than a few days. That was true. But he was different. I don't know how or why, he just was. "I trust you with my home and my customers, my business reputation."

With my heart.

That thought pulled me up.

Jayden's eyes never left mine, and if he saw the truth in me, I couldn't tell.

"Give me a list of anything you need," I said. "And I'll grab it for you. I have to go to town. Jayden, I have no problem leaving you here in my place." I shrugged. "Actually, it's probably better that I go because, if you're here, you can do what I do, no worries. Which so far has been to answer a few questions, linen supplies, checking the fires, and making sure everyone's happy. But I can't do what you do." I gestured to the breakfast things he had on the counter like it proved my point.

"You would do this just fine if you had to," he said.

"No, I wouldn't—"

"You would cope, Cass," he said flatly. "Like you've coped with everything else. Which is very well, I might add. But right now, I need you to go do what you do. Unless you want to fry some bacon, scramble some eggs, and make some toast." He checked his watch. "In five minutes."

Shit.

"I can make toast." It was honestly about all I was good for while he zipped around making everything else. I refilled the guest coffee pot and milk jugs and juices and made sure everyone had everything they needed.

As usual, Jayden was charming and proficient. Nothing was ever an issue with guests and they adored him. Actually, I thought Mrs Bailey had a crush on him with all the fluttery eyes she gave him, but he was nothing but professional. Sure, breakfast wasn't a complicated meal service. But still . . . he was so good at all of it.

And after breakfast was all said and done and the kitchen was cleaned to within an inch of its life, he began pulling everything out for . . . "What are you making?"

"I was going to make some lemon squares. Just small ones. Or what about some tiny apple pie cups?" He held his hand out, cupped. "They're only small and easy to make. Oh, that's a much better idea. You've got plenty of apples. Can I use a few?"

"I didn't even know I owned that, so sure."

He disappeared into the storeroom and came out with the can in question and one of his clipboards. "Here's my list of what I need."

I gave it a quick once over. Everything was categorised by section, brand names, weight and size, and he'd even written down the rough price. "And if they don't have that brand?"

"Something close will be fine." He held out a little white cloth bundle. It fit in his palm, was kind of round, tied off with twine. "This is for Carl. Please tell him it's from me and I hope he enjoys it. It's in a little foil ramekin. Please don't tip it or the sauce will spill."

He gave it to me and I was surprised by how heavy it was. And how good it smelled. "Is this the steamed cake?"

He nodded. "Yep. No stealing it because I will ask him when I see him at the festival tonight. Which I'm excited about. I can't wait. Have I told you I'm excited for it?"

I laughed. "I think you may be a little disappointed. It's nothing crazy."

"Small town, snow, Christmas lights, happy people, and

street food. What is there not to like?" He shooed me out of the kitchen. "Now get. Unless you plan on kissing me again, you need to leave. I'm busy."

I pretended to consider it. "Hmm. I could . . ."

"Don't tease me, Carter."

The full name surprised me. "What happened to calling me Cass?"

He raised an eyebrow. "Carter."

I listened to the house for a brief second, and knowing we were alone for the time being, I stepped over to him, right up close so he had to look up at me, and I kissed him again. "That better?"

He smiled. "Cass."

I grinned victoriously. "Call me on my cell if you need anything. I won't be long."

I drove into town with his cute little cake and shopping list on the seat beside me, smiling, feeling genuinely happy. Not just about the customers and being finally open for business, but because of Jayden.

I'd kissed him twice today. Just sweet and soft, nothing hot and heavy like the other times. But just a quick, familiar kiss, as though we'd shared a thousand of them.

And this sounded a little crazy. Yes, nights of sex with him would be amazing. No doubt whatsoever.

But what I wanted more than that?

Was to pull him in for a hug, to hold him, and to feel his arms around me too. Just in my kitchen or by the fire. To feel that kind of intimacy. I didn't want just meaningless sex. I didn't want anything meaningless with him.

I wanted sweet and tender. I wanted to be close to him. I wanted hugs and cuddles, to hold hands, to kiss and to laugh.

My heart already knew what my head was trying to out-reason.

I wanted romance.

I wanted to fall in love with a man. I wanted to be loved by a man in return, to know what that felt like.

I wanted it with him.

This had disaster written all over it—he was leaving town soon—so there was no future for us. And I was technically his employer. It couldn't possibly end well.

No matter all the well-intended reasons my brain could throw at me, my heart was telling me to do it anyway.

What did Ren say the other day?

To take the chance.

Take the chance. If it lasts a night or a week or a lifetime, take the chance on happiness whenever you can.

I sighed. Dammit.

CHAPTER THIRTEEN

JAYDEN

"ARE YOU READY?" I asked.

Cass had just finished making sure the fires were okay and the grills were securely in place. The last of the guests had already left, daylight was fading fast, and the house was very quiet.

"I am." He eyed what I was holding. "Whatcha got there?"

I opened the takeout container to show him. Inside were two small steamed chocolate lava cakes surrounded by a few of the mini apple tarts. He went to reach for one and I smacked his hand. "They're for Wyatt and Charlotte."

His head jerked up, his eyes curious and cautious. "What?"

"You said they'd be here tonight, at the light festival. And they wanted the little chocolate cakes when they were here but they weren't done steaming. And I thought they might like the apple cups. I hope you don't mind."

"No, I . . . I just didn't . . . that's really nice of you."

"I'm a nice guy."

His eyes cut to mine. "You are."

That look, that tone of voice, went straight to my belly, twisting and swooping.

"Maybe I could have another one of those little apple things . . ."

I put the lid back on. "Uh-uh. How many did you have this afternoon?"

"Not enough."

I laughed. "Come on, let's get going. I don't want to miss anything."

"I can assure you. You won't miss anything."

We went into the mudroom, I put the takeout container on the bench seat, and we put on our boots and coats. "Mrs Garza told me she's been to a few of these light festivals, and she said it's one of her favourite nights of the year."

"Mrs Garza told me she doesn't get out much." Cass handed me my scarf and beanie. "So I'm not quite sure if that's the compliment you think it is."

Chuckling, I pulled on my beanie and then my gloves. "Well, I'm still excited. What time are Kendra and the kids getting there?"

He checked his watch. "About now."

"So let's go!"

He smiled and held the door for me. It was cold outside, there was a decent amount of snow on the ground, but there was no wind. I waited for him to lock the door and enter the code, and when he was done, I began for the steps. "Oh, wait one second," he said.

I stopped, wondering what on earth he'd forgot, but he cupped my face in both his gloved hands and kissed me. Soft at first, and again, this time with a tiny nose nudge that woke the butterflies in my belly. Then he lifted my chin and kissed me deeper, his warm tongue tangling with mine.

Lord, this man could kiss.

The kiss slowed and he pulled back, a smug but happy smile on his face. "Now I'm ready."

My head was still spinning. "We don't have to go at all, if you don't want." I nodded to the back door. "It's just a light festival . . . I'm sure we could find something to do all alone in the house. We should probably stay . . ."

He laughed and took my arm. "Light festival first."

We walked to his truck, and he started the engine and cranked up the heat. His words then dawned on me. "First? You said light festival first, as though we might find some alone time afterwards?"

He put the truck into reverse and smiled as he looked over his shoulder. He was even more handsome by the dash light against the dark. "I was thinking maybe we could."

Well, shit.

"Well, shit."

He laughed, shifting in his seat as he drove us down the long drive. "Is that still okay with you?"

"Where have you been? Of course it's okay with me."

"I just wanted to make sure."

I was positively giddy. "Why the change of heart?"

He was quiet for a moment. "I tried to say no. Then I tried to set a time frame after Christmas, right? Because that was sensible. But then I kissed you, and now I can't think about anything else." He shook his head. "And what Ren said the other day was right. I shouldn't waste a day. I was a fool to say no."

"You're not a fool for anything," I replied. "And for what it's worth, I'd prefer you wait until you were comfortable."

He smiled at me. "Thanks."

"So what are we talking about anyway?" I asked. "In this alone time tonight."

He laughed. "How about we just see what happens?"

"I'm down for that." So down. So very down for this gorgeous man to do whatever he wanted to my body. Hell yes. I was going to have my way with his body too, don't you worry about that.

And I was lost in the best part of my imagination for a few seconds until I noticed the world outside the truck.

Main Street was awash with lanterns, Christmas decorations and colourful Christmas lights. There were so many people, families and kids, smiling faces. It was something out of a movie.

"Oh, Cass," I whispered. "This is magical." My excitement ramped up a notch or two.

The main block was closed off, so we turned up Bridge Street toward the Home Mart where we found a parking spot. "We'll need to walk from here."

As we walked back to Main Street, I realised the reason why they closed off the street at the main block was because they had a kiddie train ride, a Winterland scene for photos, snowmen, Christmas trees, and carollers.

I'd never seen anything like it.

And of course Cass knew every person we walked past or looked at. They waved or said hello and gave me a curious second glance. One lady even went so far as to look directly at us, nudge the woman beside her, and mumbled something to her.

Cass inhaled and gave a curt nod. "Natalie," he said.

But we kept walking. "Know her?"

"Went to school with her."

I hated that for him. They all knew he was gay, apparently, and this was his first time being in public with a man. We weren't even together. We weren't holding hands. We weren't touching in any way.

"Ignore them," I offered. "They're only staring because you're hot."

He shot me a look that was a little nervous, a little relieved, somewhat bewildered. "I don't think that's it."

"Well, think of it this way," I said as we walked. "They'll look this time, and next time you bring some lucky guy out in public for real, they won't even notice."

Something flashed behind his eyes, but before he could say anything we were interrupted. "Cass! Over here!"

The woman calling out was middle-aged, with an ash-blonde bobbed haircut and a long camel-coloured coat. She was waving and smiling and standing next to a tall man who was an older replica of Cass.

His parents.

Okay, then.

Meeting the parents doesn't mean anything when you're not a couple, Jayden.

It didn't help quell my nerves at all.

But they were also standing with Kendra, Wyatt, and Charlotte.

"Daddy!" Charlotte called and ran to him. He collected her in a big hug and lifted her up, carrying her the rest of the way.

"Evening," Cass said to everyone. "Great night for it."

"Oh, it's perfect," his mom said. Then she looked right at me, curiously, like I was a new species. "Hello."

"Uh, hi!" I said.

"Mom, Dad, this is Jayden. Jayden Turner. He's the chef I was telling you about. Jayden, this is Catherine and Miles Campion."

"Oh," his mom said. She was either relieved or surprised by the professional connection to her son. It was hard to tell. "Oh, Kendra was just telling us about you."

His dad offered me his hand. "Nice to meet you. How are you finding it?"

"I'm loving it," I replied. "This town is so charming; it looks like a Disney movie right now. And the house is amazing." I turned to Kendra and held out the takeout container. "This is for Wyatt and Charlotte, and you. I hope you don't mind."

She was a little taken aback but took the container with a smile. "Uh, thank you."

I opened the lid while she was holding it. "It's two of the chocolate cakes they helped make when they came over. They're steamed, kind of taste a bit like a mud cake. And lots of these mini apple tarts I thought you might like."

"Aw," she said. "Thank you. That's so sweet of you. They look like little Christmas ornaments."

"They're really good," Cass said. "Kinda apple, kinda caramel, shortbread, all in one bite."

I rolled my eyes. "He ate so many he's going to have diabetes."

"Show me, Mommy," Wyatt said as both he and Charlotte peered into the container.

"You can only have them when your mum says so," I told them.

It was then I noticed Cass's parent's watching me, and watching me and Cass together. It was a little awkward, and I felt bad for Cass. "Sorry, I didn't think to bring any for you," I said. "I'll set some aside and Cass can take them to you on Christmas Day."

"Aw, that's terribly kind," his mom said.

"Daddy, can you take us on the train?" Charlotte asked. Cass looked to Kendra. She nodded and Cass gave me an apologetic glance over his shoulder as he got dragged away by his two kids.

'm so sorry," I said to Kendra. "I should have asked you about the sweets before just handing them over and announcing that they were for Wyatt and Charlotte."

"It's fine," she said with a smile. "They had a lovely time the other day. And I got all their gifts bought and wrapped, so it was a win."

"Cass had a great day too." As soon as those words were out, I felt stupid for saying that. I was talking like I was his boyfriend. Which I most definitely was not. Even if I did just have his tongue in my mouth with a promise of more later on tonight.

"How are the first guests settling in?" Miles asked. My god, he was just like Cass.

"Oh, they're great. All very lovely. And everything's run smoothly so far. Well, from what I can tell in the kitchen. Cass takes everything in stride, and they all love him."

"So, Jayden," Miles hedged. "Where are you from?"

We chatted for maybe five minutes, just boring small talk about travelling and how I'd settled into the States, until a woman arrived who turned out to be Kendra's sister. And as our little circle got bigger, I felt a bit more awkward and kept glancing over at Cass to see if he could come save me.

First, he was waiting in line for the small train, then he was *on* the small train, and I did notice him looking over at us a few times—or more specifically, me—but then I spotted another familiar face across the street. "Oh, excuse me. It was really nice to meet you all. Have a great night," I said, making my excuse to leave.

Ren and Hamish were strolling along, Ren's arm around Hamish, both smiling and clearly in love. I was a little jealous. "Hey," I said, walking up to them.

"Oh, hi," Ren said. "We wondered if we'd see you here."

"Have you ever seen anything like this?" Hamish asked.

I shook my head. "Never. How gorgeous is it?"

"It's my third time," Hamish said. "I missed it by two days my very first year here, but it gets more wonderful every year."

"It's like a Disney movie," I said.

Hamish and Ren laughed, but Ren said, "Hamish is convinced his life here is a Hallmark movie and we're all actors, and he's the only one who doesn't know."

"Like the *Truman Show*," Hamish said. "Except Hallmark."

I laughed. "I could believe that."

"So, you're loving it here?" Ren asked. "Enough to stay?"

"Oh." I let out a laugh. "I don't know about that."

"You need to stay," Hamish said. "To double the number of Australians here. Purely for immigration statistic purposes only. It has nothing to do with the quaint town, the lovely people, and the eligible gay men."

I laughed at that. "Right, of course."

"Speaking of eligible gay men," Ren said, nodding over my shoulder.

I turned to find Cass walking toward us. He was grinning, his beanie pulled low. "Sorry for leaving you," he said to me. Then he greeted Ren and Hamish. "Hey. Nice night for it."

"Perfect night," Hamish replied, smiling warmly.

I put my hand on Cass's arm, then remembered where we were. I pulled it back. "You absolutely should do tiny train rides with your kids," I said. "That's what nights like this are about."

He smiled. "Maybe later. They're playing with friends right now."

"We were just going to grab something to eat," Ren said. "Apparently Carl's chilli bread bowls are a hit this year. And the beef brisket burgers. Did you guys want to come with us?"

I looked up at Cass and he shrugged. "Sure."

Cass called out to his dad, saying he was just going to Carl's. His dad waved, and we began walking over to Carl's Diner. There was a stall out the front, decked out with Christmas lights, and a decent line of people.

But the smell was amazing, and everyone was leaving with their hands full and wide smiles. I was certain the entire town of Hartbridge was enjoying the show. It was a real community night, people talking and laughing, kids laughing, snow fights, Christmas carollers were singing.

Cass nudged my shoulder with his. "Can you smile any wider?"

I laughed. "This is the best night ever."

"Wait for the lighting of the tree," Hamish said. "It's awesome."

That was down near the bridge by the river, on the very aptly named Bridge Street, which was pretty much the only intersection along Main Street. There was a big tree, apparently, that had the honours of becoming the town's Christmas tree.

Everything about this place was so cute.

Ren put his arm back around Hamish and asked Cass all about how his first guests were faring. It was so casual and innocent, but I ached to touch Cass like that.

I had to stop myself. I shoved my hands into my pockets instead.

"You cold?" Cass asked me.

"A little." It wasn't a lie exactly.

"Oh god, I'm still not used to the cold," Hamish said. "I'm better than I used to be."

Cass rubbed my back, which was strangely intimate. That was something you only did to people you cared for, right? "Did you want to go inside?" He nodded toward the door of Carl's Diner.

I smiled at him. "And miss all this? I'll be okay, thanks."

We were next in line anyway, but his hand sure felt nice on my back. I ignored the looks Ren and Hamish were giving me and was relieved when Carl saw it was us. "Oh, look who it is!" Carl said. He came around the side of the stall and hugged me. "I got my gingerbread cake, thank you so much."

I was not expecting that. "Oh."

"I took a little peek," he said, letting go of me. "But I'm saving it for Christmas Day."

"Well, you're very welcome." I found myself shrinking back to Cass's side. I wanted to hide behind him but didn't. "Have it with some creme anglaise, maybe a touch of brandy."

"Ah, I will. Just don't tell my wife. Now, what can I get you? Ren, you have the brisket, yes?"

"You know me well," Ren replied.

We ordered ours and paid, I opted for the chilli bread bowl, and we said our goodbyes. We moved down the sidewalk a little to eat out of the way of the other people in line, and we devoured the food. It really was amazing.

"Carl likes you," Ren said.

"Cass brought me here the other night. Promised me a night of Hartbridge's best dining experience, and I have to say, he's not wrong."

Cass nudged me with his elbow. "Then Jayden here

made Carl a mini, steamed Christmas cake, wrapped in cheesecloth and everything. It totally made his day."

"Ah," Hamish said. "You absolutely are going to stay in Hartbridge. You're almost a local already."

I laughed, but Cass shot me a funny look. "What's that?" he asked.

I shrugged. "These two are trying to convince me to stay."

Cass's eyes flashed to mine, but before he could say anything, a commotion broke out behind us. There was a bit of a crowd at the back of the stall, and . . . wait, was that Carl on the ground?

"I'm okay, I'm okay," he said. He managed to get to his feet, albeit very slowly, but he was favouring one leg. "Just twisted my old knee." But then he tried to put weight on it and yelped. Cass and Ren grabbed him.

"Come on, let's get you sitting down," Ren said.

"But—"

Cass looked over at one of the women who was standing by, concerned. "Shirly, can you please see if Doctor Booker is around? I think I saw his wife down by the train."

They got Carl inside and sitting down, but he was clearly upset. "I have my stall and all the customers," he said, waving his hand. "I have more brisket in the oven."

Christa was there in an instant with a bag of ice. "I'll tell them what's left is all there is. Don't you worry."

Ren pulled another chair and gently lifted Carl's leg up onto it. He wasn't doing much of anything else tonight.

"I can do it," I said, volunteering myself.

Cass, Carl and Christa, Ren and Hamish all stared at me.

I shrugged. "This is what I do. Carl, is the brisket pulled apart?"

"No . . ." he said. "I was coming to do that when I turned and my knee didn't turn with me."

"I can do that. Christa, you keep serving."

She smiled and gave a nod, going back out to the stall, and I headed for the kitchen. I took off my scarf, coat and gloves, and there was an apron on the counter so I put it on. I washed my hands, put on latex gloves, and began to work. It was all straight forward, and to Carl's credit, he had most of it organised anyway. I took the brisket out of the oven and began the pulling-apart process. It was so tender, it just about fell apart. It took no time at all.

I carried it out to the stall, then refilled the bread bowl supply, then the tray of chilli, and then I helped Christa serve the customers and we got through them twice as quick. We worked well together, not getting in each other's way at all, and she smiled at me a few times between the never-ending line of customers.

I didn't see the doctor arrive but I saw him leave, and soon after that, Carl's wife arrived. Like half the town, Cass's parents came up to see what all the fuss was about, as did Kendra and the kids.

I saw Cass talking to them and he disappeared with his kids for a while, which I was glad for. He should be spending time with them, and I was busy anyway.

And, I reminded myself, we weren't together.

He didn't owe me every second of his time, and he missed his kids so much. He knew where I was, he knew where to find me.

Before long, it was clearly time for the lighting of the Christmas tree, because the line all but vanished and everyone headed down the street. Except for me and Christa. "We can take it all inside," she said. "The crowd usually dies off now."

"Okay. Let's get it done."

We carried all the trays in, packed up the stall, and cleaned absolutely everything. It took some time and a decent amount of elbow grease, but we got it done. "Is the food cart right to be left outside?" I asked.

"Oh sure," she replied casually. "No one would touch Carl's cart."

I laughed to myself. I'd really been in the city too long.

"I hope Carl's okay," I said, wiping down the sink. We'd heard it was just a twisted knee, which wasn't great for anyone, especially a man of his age, but it could have been worse.

"Yeah, he's an old workhorse, no doubt about it. But this might slow him up. He'll still be here at 5am. tomorrow though." Christa stacked the last of the clean trays. "He'll be very grateful to you. As am I. You really helped us out tonight."

"It's no problem. It was fun. And only two hundred people asked me who I was and what I was doing working at Carl's, and another two hundred just gave me the side-eye."

Christa laughed. "That's a small town for ya. They'll get used to seeing you around. I mean, you are staying, right?"

Just then, there was a soft knock on the front door. Christa poked her head around and raised her eyebrow, then smiled at me. "I think it's for you."

I went to the door, not sure what she meant, and found Cass peering in. He grinned when he saw me, the kind of smile that squeezed my insides. I unlocked the door and let him in. "Come in out of the cold."

He stepped inside and pulled off his beanie. "You got everything cleaned up pretty quick."

"He's a fast worker," Christa said. "Makes me look bad."

Cass was still looking at me. "I know. He knows his way around a kitchen."

"We're just about done here," I said.

Christa picked up her bag. "Yep, backdoor is locked, money's in the safe, ovens are off. We're good to go."

"Is it all over outside?" I asked.

"Yeah, Santa had to get his sleigh back to the North Pole," he said with a smile. "Everyone's going home."

"Oh, I missed the tree?" I was disappointed, no point in denying it. "That's a shame."

Cass made a face. "I'm sorry."

I put my coat on and found my gloves and beanie. "It's okay. Did the kids enjoy it?"

"Loved it. Had the best time. I just walked them to their car. They'll be asleep before Kendra drives to the end of the street."

"I didn't realise it got so late." I put on my gloves. "But I'm glad you got to spend tonight with them."

"Me too."

"You boys good to go? I need to get off my feet." Christa held the door open for us and we waited for her to lock it before we said our goodbyes. She thanked me again and waved us off as she pulled up her coat collar and walked away.

I turned in the direction we had to walk and sighed. The street was as good as empty, save the train people packing up and a few stragglers. A light snow was falling, flurrying in the pale streetlights. The colourful Christmas lights looked dimmed. "You know," I murmured. "I think it's prettier now. Certainly more peaceful."

"You were really great tonight," Cass said. "You want to be careful. People might start thinking you fit in here."

I chuckled. "You know, you're not the first person to say that to me today."

He was quiet as we walked. "You do fit in here," he said. His tone was going for casual, I could tell. But there was something else there. "In Hartbridge, that is. You have Ren and Hamish baking you welcoming cookies, you made an old-fashioned steamed cake for Carl, and then you stepped in to help him out. That's what locals do." He put his hand to his chest. "I mean, no one baked me welcome cookies. But they did for you."

I chuckled. "It's been nice," I allowed. We stopped walking at the corner. "I do like this town."

He studied my eyes for a long few seconds and I thought he might ask if I'd ever consider staying. But he didn't. A flurry of snow swirled around us and he smiled. "Come this way."

We walked in the opposite direction of the truck and headed out toward the bridge. It was cold and dark but somehow still beautiful, and even though I was tired, I was happy to spend time with him.

And then I saw the tree.

Hartbridge's Christmas tree was at least thirty feet tall, and completely decorated from base to tip. Christmas lights glowed and huge baubles glinted in the night, the snow making the entire scene perfect.

I stopped and gasped. "Oh, Cass. It's . . . it's beautiful."

He grinned and took my hand, walking me closer to the tree. "I wished you'd seen it when they switched the lights on."

I just could have cried. It was so stunning, so perfectly Christmas, it made my heart ache. Which was stupid. "It's . . . I don't know what to say."

Cass glanced at me and his smile faltered. "What's wrong?"

I shook my head, blinking back stupid tears. "I don't even know," I said with a laugh. "It's just so perfect. I could never imagine a Christmas like this . . ."

He put his hand to my face, his glove warm on my cold cheek. And there, in the light of the tree in a dusting of snow, he kissed me. Where anyone could have seen us, not that anyone was around, but he clearly didn't care.

His arms went around me, his body, his hands, his mouth were the perfect heat against the cold. And he kissed me, deeper and longer, but oh so tender.

If I dared to let myself believe it, I could taste emotions on his tongue.

A shiver ran through me that had nothing to do with the cold, but he ended the kiss and pulled me into him, my face in the crook of his neck. "Let's get you home."

I could have stayed right where I was all night, but then I remembered his earlier promise. "Hmm. Stay here? Or go home to have you in my bed? I can't decide."

He grunted low in his throat, right next to my ear. But without a word, he took my hand and never let go the whole way to his car. Our gloves made it skinless contact, but it was still sweet, and I began to feel nervous, excited, and so ready.

He cranked up the heat in his truck as it rumbled to life, and we began the slow drive home. I tried to make small talk about hoping Carl's knee was okay and how working with Christa had been fun and how every single person in town had looked at me like the stranger I was.

Cass didn't say much, just smiled a lot, and I wondered if he was as nervous as me.

There were a few lights on in the house, but all was

quiet. Cass tended to the fires and I watched, wondering how this would work. "I should probably shower," I suggested. "I smell like brisket and grease."

Cass walked toward me. "You smell great to me," he whispered. He took my hand again, threading our fingers. The warmth, the strength of his hand tightened the ball of anticipation in my belly.

"So . . ." I breathed. "My room?"

Without a word, just a heated stare, he led me down the hall. When he opened the door and waited for me to walk in first, I thought I might burst into flames. Then he closed the door behind us and pushed me up against it and claimed my mouth with his.

My mind went blank, my body melted against him. He hitched my leg up over his hip, and then, like I weighed nothing, he carried me to the bed.

My blood caught fire, my bones melted, and when he lowered his bodyweight on top of me, when he settled in between my legs and I could feel how aroused he was, I thought I might expire.

I'd never wanted anyone like I wanted him.

A heady mix of wanting all of him right now and wanting it to last forever washed over me, and I gasped. "God, Cass."

He kissed down my neck, beneath the collar of my shirt. "You feel so . . ." He nipped at my collarbone. "Right."

It reminded me that this was kinda new to him. Not any kind of sex with a man. I knew he'd done stuff. But he'd said he'd never taken it slow before.

"Did you need to slow it down?" I asked.

He leaned up on his knees and pulled his sweater off.

"I guess that's a no," I said with a laugh. I ran my fingers through the hair on his chest and groaned. "Fuck yes."

Then he sat me up and pulled my shirt off over my head, and when he pushed me back down, there was a new light in his eyes. "I don't want to wait for anything," he whispered. "I've waited all my life for this."

I took his face in my hands and brought him down for a kiss. He let me lead this time, and I kept it slow, teasing, sensual.

Until he rolled his hips and sent a wave of pleasure through me. I couldn't stand my jeans on another second. I needed to feel him. I slipped my hands in between us and tried to pop the button but we ended up breaking apart and laughing.

I pulled the button and fly down, but too impatient to take my jeans off so I slid my hand under my briefs and gripped my erection. I looked up at Cass, still kneeling between my legs. His jeans were undone, his thick cock in his fist.

The sight of it, of him, of knowing where he might put it, made me ache in all the right places.

"God, Cass. Please."

He fell forward, holding his weight on one hand beside my head. He aligned our cocks and took them both in his hand. And . . .

Oh.

My.

God.

Fireworks exploded behind my eyes, at the base of my spine. I clung to him, to any hope of lasting another second. But he thrust and grunted, trembling above me, and he came. Thick spurts of his come hit my belly and slid down over his hand, onto my cock.

His hand squeezed as his orgasm took hold of him, and I fell right over the edge with him. My back arched, my cock swelled and spilled, and he pumped me, wringing out every drop of ecstasy.

The room was still spinning, my bones were still sponge, when Cass lowered his body on mine and held so tight while he kissed me. This kiss was different. This kiss was something . . .

Hard, deep, all tongue, clash of teeth, and his arms wound around me a little too tight. At first I thought something was wrong, but the longer he kissed me like that, the more I realised something was very right.

This was pure emotion.

Eventually he let me breathe and rolled us onto our sides. He pulled me into the crook of his neck and held me, our chests rising and falling in sync. "You okay?" I murmured.

"Hm." He sighed and rubbed my back. "Jayden . . ."

I pulled back. "Yeah?"

"Thank you."

I smiled. "What are you thanking me for? You did all the work."

He chuckled and traced his finger along the corner of my eye. "Nothing has ever felt this right."

My heart soared, blooming in my chest at his words. Was that a declaration of some kind?

"What I've done with other guys," he explained. "Hasn't been like that. Normally just a quick hook-up. No real touching, no kissing. But this? With a guy?" he scanned my eyes. "I like this."

So not a declaration of his undying love. I felt stupid for thinking it could be, foolish for thinking that's what it ever would be. But I realised, lying there in his arms, that I wanted it to be.

"I like this too," I replied.

It wasn't a lie. It just wasn't the whole truth.

I did like it. A whole lot. But it was more than that. Part of me yearned for this, wanted nothing but this, this right here with him. Not just for tonight or for a few days or until I left town.

Part of me loved it. Part of me was falling in love. Part of me had already fallen.

I closed my eyes and snuggled into his neck, into his arms. Safer than I'd ever felt.

In the morning, I woke up alone.

CHAPTER FOURTEEN

CASS

I'D SLEPT BETTER than I could ever remember sleeping. I'd fallen asleep in Jayden's bed, in his arms, and woke up just after three in the morning. We'd fallen asleep, still sticky, and I woke up all dried and crusty.

I watched him sleep for a minute, so peaceful, so beautiful. But I needed to piss, so I pulled on my shirt and headed up to my own bathroom. I cleaned myself up as much as I could, at bleary-eyed o'clock, and climbed into my bed for maybe another two and a half hours sleep.

Jayden was in the kitchen when I went downstairs. Mr Cantrell was already in the dining room, talking Jayden's ears off by the sound of it. But Jayden had started the coffee machine, thank god, so I poured two fresh cups and opened the door.

"Morning," I said. "Sorry to interrupt, but Jayden, I have a quick question about a delivery we're expecting this morning."

Mr Cantrell smiled cheerfully and went to the coffee machine. "Go ahead. I'll have a sneaky cup before Judith finds me. Maybe even one of those pastries."

I pulled Jayden into the kitchen and handed him his coffee. "Morning."

His eyes went to mine but they were a little guarded. "Morning. I wasn't sure how you'd be with me this morning."

Panic struck me. "What? Why? Did I do something wrong?"

"I woke up alone. I didn't know . . . Is that . . . ?"

"No, I woke up and needed to pee. I just went up to my bathroom to clean up a bit. Kind of a mess," I whispered. "That's all. Jayden, I don't know what the protocol is. I don't know how to navigate any of this."

"I don't know either, and I don't want to overcomplicate things, but I thought this morning when you weren't there that you'd decided it was a one-time thing or that you regretted it. I wasn't sure."

"Oh, no regrets," I whispered. "None at all. You?"

"Regrets? God, no."

I chuckled. Thank god. "And as for it being a one-time thing . . ."

His gaze shot to mine. "Yes?"

"Well, I'd prefer if it wasn't."

His smile became a grin, but we heard Judith in the dining room next to us. "Oh, Charles. I thought I'd find you here. You're supposed to be watching your cholesterol."

Jayden stifled a laugh. "I better cook him his egg white omelette."

I stared at him, wondering for that split second how much alone time we had. Then I thought *fuck it*. I lifted his chin, knowing he loved it because it made his eyes flutter, and I planted a soft kiss on his lips.

I could get used to this.

So used to it.

"The K is now included in the D-duty rule," I said. "I can come in here if I plan to kiss you. You said that was okay."

"It's more than okay," he whispered. "Any time." Then he brightened. "Oh, maybe we could add an F to that list. You know, in case you want to—"

I put my hand up. "Yeah, I'm pretty sure I know what the F stands for."

He grinned just as the dining door opened inward and Mrs Cantrell poked her head in. "Could I trouble you for some more soy milk?"

"Oh, of course you can," I said. "It's no trouble at all. I'll bring it out for you."

Jayden got busy with breakfast, and I got busy with helping and with guests and with fresh linens, and before I knew it, the day was over and it was almost dinnertime. Not everyone would be at home tonight, visiting their families or whatnot, so I set the table with some bonbons and a few Christmas centrepieces.

"Oh, what's this?" Jayden asked, walking out with the fresh juice.

"It's Christmas Eve tomorrow," I explained. "Time to bring out the special table decorations."

"Well, it looks lovely." He put the glass jug of juice on the sidebar with the clean glasses. "The Nicholsons and the Garzas won't be here tonight."

I nodded. "That's okay. The full table decorations go out tomorrow."

"Everyone loves the small touches." Then he put his hand to his chest and murmured, "Personally, I'm all for your small touches."

My phone buzzed in my pocket. Caller ID showed it

was the Hartbridge Motel, which was odd, so I took the call. "Arabella Bed 'n' Breakfast."

"Hi Cass, it's Denise."

"Hi Denise. How's everything?"

"Oh, busy. You know how it is. Look, I know it's a long shot but I have a gentleman here who needs a room, and I've got nothing. I was wondering if you have anything. He has his elderly father with him and he didn't want to drive down the mountain tonight."

Oh man.

"I don't actually have any more rooms, sorry."

"Yeah, I thought as much but just wanted to try."

Jayden frowned at me. "Yes you do."

I was confused. "Sorry, Denise, just give me one second." I put my phone to my chest. "A man needs a room for him and his elderly father. I don't have—"

"They can have my room."

"Your room? And where will you . . . ?" My words trailed off because I was pretty sure where this was going.

He grinned, his eyes dark and playful, and he whispered, "Your bed. All night long."

I considered it. *Christ, I was considering it.*

Jayden nodded and I almost laughed. I put my phone back to my ear. "Ah, Denise? Actually, as luck would have it, I have a room."

GUNTER ZUNIGA ARRIVED and was so grateful for the room, he was almost on the verge of tears. His father was a short, frail man who was easily ninety years old.

Gunter explained the trip had taken much longer than expected because of his dad, and with the snow he didn't want to risk the drive down that dreadful mountain to Mossley.

As soon as I'd ended the call with Denise, Jayden packed up his belongings in no time at all and helped me strip the bed and linens. We remade the room together in record time and I took Jayden upstairs.

He'd dumped his bags in the corner of my room and looked around, eyeing the bed in particular. "God," he'd groaned, then readjusted his dick. "I've never looked forward to bedtime before. You're gonna do me so hard tonight."

God.

All the blood in my body pooled low in my belly. My cock was half-hard for the rest of the night. Not even going out into the cold to help Gunter bring his dad in from the car made any difference.

We helped Mr Zuniga to the couch in front of the fire and Jayden gave him a small mug of hot bouillon to sip. The older man smiled up at him. "Very kind of you."

I helped Gunter get their bags and showed him to his room. "It's just one queen size bed," I said, pointing out the obvious, trying very hard not to think of what Jayden and I had done in that very bed the night before.

"I hope it was no inconvenience," he said. "I'm just so thankful."

I turned the heater on for him in their room. "No inconvenience at all."

Aaaaand I was back to thinking about how Jayden would be in my bed tonight.

All night.

Images of him last night flashed through my mind: underneath me, his face, his groans, his body, his face when he came . . .

I cleared my throat and gestured to the bathroom door. "You have your own private bathroom, and if you need anything, please just ask me."

"Thank you," he said again. "And please thank your partner for me. It was very nice of him to offer the soup."

My partner . . .

There was no judgement in his eyes at all, and I didn't want him to feel bad should I correct him. So I didn't.

"I'll let him know."

I left him to it and went back to help Jayden get ready to serve the evening meal. Everyone loved the table decorations and Gunter and his father joined everyone else, and, of course, dinner was a smash hit.

Bison medallions and roast vegetables with an apple pie for dessert.

It was all amazing.

The Baileys and the Ochoas, who had never met before staying here, settled into the sitting room for a night of poker. The Garzas played chess in the reading room, and when the Nicholsons came back, they opted to watch a movie in the family room, and Gunter and Mr Zuniga thanked us again and said goodnight.

Jayden had once asked if it was strange to have people in my house. And I'd be lying if I said it wasn't a little odd. But it was a nice feeling too. Especially at Christmastime. Everyone was festive and cheerful, and sharing my home with them lifted my spirits too.

Or maybe that was because of Jayden.

"Oh," I said, drying a tray as Jayden washed up. "Uh, this is probably going to sound weird, but Gunter assumed we were . . . you know, partners. I didn't have the heart to correct him. He looked like he's had a rough day."

Jayden smiled. "Is that right?"

"Just in case he says anything to you," I added. "That's all."

He dried his hands on his apron and leaned his arse against the sink. "He did look like he'd had a rough day. His dad is really sweet, though. Pre-dementia, I think I heard Gunter say." He shrugged. "So, for what it's worth, I'm glad I gave up my room for them."

"I'm glad you did too." He was being sweet and I could only think of getting him into bed. *God, Carter.* I ignored the ache in my balls. "I mean, for their benefit. Not mine. Or ours. Jesus." I ran my hand through my hair.

Jayden laughed. "Looking forward to it, I gather."

"Very much." I needed to palm my dick so badly, so putting any embarrassment out of my mind, I did. Of course Jayden saw, and of course he grinned. "I can't help it. I'm sorry."

"Oh, don't apologise," he murmured, a cheeky smirk on his gorgeous face. "I can't wait." Then he stepped in real close and whispered in my ear. "When I think about what you're gonna do to me tonight, it makes my arse ache with want."

Fucking hell.

Then he brushed his lips against my ear and my knees almost buckled.

He laughed and stepped back just as Gunter knocked on the door frame. "Sorry to interrupt. I just wanted to let you know that I've sent the payment through, and I spoke to my husband and told him how beautiful this place is and how kind you both are and told him we'll need to re-book for a weekend getaway this springtime."

"Oh, uh, thank you." I wasn't sure what else to say.

He had a husband . . .

"You're very welcome," Jayden said, like he heard these

kinds of things all the time. "And keep an eye out on the website for spring specials for romantic getaways."

Gunter smiled. "I will. Thanks again."

I waited until he was gone and turned to Jayden. "Romantic getaways in spring? Is that something I do?"

"It is now." He shrugged. "And you should look at catering for weddings and events."

I stared at him. "Do you know how difficult weddings are? All that linen and the tables and chairs, the catering, and the staff—"

"I know exactly what's involved. I've catered for a hundred of them. And you have the perfect place for that. Set limits to small weddings, say maximum of twenty or thirty people." He tilted his head. "Have you started planning Valentine's Day?"

"Uh . . ." I cringed. "I just needed to get through these holidays first."

Jayden sighed, but he smiled and rubbed my arm. "You'll be right. Don't panic. You'll find your feet. We just need to start making a list." He took a new bag of potatoes out of the storeroom and set them on the counter. "But for now, I'm going to peel all these and get them ready for tomorrow. You go do the rounds and see if anyone needs anything. When I'm done here, I'm going up to your room to shower and get ready. Then I'm going to lie face down on your bed and wait. Don't keep me waiting, or I'll start without you."

I groaned out a laugh, ignoring how my dick twitched. "It's gonna be the quickest event in history at this rate. It'll be over before it even begins."

"I'm not opposed to encore events." He wiggled his arse. "In fact . . ."

"On that note," I said. "I'll go do the rounds." I needed

to readjust my dick again and take a deep breath before I walked out of the kitchen. "God help me."

I could still hear his laughter as I went.

I THOUGHT the night would never end. I didn't want to seem rude but as soon as the last couple called it a night, I flipped the lights off and opened the door marked 'private' and locked it behind me. I certainly didn't want anyone accidentally wandering up and seeing what I had every intention of doing to Jayden.

I took the stairs two at a time and stopped just inside my bedroom. He was in my bed all right, face down, presumably fully naked but I could only see where the covers stopped just above his arse.

It took my breath away.

His smile disappeared into the pillow as he stretched. "Was beginning to wonder where you were," he said. Then he looked back at me, almost shy. "Hope you don't mind, but I did start without you. Just working some lube into all the right places."

Fuck.

There was a bottle of lube and a few condoms on the sheet next to him. My heart rattled in my chest and the rush of hot blood made me dizzy. I was struck momentarily, unable to move or speak. Just seeing him in my bed, knowing I was about to be inside him . . .

Move, Carter. Don't just stand there.

I pulled my sweater off over my head, tossing it somewhere. Then I unbuttoned my jeans and pulled them down with my briefs, my cock now fully hard and wanting.

So wanting.

"God, Jayden," I murmured, kneeling on the bed. I pulled back the covers to reveal his fully naked body, his well-rounded perfect arse. I bit back a groan. "You're so beautiful."

He arched his back a little, preening at my compliment. "I'm ready for you."

The only times I'd ever been with men, there had never been any care for tenderness or time, and I wanted to savour this. I leaned down and kissed his shoulder. "Can I take a few moments to appreciate you?" I kissed between his shoulder blades. "I've never had a man in my bed before."

He froze for a split second, then stretched his neck, so I kissed there too. "Keep doing that and you can take as long as you need."

I smiled as I kissed down his spine. I ran my hands over his shoulders, up his arms, down his sides, and over his arse. He responded to every touch, his deep groans, his hard muscles so different to the softness of a woman.

I wanted to remember every second, but someone else wasn't so patient. He slipped his hand underneath himself and raised his hips. Was he stroking himself?

Oh god.

"Yeah, I'm gonna need you to hurry," Jayden said with a pained laugh. "You've got me so turned on right now. You can take your time next round. I need you inside me."

I scraped my teeth up his back and nipped at the skin behind his ear. "I like how you think you're in charge."

Then I gripped his hips and flipped him over, his shock and surprise, his desire disappearing when I leaned down, my nose to his. "I want to kiss you. I want to see in your eyes when I push into you."

He gasped. "Fuck."

"I plan to." Resting back on my knees, I took a condom

and rolled it on. I was painfully hard. Giving myself a squeeze actually felt good. I poured more lube onto myself, then used my slick fingers to rub more lube over his hole.

Jayden spread his legs wider, lifted his hips, giving me all the access I needed. I pushed a finger into him, then another. But he shook his head. "No, baby. I need you in me."

Baby.

He called me baby.

I leaned forward, claiming his mouth with mine, desperate and hot. He lifted his knees to his chest and blindly, probably clumsily, I positioned my cock at his hole and pushed in.

He broke the kiss to gasp, and I got to see the fire in his eyes. He whined as I pushed in deeper, his eyes rolling closed and his fingers digging into my shoulders.

He was so tight, so hot. He felt so good. So right. Everything about him was right for me.

I kissed him as I began to slowly thrust, our tongues and groans tangling in a beautiful dance until we found a rhythm. A perfect beat. His legs went around me, his arms lay above his head as he let me have complete control.

I wanted to go deeper. I wanted to crawl inside him, to fill every part of him.

I made love to him.

He felt what I felt. I knew he did. When he brought his arms around me, he held me tight. He kissed me with such passion, he arched his back, wanting, needing everything I gave him.

His groans got deeper, more desperate, and his grip on me tightened; the hold on my own pleasure was tenuous. I was so close.

"God, Cass. I'm gonna . . . I'm gonna come with you

inside me." His wide eyes drew me in and I saw the pleasure there as he succumbed to his orgasm. I felt the splash of his come, the squeeze of his arse around my cock, and I thrust hard, once, twice, and I came.

So hard, so deep. I'd never felt pleasure like it. Sex had never been so good, so complete, and so whole.

I collapsed on him and he held me, clung to me, and without a word, we basked in what we'd just shared.

It took an age for my heart to stop hammering, though I think it now knocked on my ribs for a different reason. For the man in my arms, for the man I was still joined to.

With a hiss, I pulled out of him and discarded the condom before pulling Jayden back into my arms. He put his hand to my face and studied my eyes for the longest time before he kissed me. "More?"

I laughed. "Might need a few minutes. Or hours. I'm not sure. Think I'm having an out of body experience right now."

He chuckled and snuggled into my neck, letting himself be completely enveloped by me.

I wrapped him up as tight as I could and that was how we fell asleep.

And this time, when I needed to get up to pee and clean us up a bit, I climbed back into bed and he snuggled himself to me again, mumbling in his sleep. I ran my fingers through his hair until his breathing evened out and I kissed his forehead.

I wanted this so bad.

I wanted this life. To have someone, a man to share my bed with, to kiss and cuddle, to take care of, to laugh with. To share things with, the highs and the lows, all of it.

I wanted it with Jayden.

Was it crazy that I could feel something so strong in

such a short space of time? Yes. It absolutely was. But when he was lying in my arms, in my bed, I couldn't bring myself to care.

And I didn't care when he pulled me into the shower at 5:30am for mutual soapy hand-jobs and wet kisses. It was the only rightful way to start a Merry Christmas Eve, he'd said with mischief in his smile and the devil in his eyes.

I didn't care when he made me coffee in the morning and when he left me to get cornered by Mr Cantrell. I certainly didn't care when he made me do the dishes while he cleaned up the dining room and made another inventory of a few items we needed in town.

I didn't care one bit.

What I did care about was bubbling inside my chest, making me nervous and anxious until I couldn't stand it for one second longer. I was at the sink with my arms in sudsy water and he took the eggs out of the fridge.

"You're going to scrub the Teflon off that pan if you keep scrubbing it like that," he joked.

I stopped and let my head fall forward, trying to catch my breath.

Jayden grew concerned. He put his hand on my back. "Cass, what is it?"

I turned to face him. It was far too soon, it was crazy, but it was now or never.

"Stay here in Hartbridge."

He blinked. "What?"

I swallowed hard. "Look, I don't know what I'm doing, and I don't even know what this is." I gestured between us. "But it's good, right? And to be honest, Jayden, the idea of you leaving in three days makes me feel . . . things."

He stared at me, then shook his head. Not in a *no* type

of way, but in a *too-much-to-process* type of way. "You want me to stay? Here?"

Well, shit.

"Okay, well, I don't know about here, in this house. That's probably up to you. I didn't think that far ahead. I just stared at the ceiling last night, with you sound asleep there with me, and I remembered you were leaving. And I realise this is crazy, and it doesn't have to mean anything . . ."

Then it occurred to me, like a fool in slow motion, that maybe it didn't mean anything to him.

He'd said from the very beginning that anything that happened between us would just be for fun.

Oh.

The stab of rejection, the hit to my pride, took me by surprise. I tried to get my mouth to form words when it felt like I'd swallowed sand. "Sorry, I'm so out of practice. I should have read the signs. I just thought . . . you know you should stay here anyway, in Hartbridge I mean. Not for me, or because of me. Just in Hartbridge in general. I think you'd like this town if you gave it the chance. You'd fit in here, and everyone already seems to like you."

Jayden put his hand on my arm. "You wanna take a breath for me?"

Had I breathed at all in the last few minutes? I couldn't remember. I took a few deep breaths. "Sorry, I, uh . . ."

"I like Hartbridge," he said with a shrug. "I had planned to go toward the coast. I don't know why. I'm not expected anywhere. It's not like I've lined up another job or a place to live."

This was starting to sound hopeful?

"But I hadn't considered staying. I had no plan to stay

here." He bit his lip. "But I also hadn't considered meeting you."

I met his gaze. "Jayden, I shouldn't have just blurted it out like that. I'm sorry. I was about to lose my nerve and I panicked."

He chuckled but then he looked up at me, his eyes like a puppy. "It's not a yes, but it's not a no. I need some time to think about it." He put his hand to my face. "Can you give me that?"

I nodded. "Of course."

CHAPTER FIFTEEN

JAYDEN

"MUM, HE WANTS ME TO STAY."

My mother gasped down the phone. "Honey, what will you do?"

"I don't know."

"Do you like the man?"

"Yes. He's actually kind of great."

"Do you love him?"

That stopped me. "I don't know. I think I could, one day. Is it too soon? I've known him for like four days. I feel *something* . . . I just don't know. Mum, he's perfect, and I've met his family, briefly. And I could see myself with him."

"It sounds like you know your answer."

"But I wasn't going to stay here. I don't know about work. What would I even do here? There'll be no work here when there's no customers, and you know what they say about mixing business with pleasure."

"Hmm, well, that hasn't worked out too well for you in the past."

Wow.

"Gee. Thanks, Mum."

She sighed, still half-asleep. "Make a list, love. Write down the pros and cons. Make an informed decision once you see it all written out in front of you."

I smiled at the list idea. Cass was always making comments about my lists.

"I might do that. Look, I have to go. We're heading into town to pick up a few things. I just wanted to speak to you. I'm sorry for waking you up. Merry Christmas, by the way. I'll call you later and speak to Dad."

"Okay, love, be good. Merry Christmas to you too."

I smiled as I pocketed my phone, and I changed my shirt to something that didn't have flour on it. I skipped back down the stairs and found Cass in the laundry doing another load of towels. "You ready?"

"Yep. Just let me lock the door to upstairs." He went and did that while I put my boots and coat on.

When he came back, I asked, "You sure you're okay with us both leaving? I can stay if you'd prefer."

"No, it's fine. We won't be gone long, and it's only the Baileys and the Garzas here. The Ochoas have gone to some Christmas market stall in Mossley."

We walked out onto the deck and I noticed the Zuniga's car was also gone. "Did Gunter and his dad get away okay?"

Cass nodded. "Yeah. He's a nice guy. His dad is the sweetest. He was so thankful and kept saying how impressed he was."

We climbed into the truck and began down the drive. "Oh, did you bring your list?"

I took it out of my pocket. "Of course I did. And I called my mum. I woke her up. It was like half-past three Christmas morning over there, so I'll be super popular when I call her back later."

Cass laughed. "I bet."

"I told her you asked me to stay."

He whipped his head around so fast I thought he might hurt himself. "And what did she say?"

I grinned. "She told me to make a list."

"Of course she did. Is that where you get it from?"

"Being organised isn't a bad thing. And neither is a list of pros and cons."

Cass chewed on his bottom lip for a half a mile. "And what would be on the pro side?"

"Well, you. And your killer smile and amazing kissing skills. And let's not forget the magic dick."

He laughed. "Magic?"

"It's totally making the list."

He grinned at me. "I think I'm flattered?"

"You should be."

"Do I want to know what will make the con side of the list?"

I sighed. "Well, I . . . I don't know. Work, probably. Or the lack of it, I should say. You won't be needing me every week. And a place to stay. I was looking forward to getting my own place. I shared an apartment back in Missoula and I'd rather not do that again."

He nodded slowly. "Yeah. I guess. I can see that. But that's just two things, and the pro side of the list had three."

"True. But does the Home Market sell Vegemite?"

"Uh, no. Why would it?"

"I'm just kidding. I was never really a fan."

That made me chuckle. "What about a cinema? Does Hartbridge have a cinema?"

Cass made a face. "Uh, well, no. The theatre shut down about five years ago. I think cable TV and Netflix sealed its fate."

I sighed dramatically. "Well, I can't hold the war on capitalism against the town."

He laughed. "Good to know."

I held my hand out and he glanced from the road to my hand before he realised what I was asking. He slid his hand into mine and I squeezed it. "Um, hand-holding is going on the list."

We pulled up at Home Market and grabbed everything we needed. Rosie, behind the counter, recognised me straight away. "Oh, Jayden. Heard you stepped in and helped poor Carl out the other night. That was so very nice of you. Such a shame he had to close today."

Cass gawped. "Closed? He's never closed."

Rosie nodded. "Just until his knee is better. He'd be shut tomorrow, anyway, but he's hoping to be open again before New Year's. Twisted his knee pretty bad, apparently."

"That's terrible," I said, frowning. "I hope he's okay."

"He's never been shut in all the years he's been here." Rosie studied me for a second. "Say, how long are you in town for?"

I looked at her, then looked at Cass. "Uh . . ."

Cass laughed and stared at me. "Funny she should ask that."

I withheld a sigh.

"Oh," Rosie said, being all smug and conspicuous. "Has someone been suggesting you should stay?"

"Something like that."

Cass's cheeks were red, but his smile was aimed right at me. "Yeah, something like that."

She laughed. "Then I suggest you give Carl a call. He's a stubborn old goat, worked twelve-hour days for fifty years.

But he's laid up for a while this time. You never know . . . he might just need some help."

Cass took a box of chocolates from a nearby stand. "And we'll take these too."

We took our groceries and loaded them into the back of Cass's truck. He was being way too cheerful, trying to press his lips together so he didn't smile too wide.

"Don't say a word."

He laughed. "Not a peep."

But when we drove off, he went the opposite way down Bridge Street, away from home. "Uh, where are we going?"

"Just out a ways."

"A ways?" I shot him a confused look. "Is that an actual imperial unit of measurement?"

He laughed. "Yep."

He slowed to a stop outside a particular house, a quaint bungalow style with a snow-covered lawn and some Christmas garland along the front window frame.

"Who lives here?"

"Carl."

"Uh, what?"

Cass grinned. "We got him some 'get well soon' chocolates. Best hand-deliver them."

He climbed out and I followed him down the path. "I can't believe you're doing this. This is entrapment."

He laughed and knocked on the door, and an older woman with dark hair and a kind smile answered a few seconds later. "Ah, Mrs Olsen," Cass said. "We've come to see how the patient is doing."

"Oh, you're so sweet," she replied. "Come in, boys."

"Mrs Olsen, this is Jayden Turner," Cass said.

"Oh." Her eyes lit up with recognition. "And you helped Christa close up the store!"

I nodded. "I did. How's Carl?"

"This way," she replied, leading us through to the living room.

Carl was perched up in a recliner by a heater, looking about a decade older than he had the other day. His leg was propped up, and even through his lounge pants I could see his knee was either very swollen or heavily strapped. Possibly both.

"We were just in town and wanted to come see how you were getting along," Cass said. "Rosie said you couldn't open the store today."

Carl deflated. "Nah. Sad old day, for sure. Never had to shut the doors before. Might be shut next week too. Doc said m'knee's no good. Supposed to stay off it for a few days." He looked up at his wife. "How am I supposed to bake Christmas pies this year?"

Mrs Olsen rolled her eyes and smiled at us. "Like I haven't helped him for forty years. I can do it by myself this year, Carl. The kids won't even know the difference."

He grumped at that.

"He's a misery," Mrs Olsen said.

Cass handed him the chocolates. "These might cheer you up. If not, the grandkids will take care of them."

Carl's face softened. "That's very thoughtful of you." Then he looked up at me. "Thank you so much for helping Christa the other night. She spoke very highly of you. And that's a lot coming from her. Takes a good worker to impress her."

"It was no problem. You'd already done all the hard work. I just had to make sure it went out okay."

Cass nodded and he gave Carl a determined nod. "About that, Carl. I don't want to overstep, but if you need someone to help at the store next week while your knee is getting better, Jayden's more than capable and he'll be finished up at my place by then."

Carl was no fool. His heavy brow deepened as he looked at Cass, then at me and back to Cass. "Is this some kind of ploy?"

Cass laughed. "Not at all. Just hate to see your diner shut when it doesn't need to be. You know he's capable. You'll still need to be there, probably, to tell him how you make everything. But at least you can stay off your leg." He gave Carl that blinding, charming smile. "No pressure. Just think it over. He's staying at my place, so you know where to call."

I was kinda dumbfounded. I didn't know whether to be impressed or offended that he'd just done all this without so much as asking. I was leaning toward offended, but then Mrs Olsen walked us out and she was so grateful for the offer, and Cass was just beaming as we got back into the truck.

"Want to tell me what all that was about?" I asked.

He grinned as he started the engine. "That was me taking care of your list. I think your con list only has one thing on it now."

I scoffed, shaking my head. "I can't believe you just did that."

He was unfazed. "Look, in this town, if you want something, you just need to put it out there. It's how things get done."

"What if I don't want to work at Carl's?"

He shot me a quick glance as he drove, then frowned. "Oh. Well. Well, I guess you can just say no."

I sighed. "I'm trying to decide if I'm mad at you."

Cass kept his eyes ahead, but he shifted in his seat. "I'm sorry. I just thought . . . strike while the iron's hot, ya know?

You said you'd need more work and suddenly there was more work. I thought . . . I'm sorry. I should've asked."

"Well, yes, you should have." The thing was, I wasn't really mad. I should have been. But he wanted me to stay. And I wanted to stay as well, if I was being honest. Not sure for how long, but another week wasn't a life commitment. And he clearly felt bad and somewhat panicky. I kept forgetting this whole dating thing was new to him. I decided to lighten the mood. "Guess you'll just have to make it up to me."

He risked a glance at me. "Like how?"

"Your magic dick."

His eyes went wide. "Oh, right."

"Or maybe we should see what kind of dick-sucking skills you have."

He went red from his hairline to underneath his coat collar. "I, um . . . I, uh . . ."

"Oh, you've never?"

He shook his head and I laughed. "Well, my dear man, you're going to get some practice tonight."

CHRISTMAS EVE DINNER was a lovely affair. Cass put out more table decorations and had even organised small gifts for each couple. Tiny pots of locally produced honey and small jams, which was such a personal, professional touch. The Baileys and the Garzas were spending the night with their families in town, but everyone else absolutely appreciated Cass's personal touch.

Dinner was prime rib with mashed potatoes and gravy with sides of honeyed carrots and fresh baked bread. My gingerbread cake with caramel sauce for dessert was a hit, much to Cass's surprise. Though there was still apple pie for anyone who wanted it.

Christmas music played in the background and later on, Christmas movies on the TV. The fires roared, the guests drank some wine, and I served some cheeses and fruits to finish the night.

I wanted it to be perfect.

It was.

I kept two full plates aside in the kitchen while the guests ate and I cleaned up. When it was all over, Cass snuck in and we sat up on the kitchen counter and ate our Christmas Eve dinners. Just us, hidden away from the others, him smiling happily, me covered in flour and grease. Not that he seemed to mind.

Keeping him busy all afternoon was a great distraction from missing his kids. He did call them, and his "be sure to go to bed early, Santa's watching" made me smile. It can't have been easy for him—missing the Christmas Eve ritual with his kids—but he put on a brave face and made himself busy with the guests, with linen, with making sure they had everything they could want.

Last year, when he wasn't busy, when he was all alone, must have been awful.

I was alone last Christmas too, and the six before that. But it didn't compare to a parent not having their kids, not hanging stockings, or reading books by the fire or tucking them in.

My heart hurt for him. I never wanted him to be alone again.

Even now, there was a hint of sadness in his eyes that I wanted to make better.

"You got through your first holiday period," I said.

"Thanks to you."

We did make a good team.

"You should give yourself some credit too."

He raised his wine glass and waited for me to clink mine to it. "Merry Christmas, Jayden," he said.

"Merry Christmas, Cass."

"This food is amazing."

"Thank you."

"No, thank *you*. For all you've done. For me and for the guests." He nudged his foot to mine. "Mostly for me."

I chuckled. "Anything in particular your favourite."

He shoved in a forkful of potato and chewed with a smile. "Oh yes."

"Well, what is it?"

He stabbed a piece of meat. "I think the kitchen kisses."

That surprised me. "Not what we did last night?"

"Oh, don't get me wrong. That was amazing. Incredible, even." He shrugged. "But just to kiss you in here, like it's something we do every day, like it's something I would do every day if you were here all the time . . . well, that's my favourite."

His words made my insides all warm, my heart squeezed a little. "You're such a romantic."

He laughed. "I am. Always have been a dreamer." He looked around the kitchen and sighed. "Maybe that's why I took on this place."

"You turned your dream into a reality."

His eyes cut to mine. "Not all of them."

The air was suddenly a little thick. "Oh yeah?" I tried to sound calm. "And what's left?"

"To share it with someone."

I felt warm all over and my ribs were two sizes too small. "Oh."

Cass smiled at his plate. "One day."

God.

I wanted to say *yes, please.* I wanted to say *one day, starting now.* But I really felt in over my head. "One day," I whispered.

He gave me a guarded look. "When he's ready."

My breath left me in a rush. *When he's ready . . .*

Why wasn't I ready now?

A thousand thoughts spiralled in my mind. I wanted to be ready. I wanted this. I was just too scared to take that leap.

"How's that list coming along?" he asked.

I put my plate aside and sipped the wine instead. "It's still a mental list at the moment. I haven't actually put pen to paper yet."

"Maybe you should do that tonight. You know, so Santa can make your wishes come true."

I chuckled. "It wasn't really a wish list."

His eyes locked onto mine. "And if it was a Christmas wish list, that is, what would be the first thing on it?"

I couldn't look away. "I can't tell you. Then it won't come true."

He almost smiled. "I won't tell Santa I know."

That made me laugh. "Well, I think the first thing on the list would be a lot of dick-sucking practise for you."

He burst out laughing. "Shouldn't that be on my list?"

"It can go on both. It's mutually benefiting us both."

"Right."

"And then after that, I'm not sure. I should probably add something like ending world hunger or something like that. For the betterment of all humanity and not just me."

"Very honourable."

I jumped down and took his plate, but he stopped me. "I'll clean up tonight. You've done enough."

"This is my job."

He made a face and slowly slid down from the counter and leaned against it instead. "And if it wasn't your job?"

"Are you firing me?"

His eyes shot to mine, alarmed. "No!"

I laughed. "I should hope not."

He let out a long breath. "But when you don't work here anymore. If you decide to stay. Would having dinner with me feel like work?"

"Depends."

"On what?"

"What you expect me to cook. What if I want you to cook me dinner?"

"Then I absolutely would. I just hope you like eggs on toast. Or maybe a steak and some boiled vegetables." He grimaced. "You know, cooking is not my strong suit. And what if we made a deal that if you did all the cooking, I'd do all the cleaning up afterwards?"

"And the magic dicking."

He smiled. "And that."

"And you will master the art of fellatio."

He raised his hand like a scout. "I will do my best."

"Starting tonight."

"Absolutely."

I put my hand to his chest. "I'm just joking about that. If you don't like it, you don't have to do it."

He cleared his throat. "I think it's something I would definitely like. To do, and maybe have done."

Oh . . .

"Have you ever had a guy do that to you?"

He shook his head and let out an embarrassed laugh. "Uh, no."

I held up two fingers. "There will be two lessons tonight."

He laughed and put his forehead on my shoulder. My hands went to his hips, and with a deep breath, he fell into me, and we embraced. His warmth, his strength, his whole body felt so right. Like something slotting into place. What that was, I didn't know.

But this was most definitely something.

Whatever it was between us was something special. Like nothing I'd ever felt so soon, so much. My mother's voice echoed in my mind . . .

Do you love him?

"Shit. I have to call my mum."

Cass chuckled and pulled away. "Go do that. I'll wash up these last few things. Then I'll finish up here and come up." He smirked. "Maybe you should start that list. Santa comes tonight."

"He won't be the only one."

"YEAH, that's it, suck it like that," I said with a groan.

He might not have ever done this before, but he knew what he liked and he knew how to put that into action.

I was lying on the bed, still a little wet from the shower. Apparently Cass liked that because he'd taken one look at me and his brain had short-circuited. But I had him kneel between my legs. That way he could set the pace and take as much or as little as he wanted.

At first, he'd fisted my erection, sliding it up and down, inspecting it as though I was the holy grail. I told him to start with a lick, then a taste, and he did, but without further prompting, he took me into his mouth.

It took all of my self-control not to grip his hair and fuck his throat. He wasn't up for deep-throating, but he gripped the base and pumped and pulled on my balls.

"Fuck." I hissed. "Cass."

He pulled off, his lips swollen and wet. "I like this. It's hot."

"You're gonna make me come soon. So when I say, pull off, okay?"

He nodded, smiling like the devil, and went back to torturing me. After a few more passes, I ran my fingers through his hair, making him look up at me with my cock in his mouth, and that was all it took.

"Cass, gonna come."

He pulled off me and pumped me to orgasm. Spurts of come splashed my belly and he kept pumping me to drain every drop.

The room spun and I lost all sight and sound until his warm laughter rumbled on my hip. "I think I found a new favourite hobby," he mumbled.

I groaned. "Fucking hell. Get your dick up here. It's my turn."

He was clearly shocked by my words, but I shuffled up to lean against the headboard. "Straddle my chest," I said.

He was wearing nothing but briefs, which did very little to hide his erection, and he scrambled up my body, his knees either side of my chest. I peeled down his underwear and let his cock out. I gave him a few strokes and a pearl of precum glistened at his tip. "Oh yeah."

I looked up to find him staring at me, so I opened my mouth and stuck out my tongue, then guided his hips to feed his cock onto my tongue.

"Jayden," he cried out.

I pulled his hips back, then brought them forward again,

and he got the hint. Then I could use my hands on his shaft and balls while taking him in as far as he dared thrust.

He didn't last long. I didn't expect him to. And when he crumpled in a heap on the mattress, I chuckled and tapped his chest. "Let me know when you're good for round two. I wasn't going to have you in my arse tonight, but now I want it."

He groaned out a laugh and covered his face with his hands. "You still think you're in charge?"

I laughed. "Because I am."

He pulled my leg over, turning me onto my belly, and kind of dragged me toward him. Then he pressed his body weight down onto me, widening my thighs with his, his half-hard cock against my arse, and he kissed my shoulder. "We'll see about that."

Holy hell. That was hot.

Ten minutes later, he had me begging, my arse in the air with my face in the covers, begging for him to be inside me. I didn't want his fingers. I didn't want him teasing me. I wanted every inch of him, to the hilt. I wanted to feel him fill the condom deep, deep in me.

If that was on my Christmas wish list, I got every single thing I wanted.

CHAPTER SIXTEEN

CASS

CHRISTMAS MORNING WAS A BUZZ. Everyone was most excited, but ultimately they wanted a quick breakfast before heading off to spend the entire day with their families.

That suited me fine.

I could do with some quiet, private time with Jayden. Not to do anything sexual—god knows we'd done enough of that last night—but I just wanted to be with him.

I wanted to hold him and kiss him. I wanted to feel a man in my arms for as long as I was able.

If he did decide to leave, then . . .

Then I'd be heartbroken, but at least I would have had something.

I'd know then what was possible.

Christmas morning without my kids was also hard. It was usually a day that started way too early with excited squealing and little feet running around the house after not enough sleep.

Birthdays were hard to miss, but Christmas . . . It hurt.

Jayden came into the kitchen carrying the two empty

breakfast jugs. "The Nicholsons are just about to leave for the day. They'll be back sometime around ten tonight. Mrs Nicholson's sweater is eighty per cent tinsel, and I have concerns."

"Uh, yeah, thanks."

He came to stand in front of me. "You okay?"

I shook my head. "I miss my kids."

He rubbed my arm and frowned. "Oh, I'm sorry. It must be hard."

I took a deep breath and let it out slowly. "Christmas Day is, yeah, the hardest."

"Can you call them?"

"Yeah, but it's not the same. And last year when I did that, Charlotte got all sad. It's hard for them too. I'm getting them tomorrow. For two days, which will be nice. It's not the same as today, but it's about them, not me and Kendra."

He smiled, but there was something hidden there. "I like that you put them first. A lot of parents don't."

It then occurred to me why he gave me a guarded look. Two days. His last days here. "Hey, I forgot to mention that I'd have my kids before you were leaving. I—"

"You don't need to tell me," he said quickly. "They're your kids, Cass. They could be here full time and it wouldn't make a difference."

It wouldn't make a difference.

Because he was still leaving, regardless.

"Oh. Yeah, I get that. I guess I just . . . you know what? That's okay."

He tilted his head and squinted. "What?"

I wanted to turn and run. I wanted to disappear and hide from the world. This day had just gotten so much worse. He was leaving and he told me today, of all days. I took a step toward the door. My heart felt as heavy as lead. "You know, I think I'll just . . . I need some . . ."

"Cass."

I shook my head and took another step. "It's fine. You don't need to explain."

"Explain what?"

Another step.

"Cass, don't walk away. What's wrong?"

"It's not a good day for this, so—"

"Oh my god, Carter, no." He strode over, took my hand, and pulled me back into the kitchen. Not roughly, but not exactly gentle. He had fire and determination in his eyes. "You wanna tell me what conclusions you just jumped to? Because I think we missed a whole conversation. Or we were having a different conversation? I'm not exactly sure what happened."

"My kids come first," I said. My chest felt all wrong. Too tight, too loose, hot and cold. "I never made a point of talking about them or mentioning how much they mean to me because I didn't think I had to."

"Why do you think that's a problem for me?"

"Because you said it wouldn't have changed a thing. If they were here full-time. I mean, what if I did have my kids full time, Jayden? What then? Would you have even looked twice at me?"

He squinted again, even madder this time. "Christ, Cass. I said it didn't matter because it doesn't. You have kids, and that makes you a package deal. Whether you have them on weekends or after school or just for holidays or full-time or whatever. For fuck's sake, what kind of person would I be if I didn't want to stay with you because you had kids?"

I opened my mouth to answer.

"Oh my god, did you think I was that shallow?"

"No. Of course not. I just panicked. You said . . ."

He sighed, half turning away from me, and pulled at his hair. "I'm trying really hard not to be mad at you. Because it's Christmas Day and you miss your kids and I get that." He put his hand to my face. "And you didn't say that because you think poorly of me. I can see that. You said it because you think poorly of you."

My eyes met his, but I couldn't get any words out.

He swiped his thumb along my jaw. "You deserve to be happy, Cass. Feeling guilty is fine. Guilt is valid, and it's okay. But it's okay to move on. Don't feel bad for letting it go, Cass. You're allowed to be happy. You don't have to live in misery as payment for ending your marriage."

I swallowed down the lump in my throat.

"You're a great dad. Your kids adore you. Lots of kids live with separated parents. It's better than living in an unhappy household. So you get your kids tomorrow and you need to make every minute count with them. Do all the fun things, play games, build snowmen. Be someone they can talk to. That's what they'll remember."

My eyes watered and my nose burned as I tried not to cry. I nodded. "Thank you."

With both his hands cupping my face, he kissed me sweetly, then rested his forehead on mine. "You're a good one, Cass."

I couldn't speak for a while. I just needed a second to breathe and to feel him close. I needed some kind of connection, on this day, of all days, and he was all that and more. "You called me Carter when you were mad at me."

He smiled. "It just rolls out so perfectly when said in anger."

I sighed, still sad. "I'm sorry your last days here won't be just us. The kids will keep me pretty busy, and then I'm back at work on the twenty-eighth. I mean, I work from home so I'll be around, but life will be back to normal and this week with you will feel like a dream. This week has been a dream. And I'm glad I decided not to wait until after today."

He swatted my arm and gave me a pouty smile. "I haven't decided if I'm staying or not. And Carl hasn't officially offered me any kind of job, so I don't know if I can. My Christmas list of pros and cons is still a work in progress."

I wasn't sure what I could say about that.

Then he sighed and leaned against the counter. "You okay, Cass? I know today's not easy for you."

I chewed on my bottom lip. I wanted so badly to ask him to please stay. But he said he needed time, so the least I could do is give him that. "I'll be okay."

"Do you need a hug?"

I laughed, ignoring the burn behind my eyes. "I would love a hug."

He pulled me against him, and as his arms went around me, as I held him in mine, the tension left my body. It wasn't even the human contact, being touch-deprived. It was him.

It was Jayden.

His touch, his strength.

We stood like that for a long time, just holding and breathing each other in. I pulled back and put my hand to his face, staring into his beautiful eyes. He seemed to be searching mine for something. A clue? The truth? Something to tell him if he should stay or go?

"You wanted time," I whispered. "Take as much time as you need. You can stay here for another week or a month if you want, while you figure out what you want to do. I'm not pressuring you. I just want you to know you don't have to leave in two days, if that was worrying you. You can stay here. In my room or in your own room. Whatever."

He smiled, just about to say something, when a car came up the driveway and around the back of the house. At first I'd wondered if one of the guests had forgotten something, but then I saw it was Kendra's car.

"Hmm."

"Are you expecting them?" Jayden asked.

I shook my head and went to put on my coat and boots. Jayden didn't follow, obviously giving me some privacy. I got as far as the back deck when Wyatt and Charlotte came running across the snow and up the steps. "Daddy!"

I collected them both in a big, squeezy hug. "Merry Christmas. Oh, I love you both so much!"

They both started to talk at the same time, telling me what gifts they got and what Santa gave them, and they were so excited.

God, it was good to see them.

Kendra walked over, smiling. "They were dressed so early to go see my folks for lunch, I thought they'd like to see you today as well. Hope that's okay?"

I gave her a hug too, my heart full. "Always. Actually, it's perfect. You just made my day. I was really missing them." I patted the kids on the head. "Who wants their Christmas presents early?"

"Meeeeee!" they cried, running inside.

"Hold on, wait for us," I said, holding the door for Kendra.

I gave them their gifts and they ripped into each one, and as we stood back to watch them, Jayden appeared. "I made some fresh coffee for you."

"Oh, thank you," Kendra said. "I've been up since before five."

Ah, the joy of little kids on Christmas morning.

I thought Jayden would join us, but he sat on the single sofa. "Show me what you got!" he said excitedly, and Charlotte and Wyatt both began going through each little thing.

Kendra and I went into the kitchen. I poured two cups of coffee and handed her one. "Thank you for bringing them here. It's a hard day without them, so I appreciate you thinking of me."

"I know. They wanted to see you too. They miss you too." She looked around. "No guests here at the moment?"

"No. They're all with their families for the day."

"And how's it all gone this week?"

"Really well. Better than I expected, to be honest. But I've learned a lot, and I know I won't be offering full catering all the time, but seeing what Jayden does has really shown me that I have a long way to go."

"He seems really nice," Kendra said. "The kids like him, and it was very sweet of him to bring us those baked sweets."

I smiled. "Yeah, I ate too many of those."

Kendra studied her coffee for a few long seconds. "So . . . he seems really nice . . ."

Oh, dear god.

She knows something. She knows.

Be honest, Carter. You owe her that.

"He is. He's kinda great."

She was quiet for too long, and when I looked up at her, I found her smiling at me. "You like him."

I laughed, embarrassed and, yes, a little guilty. "I do."

"I can tell. You blush when you're around him. I don't

think I've ever seen you blush before, Cass. Ever. What's up with that?"

I laughed. "I don't know. It's new. And it's horrifying."

She chuckled and sipped her coffee, and we could hear Jayden, Wyatt and Charlotte all laugh from the sitting room.

"I've asked him to stay," I blurted out in a whisper. "He was supposed to move on in two days. Somewhere in Oregon or Washington. But I don't think I want him to leave. God, I don't know why I'm telling you this. I'm sorry. It's probably weird and hard for you to hear." I shook my head. "Just forget I said that. Sorry."

"Don't be sorry. You can tell me this. We were always friends, Cass. We've been through a lot, yeah? School, college, first jobs, moving house, childbirth. We should be able to talk, yeah?"

I nodded, blinking back tears. I took a deep breath. "Yeah. Thank you."

She sipped her coffee. "And you never blushed for me."

I snorted out a laugh. "Um, sorry? I don't know why it's a thing now. It's not really a thing. It just happens when . . ."

"When you're around him."

I nodded.

"I'm happy for you," she said quietly. "A little sad and a little jealous, but mostly I'm happy for you."

That was fair. And completely honest. "Thank you."

"I might be seeing someone?" she said. My gaze went to hers. "It's only new, like four or five dates. But he's nice. I like him."

"Do I know him?"

"It's Trey Young. Do you remember him?"

"He was two years above us in school, right? The horse guy?"

She nodded. "He lives out on Red Cedar Road. He has horses, yes. He's a nice guy, Cass. He met the kids . . ."

God, this was hard. What did she say it was? A little sad, a little jealous? He'd met my kids . . . But what could I say? The guy I'd met and had feelings for was in the sitting room right now, laughing with my kids.

"I'm happy for you, Kendra. A little sad and a little jealous, but happy."

She chuckled and let out a breath. "Why was I so nervous about telling you?"

I studied my coffee cup. "It's been two years. You should do what makes you happy. As long as he treats you and the kids right, I'll support you. I'll support you no matter what. No matter what happens, you can come to me."

Kendra smiled at me. "You're a good man, Cass."

I sipped my coffee.

"So is he staying?" Kendra asked.

"Who?"

"Jayden, silly."

"I don't know. I hope so. But I can't make him stay."

Just then, Wyatt ran into the kitchen. "Mom, can I play pool with Jayden?"

Jayden appeared after him. "I'm really bad at it, so it'll only be a quick game. I wasn't sure how much time we had. Told him to come ask."

Kendra grinned at them. "Sure."

By the time Wyatt had beaten Jayden twice and Charlotte was three balls in front, another car arrived. This time it was my parents.

Jayden shot me a bewildered look. "Are they here for lunch? I haven't cooked anything. Did you know they were coming?"

"I had no idea! We'd planned on seeing them tomorrow when I had the kids."

"There's leftovers I can heat up." He put his hand to his forehead. "God, I can't serve them leftovers."

I squeezed his shoulder and tried not to smile. "Jayden, calm down. They won't expect anything."

"You have to feed people when they turn up, Cass," he said. "It's what you do."

Kendra laughed and the kids ran out to meet their grandparents. Mom and Dad came in, pulling off coats and gloves, then ooh'd and ah'd over the big tree in the sitting room. The kids showed them the two other trees they'd helped decorate, and then they had to show them their Christmas gifts.

It was probably a good ten minutes before they'd even had a chance to stop. "Mom and Dad, you remember Jayden."

"Yes, of course," Dad said.

"Oh yes," Mom added. "We missed you at the tree lighting the other night. Cass here said you had to help Carl in the diner. We heard he hurt his knee."

"Needs to take it easy," Dad said. "He's too old to be working like that."

I shot Jayden a smile.

"Oh, Kendra, darling," Mom said. "It's so nice to see you here. I didn't realise you'd be here. What a wonderful surprise." Her tone was totally implying that maybe Kendra had stayed here last night.

Kendra glanced at me, then smiled at my mom. "Oh yes, we just stopped by this morning on our way to my parents' place. The kids wanted to see Cass. But we have to get going now. It was really good to see you again."

"Oh yes. What a nice thing for you to do. Very considerate."

"Mrs Campion," Jayden said. "Will you be staying for lunch? I can prepare something for you . . ."

"Oh no," Mom replied. "That won't be necessary."

"Well," Dad hedged. "Cass did say those chicken puff things were good. And the steak with the . . . crust." He looked at me. "What was that?"

"It was a herb and cheese crust."

Dad nodded. "Yes, and those little apple tarts. Actually, Cass said everything was good."

Jayden's eyes grew wider with each mention of food. He turned to me. "Oh. I could do . . . something? I have the ham—"

"That's for our guests tomorrow," I explained.

"Well, I have to do something. There's some salmon—"

"We have a fridge full of leftovers."

Jayden, horrified, put his hand to his heart. "I will not serve your parents leftovers."

Kendra laughed. "Okay, kids, grab your things. We need to go." She collected a few things and I helped the kids. Then Kendra put her hand on Jayden's arm. "Good luck. Oh, and honestly, you need to stay." Then she leaned in and whispered something into Jayden's ear. His eyes shot to mine and he pulled back, but Kendra just smiled as she came over to me, leaned up on her toes, and kissed my cheek. "Have a great day. See you in the morning."

I helped the kids into the car, very mindful of leaving poor Jayden alone with my parents for too long, and also very mindful of what I said in front of the kids. "Uh, Kendra, what did you—?"

"Nope. Ask him," she said with a grin. "Kids, wave to Daddy."

I waved as they drove away, and remembering that Jayden was probably having a nervous breakdown in the kitchen, I jogged across the snow and went back inside.

He was in the kitchen. And he was flustered about something, mumbling to himself and rifling through the fridge. "Hey," I said.

He stood up, holding a tray covered with foil. "Leftovers? This is a travesty, Carter."

I took the tray from him, slid it onto the counter, took his face in my hands, and kissed him until he wasn't mad anymore. Then I walked out with a smile. "Christmas leftovers is a perfect lunch."

Mom and Dad stayed for a few hours. They'd known it was going to be a hard day for me, like the year before. They knew all the guests would be out for the day, but they clearly didn't expect Jayden to be . . . Well, they didn't expect it.

After lunch, when I walked them to their car, I knew they were going to say something.

"He's a nice boy," Mom said.

I pretended my cheeks weren't red. "He is."

"Is he . . . just the chef?"

"Mom."

"I caught you looking at him. And I know we never really talked about you being gay. We never really had to before because there was never anyone . . ."

"I asked him to stay on," I said. It wasn't exactly easy for me to admit to them, but I had to start somewhere. "I mean stay. As in here, or stay in town. But he's not sure if he will yet. I like him. He makes me happy."

"He sure knows how to cook," Dad said, rubbing his belly.

"And the kids?" Mom asked.

"The kids love him. Kendra loves him."

I love him.

"I didn't tell the kids about us, though. Obviously. There's nothing official to tell yet. But I will. It won't be easy, Mom. But it's a part of my truth, and my kids will understand. We raised them right."

Mom nodded and patted my arm. "I know. I know. I just worry. I want you to be happy, Cass. It's all I want."

"It'd make me happier if we got out of the cold," Dad said from over the roof of the car. "See you tomorrow at home. Bring Jayden." He tapped the roof. "Get in the car, Catherine. It's cold."

"Drive safe," I said. "And Merry Christmas."

I watched their car disappear down the drive and made my way inside. Jayden was picking up the coffee cups from the coffee table. "Hey," I said, taking a cup from him and putting it back on the coffee table. Keeping his hand in mine, I pulled him close and began to slow waltz in my sitting room.

"What's this?"

"Christmas Day dancing," I replied, kissing the side of his head. "Something to add to the good side of your list."

He chuckled. "Shouldn't there be music playing?"

I pulled him a little closer. "Nope."

He smiled into my neck, and we danced to some silent song for a minute. "Your dad's funny," he said. "I don't think your mum likes me."

"Yes she does. And you're invited to lunch tomorrow at my parents' place. With me and the kids."

He stopped dancing and looked up at me. "I'm what?"

"Lunch, tomorrow. At my parents' house. Breakfast is your last official meal to do. All the guests have to be out by ten, and then we're off duty." I laughed at his expression and kissed him softly. "You don't have to come with us. They offered but I know it's a lot to take in. If you'd rather not, I will completely understand."

"It is a lot."

I couldn't help but chuckle and I began to dance again. "Just out of interest, which side of the pros-and-cons list would being forced to a lunch at my parents' house be on?"

"Undecided."

I laughed. "That reminds me. What did Kendra say to you?"

He froze, stopping our dance a second time. "Oh, that was nothing."

"It doesn't sound like nothing."

He made a face. "How long have we got before anyone gets back?" He took my arm and lifted it so he could see my watch. "Shouldn't we be using this time in the bedroom? I'll have to start dinner soon."

I took his hand and raised it above his head, leading him into a twirl. Then I pulled his back to me and kissed behind his ear, slowly rocking side to side. He craned his neck, giving me better access. "That's really distracting," he breathed.

"Good." I kissed down his neck. "This is what I want."

"To dance with a guy in your sitting room? Without music."

"Not just any guy," I murmured. Then I spun him around and pulled him in close. I could feel how much he was enjoying this. "Only you."

He grabbed my face and brought our mouths together in a bruising kiss, and he pushed us backwards onto the couch. He fell on top of me and he kissed me deeper, his tongue in my mouth, rough breaths, and desperate hands . . .

Until he stopped.

He broke the kiss, keeping his face close, his eyes shut. He looked like he was in pain.

"Jayden?"

"You scare me."

I had to think about what he said. "What?"

"You scare me. This scares me."

I ran my hand down the side of his face. "Look at me."

He did, his eyes a storm of troubled thinking.

"What about this scares you?"

"I want to stay. I really do, but it scares me. Because I think you might be someone I was destined to meet. What I feel for you . . . it's crazy. It scares the shit out of me, Cass. I don't know if I'm ready for it, ya know? And then Kendra said I should stay, and she whispered, 'That man is in love with you,' and it fucking terrifies me."

That was a lot to unpack. "Why is it terrifying?"

He squinted and groaned before his eyes met mine. "Because I think I feel the same."

A slow smile spread across my face. "You do?"

He groaned and climbed off me, slumping onto the couch. "Does it not scare you?"

I tried not to laugh, but he'd just admitted to maybe being in love with me. "Of course it does."

"Everything changes. Doesn't it? I mean, it's so fast and I don't know if it's real. So should I change my entire plans on some crazy fling?"

"A fling?"

"Well, I don't know what else to call it. It feels like a cyclone, if I'm being honest. Out of control and no idea if the damage will be minimal or catastrophic. Or you know those rides at the fair. Amazing and exhilarating, but also like I could puke."

I laughed. "Wow. That's the most romantic thing I've ever heard."

He groaned. "Cass."

"Okay, real talk. One, I can't believe Kendra said that. But two, I don't know if she's completely wrong. Because I am falling in love with you, Jayden. And yes, it's crazy-fast, but I don't care about what anyone else thinks. I care about what you think. About us. And baby, honestly, it is scary. But you're worth it. I don't need a Christmas pros-and-cons list to know that."

He leaned his head on the back of the couch and stared at me. "You think you might love me?"

I nodded. "Yeah. You're kinda perfect."

His smile grew wider and he buried his face in his hands. "God, this is crazy."

I drew my fingers through his hair and he raised his head, so I pulled him in for a kiss. "It is crazy. But you know what?" I stood up and held out my hand. "Come with me."

He let me pull him to his feet. "Uh, we don't have that kind of time . . ."

I laughed and led him into the kitchen. I took one of his clipboards from the pantry hook and put it on the counter in front of him. I took the top sheet of paper.

He looked a little worried. "What are you doing? I need that."

Chuckling, I turned it over to the blank side. I drew a line down the middle and wrote pros on one side and cons on the other.

"What are you doing?" Jayden asked.

"Making you a list." Then on the pros side, I wrote:

Holding hands
Kisses

Magic dick

Then I looked at him. "What else was there? We were keeping the war of capitalism off the list, yes?"

He rolled his eyes, and with a laugh, he took the pen. "Well, on the pro side, I could write *small town* because it's super cute. But then on the con side, I could also write *small town* because, well, you know . . . small town."

Then he chewed on his bottom lip. "Then there's your family. They're kinda great. Parents, ex-wife, kids. Like it's a whole complete thing, like those cooking shows on TV, you know, when they bring out one that's already made and be like, 'look here's one I prepared earlier.'"

That made me laugh. "Is that a bad thing?"

"Oh no. They go on the pro side."

Then he actually wrote *pre-made family* on the pro side.

"So what goes on the con side?"

Jayden sighed and tapped his pen on the counter. "To do with you? Well . . . nothing. Yet. I'm sure things will piss me off eventually, and I can add them."

"So I'll come down to the kitchen and see in big bold letters *left towel on floor* on the con side and I will know I fucked up."

His eyes lit up. "That's a great idea!" Then he side-eyed me. "You don't leave your wet towels on the floor though, do you? Because that's gross."

I laughed. "I absolutely do not."

"Oh. I just remembered what it was," he mumbled, then wrote two things on the con side.

Work
Place to live

"I'll need some more consistent work, and if Carl isn't interested, then I don't know . . . And my own place."

"You can stay here," I said, brushing his hair back from his forehead. "In your own room, down at the end of the hall. So you can have your own space, if you want. Or in my room, in my bed . . ." I leaned in and whispered, "Every night. All night."

He let out a shaky breath. "I can't make that decision with you doing that. It's coercion or bribery or something."

He pushed me off him and started to write something else on the pro list.

Magic dick

"I already wrote that."

"It deserves to be on there twice."

I laughed and turned another sheet of paper over on his clipboard and wrote the heading *My Christmas Wish List* at the top.

"Oh, this should be good," he joked.

I held it up to my chest and pretended to be scribbling for ages.

"Come on, lemme see," he said.

I put the clipboard down so he could read it. It just had one word, right in the middle.

Stay

He laughed and gave me a playful shove. "I thought you were writing a whole list."

I shook my head. "It's all I want."

He sighed and put his hand to his forehead. "God, okay, okay, I'll stay."

"You will?"

He nodded, and I picked him up in a bear hug and twirled him around the kitchen. He laughed and laughed until he groaned. "Oh, here's the puking part," he whined.

I sat him on the counter instead and stood between his legs. I pulled him in close and he slid his arms around my neck, giving me smiling kisses.

"Still scared?" I asked him.

He grinned. "Petrified."

"Same. But never been happier."

He held my face and kissed me again. "Same."

EPILOGUE
JAYDEN

CASS WASN'T LYING when he said Arabella was even prettier in the springtime. The fields of green and wildflowers, the pond, the impressive mountain behind the house, and of course the house itself.

It reminded me of the mountaintop that Julie Andrews did the sing-and-spin thing on in *The Sound of Music*.

It was that spectacular.

But it was spectacular in every season. Just when you'd think it was the prettiest it could get, the seasons changed and everything got prettier, just in different colours.

I'd been here for fifteen months.

I needn't have been worried about work. Carl did call the day after Christmas and asked if I'd help for two weeks while his knee mended. Of course I said yes. It was perfect timing. Like fate or something.

But at the end of those two weeks, he had another proposition for me. Three days a week, just Monday through Wednesday. His knee wasn't ever gonna be great— it ached all the next winter—and it was time for him to start slowing up a little. The early mornings did his old body no favours anymore, he'd said.

And the three days a week suited me perfectly. Cass still did his design work on those days, so getting me out of the house gave him peace and quiet, and it gave us weekends to work at Arabella. Me having outside work not only brought in some money but it also gave us decent time apart, so we weren't in each other's pockets all the time, given we worked together most weekends and for events throughout the calendar.

We'd held weekends for Valentine's Day getaways, spring weekend specials, Memorial Day weekend, Halloween and Thanksgiving. We'd learned a lot over the year and had a few mishaps, but all in all, Cass's business was doing better than he'd ever dreamed.

But this was our first wedding.

The house looked like something out of one of the wedding magazines Cass had worked on. It hadn't helped at all that the Bridezilla expected absolute perfection. And when I say Bridezilla, I say that with all affection because Hamish had become one of my best friends.

Yes, Hamish was Bridezilla.

He wasn't horrible, just panicky and wanted everything to be perfect for his perfect day, and of course it was.

Because Cass was in charge. And we'd had almost a year to plan for this.

Hamish was visiting one day last spring when the house was at its prettiest. And I'd showed him where the ceremony could take place down by the pond and how we could clear out the recreation room and put the head table against the windows. We'd have round tables with elegant tablecloths and soft lighting and a menu to die for.

And that was exactly what we'd done.

Kendra and Trey had come to help. Well, Kendra and I gossiped in the kitchen while Trey and Cass did all the heavy lifting getting the tables inside. Kendra had become a close friend of mine, which made it sound like a *Sister Wives* thing, which it wasn't at all.

Trey had been a bit wary at first. Wary of Cass and I being together, being gay. But very early on, Cass had told him bluntly that he appreciated Trey being the stepdad to his kids, but if he intended to be in Kendra and the kids' life, he had to deal with the gay ex-husband, and there'd been some kind of mutual respect exchange after that.

Anyway, Trey had helped Cass fix an issue with the pond last summer and some fencing thing too, and now with the wedding tables. We were kind of a dysfunctional family but it really worked. The kids were thriving, happy at school, happy at home, happy to spend time with us.

Life was pretty damn great.

But the wedding . . . I'd planned a menu of seared scallops and salad for a starter, beef or salmon for the main, so I had a lot to organise and a lot to get right.

So, of course I had a list for every single thing.

Cass ran his finger down the list stuck to the clipboard. "What do you need me to do?" Cass asked.

"Uh, stay out of my way?"

He laughed. "Noted." But we'd done this enough times that he kinda just knew what to do. He carefully lifted trays for me and made sure I had all the serving gear I needed, and he cleared things away as I'd finished with them.

We worked well together.

I didn't even mind that I had to work throughout the ceremony. I stopped long enough to watch Ren and Hamish exchange vows; they both looked so handsome, so happy. Hamish's niece and nephew from Mossley were the cutest little flower girl and ring bearer you ever could imagine.

The whole day was a fairy tale for them, and I was proud to have done that for them.

I left the clean-up to watch them cut the cake and have their first dance as a married couple. The wedding was a small affair, very intimate and personal.

Very magical.

Cass had pulled me out to the dance floor, me in my chef's uniform, and along with everyone else, we slow danced under the fairy lights. It was the perfect end to a stressful day.

As the night went on and Hamish and Ren escaped to their room, Cass and I began the clean-up.

Every room was booked, so I also wanted to get a head start on breakfast. Cass brought some empty bottles of wine in and put them in the recycling crate, then he kissed the back of my neck. "We did it."

"We sure did."

"I'll sleep well tonight, now that it's all over."

He'd been so worried. "Now we need to start planning for Easter next month. And my parents will be here then too, don't forget." My parents hadn't been back to the US in years but were very keen to meet Cass and see the tiny town I raved about, and they'd be staying again for two weeks in April.

I couldn't wait to see them.

"I haven't forgotten." Cass sighed and kissed the back of my head. "Whatcha doing?"

"Just getting a head start on breakfast. There's going to be a few sore heads in the morning."

He chuckled, but it was a tired sound. "The work never ends."

I kept slicing the shallots. "And that's a good thing, baby."

"Yes it is." He gave me a bit of a squeeze. "The wedding was great, wasn't it?"

"So beautiful."

"I didn't expect Ren to cry," Cass said. "I thought it would have been Hamish."

I laughed. "Sweetie, there was no way he was ruining months of skin care preparation for a few tears."

Cass laughed from the storeroom, and when he came out, he was holding a clipboard with a to-do list on it. "Is this for tomorrow?" He turned it around quickly so I could see.

I nodded. "Most of it's clean-up. And we need to have the table cloths back to the rental company first thing Monday morning."

"Yeah, no worries. I'll take care of that."

"Oh, and don't forget we have three rooms booked this weekend. Four adult couples and three kids."

"Yes, boss," he joked.

"I need to put an order in at the market," I said, scraping all the shallots into a container. Then I started to measure the ingredients for the bread maker. I could set the timer to have fresh bread ready for breakfast.

Cass pushed the list toward me. "Anything else that needs to be done tonight?"

I took a quick glance. "No, I don't think so." I wiped my upper arm across my forehead.

"Sure?"

"Uh, yeah. I'll just separate this. The rest I can do tomorrow. Oh, do you want to check the ground coffee?"

Cass didn't move or answer, and when I looked over at

him, he had a weird smile on his face. "Sure about the list? Is there anything that needs to be crossed off?"

I put the lid on the flour and pulled the clipboard over, going down the list from the top. "No, it all looks good . . ."

Then I noticed Cass's handwriting at the very bottom.

Say yes to Cass

Say yes to Cass? What the hell? "What am I saying yes to?" I asked. "Unless it involves hot showers or full body massages, I'm not sure what else I have the energy for tonight."

He laughed and took my hand. He turned me to face him. "Marry me."

What?

What?

"What?"

"I want today with you, Jayden. The wedding, the vows, fancy suits, the slow dancing. I want forever with you."

"Cass . . ."

He pulled the list around. "It's on the list. You have to check it off."

My heart was hammering, my mind was spinning in circles. All I could do was laugh. "Is that right?"

He nodded. "Or you can make a pros-and-cons list again if you want."

I leaned in, sliding my arms around his lower back. "I don't need to do that. My wish list only has one word on it now."

He kissed me. "And what's that?"

"You."

"You have me."

"Forever."

"If you say yes."

I didn't need any wish list or pros-and-cons list to know my answer.

"Yes."

The Merry End

HARTBRIDGE CHRISTMAS SERIES

WANT TO READ MORE IN THE HARTBRIDGE SERIES?

HARTBRIDGE CHRISTMAS SERIES

ABOUT THE AUTHOR

N.R. Walker is an Australian author, who loves her genre of gay romance. She loves writing and spends far too much time doing it, but wouldn't have it any other way.

She is many things: a mother, a wife, a sister, a writer. She has pretty, pretty boys who live in her head, who don't let her sleep at night unless she gives them life with words.

She likes it when they do dirty, dirty things... but likes it even more when they fall in love.

She used to think having people in her head talking to her was weird, until one day she happened across other writers who told her it was normal.

She's been writing ever since...

nrwalker.net

ALSO BY N.R. WALKER

The Twelfth of Never (Blind Faith 3.5)
Twelve Days of Christmas (Sixty Five Hours Christmas)
Best of Both Worlds

Translated Titles:

Italian

Fiducia Cieca (Blind Faith)
Attraverso Questi Occhi (Through These Eyes)
Preso alla Sprovvista (Blindside)
Il giorno del Mai (Blind Faith 3.5)
Cuore di Terra Rossa Serie (Red Dirt Heart Series)
Natale di terra rossa (Red dirt Christmas)
Intervento di Retrofit (Elements of Retrofit)
A Chiare Linee (Clarity of Lines)
Senso D'appartenenza (Sense of Place)
Spencer Cohen Serie (including Yanni's Story)
Punto di non Ritorno (Point of No Return)
Punto di Rottura (Breaking Point)
Punto di Partenza (Starting Point)
Imago (Imago)
Il desiderio di un soldato (A Soldier's Wish)
Scambiato (Switched)
Galassie e Oceani (Galaxies and Oceans)

French

Confiance Aveugle (Blind Faith)

A travers ces yeux: Confiance Aveugle 2 (Through These Eyes)

Aveugle: Confiance Aveugle 3 (Blindside)

À Jamais (Blind Faith 3.5)

Cronin's Key Series

Au Coeur de Sutton Station (Red Dirt Heart)

Partir ou rester (Red Dirt Heart 2)

Faire Face (Red Dirt Heart 3)

Trouver sa Place (Red Dirt Heart 4)

Le Poids de Sentiments (The Weight of It All)

Un Noël à la sauce Henry (A Very Henry Christmas)

Une vie à Refaire (Switched)

Evolution (Evolved)

Galaxies & Océans

Qui Trouve, Garde (Finders Keepers)

Sens Dessus Dessous (Upside Down)

Spencer Cohen Series

German

Flammende Erde (Red Dirt Heart)

Lodernde Erde (Red Dirt Heart 2)

Sengende Erde (Red Dirt Heart 3)

Ungezähmte Erde (Red Dirt Heart 4)

Printed in the USA
CPSIA information can be obtained
at www.ICGtesting.com
LVHW090403031223
765360LV00009B/252

9 781925 886672